TROUBLE IS A FRIEND OF MINE

STEPHANIE
TROMLY

speak

SPEAK
An imprint of Penguin Random House LLC
375 Hudson Street
New York, New York 10014

First published in the United States of America by Kathy Dawson Books,
an imprint of Penguin Group (USA) LLC, 2015
Published by Speak, an imprint of Penguin Random House LLC, 2016

THE LIBRARY OF CONGRESS HAS CATALOGED THE KATHY DAWSON BOOKS EDITION AS FOLLOWS:
Tromly, Stephanie.
Trouble is a friend of mine / by Stephanie Tromly.
pages cm
Summary: After her parents' divorce, Zoe Webster moves from Brooklyn to upstate New York,
where she meets the weirdly compelling misfit Philip Digby, and soon finds herself in a series of
hilarious and dangerous situations as he pulls her into his investigation into the kidnapping of a
local teenage girl, which may be related to the disappearance of his sister eight years ago.
ISBN 978-0-525-42840-4 (hardcover)
[1. Missing children—Fiction. 2. Moving, Household—Fiction. 3. Divorce—Fiction.
4. High schools—Fiction. 5. Schools—Fiction. 6. Mystery and detective stories.]
I. Title.
PZ7.1.T76Tro 2015 [Fic]—dc23 2014040605

Speak ISBN 9780147515438

Printed in the United States of America

1 3 5 7 9 10 8 6 4 2

TROUBLE IS A FRIEND OF MINE

Of course I didn't like Digby when I first met him. No one does. He's rude, he doesn't ever take no for an answer, and he treats you like a book he's already read and knows the ending to even if you yourself didn't yet. Now, if you're a normal sixteen-year-old like I am, and you spend half your time obsessing about the future and what you're supposed to be and spend the other half reading about makeup, diets, and all the ways to change who you already are, then the stuff he hits you with is hard to take. Like Digby himself said: The truth is almost always disappointing.

Not that I need him to tell me about the truth. Or disappointment. In the last six months, I went from living in an almost-good part of Brooklyn to my parents divorcing and Mom and me moving to River Heights, a small city in the armpit of upstate New York. Trust me, it's an even bigger lifestyle demotion than it sounds like.

Here's my first confession. I hung out with cool people, sure, but looking back, I think maybe we were friends only because we were in the same classes and our parents all got divorced around the same time. Digby calls them circumstantial friends. Right place, right time—it was easy to be friends, and so we were.

My friendship with Digby, on the other hand, while circumstantially convenient—he just shows up, after all—is not easy. Nothing with that guy ever is. At first, I thought I hung out with him because I was bored and wanted to get back at Mom for moving me here. Then I thought it was because he seemed so lost and alone all the time.

But now I'm standing outside a house wired with enough explosives to blow up our entire block into a pile of matchsticks, trying to figure out the best way to get back *in,* and I realize that really, I'm the one who's been lost.

But I'm jumping too far ahead. All this began on the first day of school and we need to go back there for you to understand.

ONE

I'd been telling Mom to change the drained batteries in the doorbell since we moved in. The chimes were out of tune and dinging at half their normal speed. They sounded like a robot dying in slow agony. And now some jackass was ringing it over and over. After five minutes of pretending nobody was home, I thought I was going to snap, so I answered the door.

"Nice bell," he said.

He was my age, wearing a black suit that made him look even taller and skinnier than he already was. It was a hot morning and he was sweating into the collar of his white button-down. He held a black book and I would've thought he was a Jehovah's Witness with a Bible, but I doubted they wore sneakers when they came calling. His messy brown hair had probably once been pop-star shaggy, but now it needed cutting. His sad brown eyes turned down at the corners and he had a bored facial expression that I later realized was one of his main weapons in life.

"Sorry, not interested." Just to be safe, I yelled, "It's no one, Mom, just some guy selling something."

"Why are you pretending your mom's home? You're here alone. You guys drove off together, but you're back and her car isn't. I'm guessing she dropped you at school and you walked home," he said. "Next time, fake sick and save her the gas."

I tried another one. "Dad!"

"You only had the one car in the garage—the tires are squishy, by the way—the grass on your lawn that isn't brown is a foot tall, recycling isn't sorted, and you know . . . the door-bell," he said. "There's no dad in the picture."

I was too shocked to deny it.

"What, were you casing the place? Because I gotta tell you, we don't have anything nice." The following catalog ran through my head: letter opener in the hall drawer, knives on the kitchen counter, poker by the busted fireplace in the den, and a collection of advice from Sexual Assault Prevention Day, like: "Never let them take you to a second location."

"Casing the place? No. Well . . . technically, I guess I was casing *around* your house, but not your actual house," he said. "Anyway, I've watched you photograph yourself every morning—"

"What?! You're looking in my window—"

"I need to see the photos," he said. "Although, if you only take them at the same time every day, they probably won't tell me much because they never do anything interesting in the mornings. Then again, you never know . . ."

"I'm calling the police."

I slammed the door so hard, the doorbell started ringing on its own.

"Listen, my name's Digby. Here's my e-mail address." He slid a small piece of paper under the door that said: Digby@TheRealDigby.com. "E-mail the photos if that's less freaky for you."

Through the glass panel in the door, I saw him start to knock, so I grabbed the letter opener and flashed it in an I'm-gonna-stab-you way. I guess I was convincing, because he said "Whoa" and backed away. When he got to the sidewalk, he looked up to my bedroom window, then stared at the mansion across the street for a long time.

And that wasn't even the weirdest thing that happened that day. I'd just started as a junior at River Heights High and didn't know they phoned parents of absent students after first period bell. They called it the Ferris Bueller Rule. Apparently the school board made the new rule after a girl disappeared during summer vacation. Marina Jane Miller (TV news always used all three of her names) had been kidnapped while friends were sleeping over in her room. They hadn't heard a thing. The whole of River Heights was freaked, especially the rich people, because Marina Miller was rich.

The school called Mom at work and she called me, but when I didn't pick up, she rushed home only to find me napping. Naturally, she had a mini conniption fit but much worse than that was the fact that cutting school landed me in an early intervention meeting with thirteen other kids who got busted that day.

Which is where I saw Digby again.

TWO

The truancy officer was a hard-ass named Musgrave. He was the kind of man about whom Mom would say, "Poor thing wasn't held enough as a baby." He sat us in a circle and slowly walked around outside it. When I was first summoned to the meeting, I didn't think it was going to be a big deal, but Musgrave's black uniform and shiny badge were intimidating.

Meanwhile, our guidance counselor, who introduced himself as "please-call-me-Steve," stood in the middle of the circle handing out chocolate chip cookies he'd baked for us. He'd also made HELLO, MY NAME IS stickers. Mine had ZOE WEBSTER in swirly red ink like all the girls'. The boys' were done in blue.

Musgrave scowled when Please-Call-Me-Steve offered him a cookie. Funnily, the two of them looked evil-twin/good-twin alike. Both were short, dumpy men with bad haircuts and red splotchy faces, but where Steve's was red with sunburn from riding his bike to work, Musgrave's was red from, I'd guess, drinking and rage.

Musgrave was halfway through his threats about unexcused absences and summer school when Digby arrived. It had taken Musgrave twenty minutes to wind up to this climax, so he was totally derailed when Digby sauntered in.

"You must think you're a funny guy, almost missing a disciplinary meeting on truancy," Musgrave said. "Grab your name tag and get your butt over here."

Digby had to write his own tag, which he did in swirly red letters. Then he sighed and dragged a chair to the circle. The metal legs screamed the entire way. The other truants clapped and laughed. To my horror, Digby parked himself next to me and greeted me like we'd planned to sit together.

I tried to look saintly and refused to acknowledge Digby's muttered asides. He stage-whispered things like, "It's nine a.m.—he smells like jerky. Discuss," and, "Do you think it's fun to stay at the YMCA in that outfit?"

I sat, frozen, but Musgrave threw me the same evil stare he pointed at Digby. As far as he was concerned, we were in it together. Finally, after repeating the policy on truancy and summer school twice more, Musgrave ended the meeting.

"Okay, everybody," Please-Call-Me-Steve said. "Please come and leave your information on the sign-up sheet here. Make sure you take a look . . . and help yourself to some snacks. Give pepitas a chance!"

Meanwhile, Musgrave cornered Digby and me.

"How's it going, Harlan?" Digby said to him.

"Welcome back to River Heights, Mr. Digby," Musgrave said. "I haven't gotten your file from your school in Texas.

Did they teach you manners there or are you and I gonna have problems?"

"Harlan and I go way back . . . before his demotion, when he was an actual police officer," Digby said.

"Guess that answers my question about manners," Musgrave said.

"Don't be sad, Harlan. You should learn to see the positive in this new job . . . after all, I believe children are our future," Digby said.

"You will call me Mr. Musgrave," he said. "And you, Zoe Webster, your fancy Manhattan psychiatrist called." Everyone in the room was listening. Musgrave checked his clipboard. "Didaskaleinophobia? That's a mouthful. Fancy way of saying you don't like school. That's a thing now? When did that become a valid excuse?"

"That's confidential student information," Digby said.

"Excuse me?" Musgrave said.

"I'm pretty sure if she told her parents you read all that to her classmates, they'd call their 'fancy Manhattan' *lawyer* and sue you and the school board for violating her privacy," Digby said.

"Still a troublemaker," Musgrave said. "I remember you were fractious and disruptive to our investigation. Nothing's changed, I see."

"And might that be more confidential student information you're revealing?" Digby said.

Musgrave's left eye twitched but, thank God, Please-Call-Me-Steve called him to the other end of the room.

"What are you doing?" I smacked Digby's arm.

"You wanted him to announce your private business to the whole room?" Digby said.

"Stop helping and get away from me, please—I don't want him to think we're friends."

"Don't knock it. Spend some time in River Heights and you'll know it ain't easy making friends around here."

"I'm serious. I can't get in trouble. I need a clean transcript or I'll never get out of here."

"Which makes your decision to skip school super-interesting," Digby said. "Are you transferring out of this fine establishment?"

"Hope to."

"To where?"

"A school in New York. The Prentiss Academy."

"Sounds uptight."

"It's a feeder school for Princeton."

"Princeton? You wanna go there?" He was laughing at me.

"Not that I have to explain myself to you, but I have the grades."

"Your answer to having school phobia is applying to a really hard school so you can get into a really, really hard college?"

"I'm not phobic anymore."

"Were you ever really?" Digby took a bite of cookie. "Hey, these cookies are good."

"Yeah, the guidance counselor made them."

"Wait. He said he physically *made* them?"

"Yeah . . ."

Digby rifled through the tray of cookies. A few of the kids standing near us groaned in disgust.

"You're touching all the cookies. That's gross," I said.

Across the room, Steve and Musgrave argued loudly.

"Wanna get out of morning classes this semester?" Digby said.

"How?"

"Think fast—Steve's losing against Musgrave—are you in? Now or never, Princeton."

I meant to say no, but as I later found out, something about Digby makes me do the exact opposite of what I know is the right thing. Over and over again.

"I guess . . . I'm in?"

Digby ran over and inserted himself into their argument.

"Steve, I gotta talk to you about our independent project," Digby said.

Steve looked blank but played along. "Oh?"

"What independent project?" Musgrave said.

"Our approval form's right here," Digby said.

"It's new," Steve said. "Students work on projects off campus to pursue interests the curriculum doesn't address."

"They don't come to school?" Musgrave said.

"They meet with a faculty advisor, but they work on it outside the classroom. They come to school for the rest of their credits," Steve said.

"That's ridiculous! That's kids schooling themselves. Blue state liberal garbage . . . what's this project anyway?"

Digby used his extra-bored expression. "We're calling it 'Convicted in Absence.' We're looking at whether skipping class leads to criminal behavior, or whether being punished like a criminal for skipping class actually causes the criminal behavior. Bet it's the second one." It came out fast and shiny, like he'd spent time polishing up his spiel. "We're talking about securitization . . . schools as an extension of the police state. 'Convicted in Absence.' Good title, right?"

"This crap is destroying this country," Musgrave said.

That sealed it. Anything to annoy Musgrave. Steve signed the form.

++++

I caught up with Digby in the hall. "What just happened? How'd you do that?" I said.

"*Manhattan psychiatrist,* but downgraded to a falling-down house in a B-grade suburb? Your parents are divorced. C'mon, you never use divide and conquer? It's a divorce-kid classic." Digby looked at me hard. "Although . . . no makeup, no piercings, loose jeans." He looked at my butt a little too hard for my taste. "I don't see a whale tail . . . good girl who doesn't play that game? Yeah . . . that's you. The girl in the music video before the makeover."

"Half the school's got divorced parents. You had a fifty-fifty chance," I said. "What was with the cookies?"

"When Mommy, or Steve in this case, lies about storebought cookies being homemade, it means the battle for the kids' affection is not going well for her. I gave Steve a way to win the battle," he said.

"How'd you know these weren't homemade?"

"Unless they're OCD, people don't use cookie cutters on

15

chocolate chip cookies. Perfect circles." He held up cookies he'd swiped. All unnaturally round. "Plus, they're warm, so the guy microwaved them, meaning he *really* cares."

"Great, Professor Pillsbury. But now we have to actually write this."

"Read the room. Steve will give us a good grade no matter what we turn in just to freak out Musgrave," he said. "What's with *you*, anyway?"

"What's with *me*?"

"The psychiatrist. Bipolar? Plain vanilla depression? Rainbow sprinkles of phobias and anxieties? What's your deal?"

"That's personal."

"Is it like you can't get out of bed because you feel like someone's sitting on your chest, but who cares anyway because what's the point?" he said. "Or like you can't be around people because you feel like everyone *knows*?"

"*Fine*. I skipped class a bunch when my parents were divorcing, but Dad said it'd look bad on my transcript, so he called his psychiatrist friend and . . . I'm a fake, okay?"

"Just because your psychiatrist's note's fake, it doesn't mean you're not really depressed."

I hadn't considered that.

"But hey," Digby continued, "your dad's got a medical professional who's willing to falsify medical records for you, huh? That's pretty handy." He pointed at my earrings, a pair of big diamond studs. I'd wondered if I shouldn't wear them to school, but when he gave them to me, Dad had insisted that I never take them off. "Is that part of the official uniform of

16

Team Dad?" When I winced, he said, "Just kidding. They're beautiful, Princeton." Digby turned and walked away.

"Hey, wait! Now what?" I said.

"I'm gonna check out the cafeteria," he said. "Zoe Webster, right? You have a school e-mail? I'll e-mail you."

Then I didn't see or hear from him for weeks.

THREE

When we first moved to River Heights, everyone was visibly freaked about Marina Jane Miller's abduction. People didn't go out after dark. They walked dogs in groups. By mid-September, though, the local news stopped talking about her, and the "Where's Marina?" posters curled up and fell off the trees after it rained. Soon it sounded more like an urban legend and less like something that could happen to me. Before long, River Heights went back to normal—with *normal* meaning boring and lonely.

After starting some awkward conversations that went nowhere, I realized Digby was right about it being hard to make friends here. Most people gave me attitude because they expected *me* to have an attitude about moving to River Heights . . . which I sort of did, but it had nothing to do with them.

When I asked my lab partner how to turn on the Bunsen burners, she said, "Bet your old school had automatic ones, huh?" I said yes and tried to say something quippy about almost burning off my eyebrows once, but it came off as a lame humble-brag. Even I heard it. We spent the rest of the experiment in painful silence.

I told myself that since I was transferring, I didn't have to sweat the no-friends situation. Prentiss would be my salvation. Of course Mom wasn't happy about Prentiss. How could she be? She'd fought hard for my custody, and transferring to Prentiss meant I'd move right back to the city and live with Dad and his new wife. Mom accused my dad of doing an end run around the custody judge, but almost as soon as she'd said it, her therapy kicked in. She'd shut herself down, saying over and over, "It's not about me." Later, while looking for Band-Aids, I'd found a pile of Post-its in her drawer with mantras like "It's not about you" and "Transcend to transform."

I had to admit, my class schedule was sweet. Digby and I were supposedly working on our project for the first two periods, so I slept in every day. Sure, I worried about actually doing the assignment, but from September, December looked far away.

I never saw Digby at school, but with the stress of figuring out where my classes were and how to make friends, I wasn't looking for him that hard.

++++

One day, I got home to find that Dad had forwarded the application package from Prentiss. Mom hovered by the sink, looking extremely casual while she made dinner. "Baked spaghetti, okay?" She used her best transcending-to-transform

19

voice, as if she hadn't even noticed the Prentiss envelope sitting on the kitchen table.

Okay. So it was going to be a game of chicken. I slid the Prentiss application to one side and unzipped my backpack. "Ever feel like we should eat more vegetables?"

"I could sprinkle parsley on it . . ." Her eyes were now locked on the thick envelope. "So."

"So?" I was winning. But I got cocky. I started highlighting the novel I had to read for homework. Big mistake. Never wave a lowbrow book in front of an English professor. It will enrage them, distracting them from everything else.

"O. Henry? That's not what you're reading in school, is it?" She grabbed my book and flicked through it. "This is a nightmare. Why don't they just assign you *Reader's Digest*?" When she realized I didn't know what she was talking about, she said, "You don't know what *Reader's Digest* is? The nightmare deepens." The game of chicken was ruined. "For decades, it was the only contact some people had with any kind of literature—"

I ripped into the envelope my father sent me. Mom stopped talking and dumped the pasta in an oven dish, pretending to suddenly be totally into her cooking.

Looking through the forms, I realized that he'd already filled out most of them for me, even the parts about my favorite subjects and potential college majors. Economics or pre-law, he'd said.

In a separate pink pamphlet was the essay question: "Virginia Woolf said, 'Almost any biographer, if he respects facts, can give us much more than another fact to add to our collection.

20

He can give us the creative fact; the fertile fact; the fact that suggests and engenders.' Be your own biographer, go beyond fact, and tell us about yourself."

He'd answered it. In fact, he'd answered it well. I even kind of recognized myself in his answers. But reading about this go-getter fantasy daughter who volunteered and read *The Economist* was . . . confusing. Even *I* liked that Zoe better than me.

Maybe he'd anticipated the queasy feeling I'd get when I saw that he'd written it for me, because Dad had included a note on a Post-it. "Time to leave the sheeple behind, Zoe. Get ready to run with the wolves," it said. In the world according to my father, there were only two kinds of people: wolves and the sheeple (people so meek, they were practically sheep) who deserved every bad thing the wolves did to them.

"Are those samples of someone else's application?" I hadn't noticed Mom sidle up behind me. I ripped off the note and crumpled it up before she could see it. Mom read aloud from the essay section. "'I take my citizenship in the classroom seriously'? I smell your father's aggressive Wall Street bull crap. Are you kidding, Zoe? It's come to this?"

"He just rewrote a few things, Mom. It's not a big deal."

"You want to go to that school so badly, you'd cheat to get in?" Mom said.

"Oh, and you don't think the other kids get help? Tutors? Interview prep? I'm applying out of *public school*!" What I didn't say but she probably heard anyway was the reminder that she was the reason I was in public school in the first place. We were in Nowhere, New York, chasing her dream of being an English professor. "Getting help from a *supportive parent* is probably just the minimum they expect!"

I shouted the words *supportive parent* and took advantage of the emotional chaos they created to make my exit.

"Where are you going?" Mom said.

"Walk."

"When will you be back?"

"Why? Are you worried? Safe town, right? It's what you told the judge."

And with that, I left.

++++

Olympio's was a vinyl booth diner with a long counter and a weirdly huge assortment of pies arranged in an old-timey pie display. I heard a tap-tap-tap as I walked past. Digby was in a booth, knocking on the glass and waving. I went inside.

"Hey, Princeton, I was just gonna text you," he said. "We need to talk."

"Yeah, we should start our project," I said.

"Project?" he said.

"'Convicted in Absence,' you called it. Remember?"

"Oh, *that*. Later. There's something else I wanna talk to you about."

His took off his jacket and rolled up his sleeves. A stack of files lay in front of him.

"Those look like police reports," I said.

"They *are* police reports," he said.

"Why do you have police reports?"

"Four weeks ago, Marina Miller disappeared from a slumber party at her house."

"These files are from the Marina Miller case?"

"No, these are from when another girl disappeared from River Heights eight years ago."

"They're related?"

"Yup. Maybe. Definitely maybe," Digby said. "Hey, are you hungry? I gotta eat."

"Not really." I looked at a menu. "Maybe something small."

Digby held up two fingers at the waitress, who walked into the kitchen, writing on her pad.

"Uh . . . did you just order for me?"

"Yeah."

"Rude much? How do you know what I want?"

"I've had everything here. Trust me, you want the cheeseburger."

"How d'you know I'm not vegetarian?"

"Leather boots, leather bag, leather belt—if you're a vegetarian, you're the kind who doesn't mind being a hypocrite sometimes, in which case, trust me, their cheeseburger's worth being a hypocrite for," Digby said.

I looked at the table next to us. The guy's cheeseburger did look juicy.

"Anyway, the cops arrested a suspect, but they couldn't make it stick."

"Wait, the girl who disappeared eight years ago, or Marina Jane Miller?"

"Marina. It doesn't matter, though, because he's a dud—

no way he did it," he said. "David Siddle."

"Oh, you think he's a dud? Are the police aware of your conclusions?"

"Not yet. I'll call them when I know a little more."

"I thought it'd be clear I was being sarcastic."

"Oh, no, I got that."

"I seriously doubt they care what you think."

"We'll worry about that later."

"'We'? I don't know about 'we.'"

Digby passed me two photos of middle-aged men. They were probably just normal guys, but who *doesn't* look like a murderer when they're secretly photographed through a tele-photo lens?

"I don't know who these guys are. Is that all you wanted to ask me?"

"I know who they are. This one's Dr. Leo Schell. He's a gynecologist," Digby said. "Specifically, your mother's gyne-cologist."

"How do you know *that*?"

"I watched her go in his office."

"You're kind of a shady guy, you know that?"

"Schell is one of my two favorites for who took Marina."

The cheeseburgers came and Digby poured ketchup all over the bun, the fries, the coleslaw. All over.

"Can you even taste the cheeseburger under all that?"

"I can't taste. Not much, anyway."

"You can't taste? Is that, like, a genetic thing?"

"Doctors say it's the Celexa, but I think it's the Paxil. It started with the Prozac I used to be on," he said. "I usually take Adderall to get decent, but I don't use it too much because it's, you know . . ."

"Addictive?"

"Expensive," he said. "I need my stash to last."

"Ah." It's not like the kids back home didn't take meds, but Digby seemed to be on all the meds I'd ever heard of.

He bit into his burger. "My other favorite suspect is a retired principal named Kenneth Dale. But this guy, Dr. Schell, he's a better bet."

Digby pulled out a marked-up map of River Heights. "This red cross is Marina's house, the green ones are Schell's and Dale's houses, and the red lines are possible ways they might've driven away. Now, we could ask people who live in the area if they saw anything that night . . ."

"Please stop saying 'we.' I'm not knocking on random people's doors. I'm already tired just thinking about it," I said. "Besides, haven't the police already checked?"

"Yup. The police canvassed the neighborhood. Plus Marina's street is crescent-shaped, with a bank, convenience store, gas station, and library at the top of the crescent. They all have cameras. But since no photos or sketches were released, we can assume the cameras and the people didn't see anything . . . which works in our favor."

"How d'you figure?"

"Because now the cops need to get creative. And most cops are miserable paperwork drones who suck at being creative," Digby said. "They're probably just treading water,

25

hoping Marina's parents' investigators find something."

"Let me guess—you think you're gonna swoop in and solve the case for them," I said. "Superman complex?"

"Wouldn't this be a more interesting topic for our project?"

"I don't think anyone's gonna give us *any* grade for a detailed record of how we stalked and harassed random people . . . much less a good one."

"It doesn't have to be about the abduction itself. It could be a report on police procedure, say."

"That sounds even harder than the other fake project you made up."

"I'm telling you, it doesn't have to be as good as you're imagining. Steve will barely read it. Seriously."

I wiped off the ketchup blobs and looked at the map.

"What makes you think one of these guys kidnapped Marina?" I said.

"Kenneth Dale's a possibility because his house backs onto Marina Miller's. He'd fought with her dad about cutting down some trees and didn't have a confirmable alibi for that night," Digby said. "He was also forced into early retirement for sexually harassing a student."

"And Schell's a better bet than that? This Dale guy sounds like a total creep."

"Schell lives three blocks away, but neighbors said his car was parked outside the Millers' that night and was gone by morning. He claimed his car was leaking oil, he didn't want it staining his driveway, and that the space in front of the

Miller house was the only one for blocks," Digby said. "He also doesn't have a confirmable alibi for that night."

"Sounds like a coincidence . . ."

"Another coincidence is that Marina's parents didn't know she was Schell's patient."

"How do *you* know?"

"Let's just say that the way I found out was less wrong than his not telling the police she was his patient," he said. "But what interests me is that no alien fingerprints were found in the bedroom except for a whole lot of blurred ones."

"How's *that* a clue?"

"Eight years ago, just like Marina, a little girl was taken from her bedroom in the middle of the night while the rest of the house slept. No one heard or saw anything. No one knew she was gone until morning." He passed me a fingerprint analysis report and pointed at the notes. "All they found were the family's prints and the blurred prints on the windowsill."

"Blurred prints aren't clues . . . they're the absence of clues."

"But these aren't prints that got smudged. Look, they're perfectly finger-shaped. The prints are blurred on the fingers themselves."

"Like that one serial killer who burned off his fingerprints with acid." He had me going now—I couldn't believe I was getting sucked in. "Okay . . . so this is all interesting and Nancy Drew–ish, but I still don't see—"

"Some medical conditions cause blurry fingerprints, but those conditions rarely affect all the fingers," he said. "Some people get it from their jobs. Guitarists who don't use picks, people working in laundries that use phosphates, housepainters who don't wear gloves, or . . . medical professionals who wash their hands so much, they smooth out the ridges of their fingerprints."

"Schell . . ." I said. "Mom's gynecologist might be a murderer?"

"Well, technically, we don't know for sure that Marina's dead. Not yet, anyway."

It sounded big-league. "I don't think we should . . ."

But Digby wasn't paying attention to me anymore. He was looking at a table of five boys. They were a weird-looking bunch. The youngest kid's feet didn't touch the floor, and the eldest had stubble. None of them looked alike enough to be related. It didn't make sense that they were together. In their prairie folk plaid shirts and high-waisted flannel pants, they looked like an agricultural glee club.

Digby cocked his chin at them. "They live in the mansion across from you."

"They do?"

The eldest wore red plaid and the others were in blue plaid. Red Plaid looked about twenty years old and was actually kind of a tall, dark, and handsome dude if you overlooked the creepy high and tight haircut he and the other kids all had. His shirt was a size too small and his sleeves looked like a bubbling bratwurst on the grill.

At that moment, the older boys were bullying the youngest to eat his pancakes faster. The little guy's face was covered in syrup.

"You're telling me you've never noticed them walking around in their little outfits?" he said. "Supposedly, they're a rapture cult, but they don't recruit in town or even online . . . which is weird. You really never noticed them before?"

"We just moved here."

"When there's an end-of-the-world cult living next door to you, make it your business to find out what they're up to," he said. "That's, like, a basic life rule."

"Well, I do see girls in prairie dresses constantly cleaning and scrubbing. And the place reeks of chemicals."

"Okay, so you did notice. Ever notice that the girls cleaning aren't always the same ones? They go, they come back . . . the boys do too. The kids are cycling through that house."

"Are they prisoners or something?"

"Who don't run away when they're unsupervised? Nah, it's something else."

The older boys ate the little guy's pancakes to clear his plate faster, but all that did was make him cry. The eldest in red plaid, clearly their leader, slid out of the booth and dragged the little guy out behind him.

"Oh . . . I get it," Digby said.

Digby took my soda and grabbed a mop from a bucket by a wait station, leaving a sudsy streak behind him as he dragged it outside the diner.

On the other side of the door, Digby slid the mop across the handles so when the boys in plaid tried to leave, the door wouldn't open. They piled up against the glass and pushed and pulled to rock the mop loose. No joy. It was stuck and so were they. Digby sipped my soda and watched the trapped boys get more and more frustrated. He had that bored expression again and it drove those boys crazy.

The diner's manager came out to see what the racket was all about. He grabbed two boys by the collar and steered them back to their table. Red Plaid pointed at Digby, mouthed the word *you,* and punched the glass door before following the manager.

Digby slid out the mop and walked back in behind them.

"That was nice," I said. "That poor waitress would've had to pay if they'd skipped out on their bill."

But Digby wasn't even looking at the angry waitress hawk-eyeing the boys.

"But I get the feeling you don't really care about her," I said. "So why *did* you do that?"

"Who knows? Fun?" Digby saluted Red Plaid.

The manager said something about calling the police and went into the back.

Red Plaid walked to our table. I slipped my butter knife onto my lap.

"Think you're smart, huh?" Red Plaid said.

"Smarter than you, at least," Digby said.

Red Plaid kicked over a chair behind him. "Someone oughta teach you to mind your own business."

He lifted Digby by the shirtfront and would've smashed Digby in the mouth, but another, even bigger hand clapped itself around Red Plaid's fist.

Digby's savior was a tall, muscle-bound, Disney Prince Eric

type I'd usually consider lame, but this guy had it working. He was hero handsome.

"Hey, Henry. Great timing as usual," Digby said.

"Digby. I heard you were back from Texas." Henry pushed Red Plaid away. "Pay your bill, never come back. Got me, dude?"

"Next time . . . it'll just be you and me," Red Plaid said to Digby. As he left, he slapped a glass of water off our table. It smashed into smithereens.

"He has a point. Aren't you worried he'll jump you on your way home?" I said.

"Not today—I'll wait until the cops come before I take off," Digby said.

"And after today?" Henry said.

"I'll worry about it after today," Digby said.

Clearly, Digby wasn't going to introduce us.

"I'm Henry Petropoulos." Petropoulos. Like an actual Greek god. "My parents own this diner." This explained his apron and soapy elbows.

"I'm Zoe Webster. Digby and I are partners on a school project."

"She wouldn't want you to think we were on a date or anything," Digby said.

"I wouldn't want *anybody* to think we were on a date." I was surprised I had that answer lined up. Bonus: Henry laughed.

Henry saw the file folders on the table. "Damn. You're doing this again, Digby?"

"It's not 'again' if I never stopped," Digby said.

"And now you're dragging her into it?" Henry said.

"No one's dragging me into anything—"But I might as well have been a piece of furniture.

"I never dragged *you* into anything, Henry," Digby said.

"No, you just made it impossible to be around you if I didn't do what you wanted me to," Henry said.

"Tell your mom the cheeseburgers are even better than before. I don't know about shoestring fries, though, I liked the crinkle cuts," Digby said. "But then, I'm a classic kind of guy."

Henry knew he was being dismissed. "Whatever, dude." To me, he said, "Digby's a good guy and he doesn't mean to do it. He never means to do it. But if you're gonna hang with him, look out for yourself, because he won't remember to look out for you. Nice meeting you, Zoe."

Digby didn't look up at Henry waving and walking away.

"So—medical professional, parked outside her house on the night she disappeared . . . my money's on Schell," Digby said. "Speaking of money . . . you got any?"

"Not enough to cover both of us."

"Know what? That's okay—in fact, keep it. Catching a dine-and-ditch has gotta be good for a free meal."

"Wait. You sat down to eat knowing you couldn't pay? That's crazy."

"I knew something would turn up. Lookit, you came along."

"But I can't pay for both of us."

"And you don't have to because *this* came along."

Later, when I knew him better, I realized there was no point having this kind of conversation with Digby. We lived in different universes. What-if scenarios that bothered normal people never rattled him because for Digby, there were too many close calls to worry about.

"What's the deal with Henry?" I said.

"You're not his type. He's a typical varsity QB . . . he likes them blond and top-shelf generic," Digby said. "And he probably has a girlfriend—he always does. Even in kindergarten he had one. Henry brings the girls to the yard. Know what I mean?"

"What? I didn't mean that. I meant, what's the deal with *you* and Henry."

"Oh, that." Digby looked sad. "We used to be friends. A long time ago."

"And now?"

"Now I don't bother with friends. Better to travel light."

I wasn't sure if I minded that he didn't think I was friend enough to be considered baggage.

FOUR

A few days later, he messaged. "Meet 4pm parking lot ur moms gyn." Rude. I didn't answer even though I knew he could see I'd read his message. I didn't intend on meeting him. I'd just microwaved popcorn and I had a stack of magazines.

Then I realized that although he took up so much mindspace, I didn't know anything about Digby. I hadn't even googled him, which was weird because I google everything.

I'd typed in *Digby* before I discovered I didn't know his first name. *Digby* and *River Heights* was the best I could do. I thought I'd get a million random hits, but instead, I got these: "Sally Digby: Abducted!" "River Heights Girl Vanishes in the Night," and "Day 54, No Ransom, No Clues: Sally Digby Feared Dead."

Whoa. Not what I'd expected. I read the articles in order. This is how it went down.

In the middle of the night eight years ago, four-year-old Sally disappeared from the bedroom she shared with her older brother, Philip Digby. The police had problems gathering evidence because she'd had her fourth birthday party earlier and there were prints and footprints all over the house and yard. A change of clothes had been taken from her dresser. No one in the house, including Digby in the bunk above her, had awakened. No signs of forced entry. Neighbors and party guests were questioned but eventually, the police focused their investigation on the family.

It was revealed that the father had gambling debts and a mistress. Then the police shifted focus to the mother, who had lapsed in taking medication for her bipolar disorder. One expert suggested seven-year-old Digby might have killed his own sister, accidentally or maybe because he was jealous after the party, and his parents were covering it up. That theory had been good for a few headlines, but the newspapers eventually dropped Sally's story entirely.

The photos in the papers were a slide show of Digby's family falling into hell. It started with the party in the sunny backyard and ended with Digby's mother on a gurney after she'd collapsed. After seeing that, ignoring his message felt mean.

It took three tries to write Mom a note that wasn't as much pants-on-fire lying as it was just devoid of any real information about where I was going.

When I arrived, Digby was on a bench outside the doctor's building, eating a sloppy meatball sub. Even though I hadn't answered his message, he seemed unsurprised to see me.

"I got you cookies," he said.

"I'm not a cookie fan."

"You ate, what, seven of Steve's."

"But I'm not hungry now."

"You're in luck, Aldo. She's not hungry." Digby threw the bag of cookies at a homeless guy standing near us. "You remember what to do?"

Aldo nodded and dug into the cookies.

Digby pointed at a billboard looming over us that said: RIVER HEIGHTS—WE'RE A FAMILY PLACE. It showed a poster-perfect nuclear family with a boy and a daddy playing catch and a girl and her mommy setting the picnic table.

"'Family place' is 1930s lingo for no Jews, no gays, and no black people. Tells you everything you need to know about the people running this town that they kept it even though it's eighty years old and River Heights is, like, thirty percent not white now," Digby said. "Makes me wanna burn this whole place down."

"Uh . . . speaking of arson and other crimes, just to be clear, I'm not doing anything dangerous . . . or illegal."

"Define *do*."

"I'm not stealing anything, or using any kind of weapon or making threats—"

"Relax, you won't have to do any of that. You'll still get into your prissy-priss academy."

"Prentiss. The Prentiss Academy," I said. "You promise?"

"I promise you won't have to *do* anything more than just come with me."

"But I don't understand what you want from me."

"I need a look at this Schell guy, and since I clearly have the wrong plumbing . . ." he said. "How good are your improv skills?"

++++

Digby marched up to the receptionist. "Hello. My girlfriend and I are gonna have sex and we need to ask Dr. Schell about birth control."

I almost died. The look the receptionist gave us reminded me of when Grandma called her neighbor a dirty bird for peeing in the hydrangeas. Actually, the entire waiting room of women was giving us that look.

"Well, there's been a cancelation and I can squeeze you in for a fifteen-minute consultation. But only a consultation— no procedures," the receptionist said.

"We won't take long," Digby said. "We got the basics in Health. Just wanna confirm some details with an expert . . . can't believe everything on the interwebs, amiright?"

The receptionist frowned at *me*. Why *me*?

"Tips . . . techniques . . . whatnot," Digby said.

Why was *everyone* staring at me? The words were coming out of Digby's mouth.

"Yes, yes, all right," the receptionist said. "Sit down, fill in these forms, and I'll call you when it's your turn."

I took the forms and we sat down. For some reason, Digby was humming loudly.

"Should I use our real names?" I said.

"Doesn't matter, nerd. Leave it." Digby's feet stomped a beat and his hands slapped his armrests. Pretty soon, he was half singing and full-body-bopping an elaborate rhythm.

The receptionist sighed loudly to make it clear she was annoyed.

"Song in my head," Digby said. "Don't you hate that? It's stuck. Dad-dad-dad-da-dee-dee-dee-dee . . . it's SO *obnoxious!*"

He was shouting and the receptionist had to work hard not to listen to what she was hearing. The other women in the waiting room did likewise to avoid encouraging Digby's crazy. Digby got up and danced across the back of the room. Because everyone was refusing to make eye contact, no one saw him hit the PANIC button on the security alarm keypad.

The alarm was like a million harpies screeching out of sync. The place exploded. Everyone jumped to their feet. I knew where the sound was coming from and even I thought my heart was going to blow out of my chest.

Schell ran in yelling. He and the receptionist fought as she punched in the alarm code. They were so angry with each other that neither wondered what triggered it in the first place.

"What the hell, Digby?" I said.

Digby whispered, "One-two-one-three-one-zero. One-two-one-three-one-zero."

Before I could process that, the receptionist said Schell was ready for us.

Despite all the sex talk in my house in the last year while the divorce proceedings were in full swing, my own experience with sex was nonexistent. I hadn't even been to a gynecologist's office before.

On the long walk to the exam room, we passed posters like HOW TO TELL A NEW PARTNER YOU HAVE A SEXUALLY TRANSMITTED DISEASE and DON'T PANIC!: WHAT TO DO WHEN YOUR CONDOM BREAKS. When I saw the exam table with stirrups you put your feet into so your knees stuck straight up, I thought, God, I promise to stay a virgin, just please don't let anyone probe me.

"What can I do for you?" Schell said.

There was something creepy behind the suburban dadness of Schell's first impression. If he were ever found with corpses in his freezer, people would say *I knew it*. He was so pink and moist. Of course, it's possible that Digby's paranoiac distrust of everyone was contagious.

"The school nurse isn't allowed to give us the talk anymore, so . . ." Digby said.

"Surely your parents—" Schell said.

"No, I mean the talk about different things we can use, not the classic sex talk," Digby said.

Schell's eyes goggled at me out of his sweaty bald head. There were beads of sweat on his upper lip too, which was weird because the room was chilly.

"You mean contraceptives?" Schell said.

"Yeah—what we could use in addition to condoms. A pill just to make sure?" Digby said.

"She could go on a low-dose—"

"She's got a seizure disorder, so maybe you could check if it'd interact with her anticonvulsant."

"These are widely prescribed—"

"We'd be more comfortable if you checked."

39

"Anyway, you'll have to come back. I can't write the scrip without insurance information, parental consent, an internal exam . . . and I don't have time today."

Internal exam. I didn't like the sound of that.

"Please, Doc. If you'd just look it up real quick," Digby said. "But, you know . . . *now*."

Schell looked annoyed but went to his computer anyway. Digby stood behind him, spitting out questions. Thrombosis? Weight gain? Hair loss?

Digby seemed even more wired than usual and kept checking the time. A minute into this weird charade, we heard a loud wail. Most of it was garbled, but what was audible was disturbing.

"Mafawashee . . . you killed my baby . . . !"

Schell ran out of the room, cursing. Digby immediately jammed a USB key into the computer, about to type, when I pointed out a key logger plugged into it.

"Why does a gynecologist need a key logger?" I said.

"Or a cell signal jammer, but he has one of those in reception too." Digby removed the key logger.

"Get off that."

"Close the door," he said, already typing. "I can get into his patient records, but not these encrypted files. I'll clone them and decrypt later."

I was in a bind. Close the door and help him rip off Schell's files or leave the door open and get caught sooner. I would later recognize this as a textbook Digby lose-lose scenario.

I closed the door.

"Finish what you're doing or stop—I don't care which. Just get off that computer."

"Take it easy." Digby ejected the USB and clicked back to the webpage Schell had been on. I put back the key logger. "Hey, check *this* out." He climbed onto the exam table, leaned on the stirrups, and reached for a ceiling-mounted camera.

"It's for training med students." I pointed at a sign that said so with a highlighted note that CAMERA IN OPERATION WHEN GREEN LIGHT IS ON.

"The angle's weird. It'd film the patient but not the med student."

"That doesn't make sense," I said. Digby waited a second for the penny to drop. "He's filming patients . . . ?" Patients like Mom.

"What's this?" Digby reached out again but lost his balance and somersaulted off the exam table. He pulled the camera off its mount on his way down, leaving it dangling by its wires, and causing a huge racket.

God, we're dead. Any second Schell would rush back in. I panicked. I bolted out the door into the waiting room, where I barely registered that Schell was arguing with Aldo, the homeless guy Digby was talking to outside. "Hey, girlie, where your cookies at?" Aldo said as I ran past him.

I ran out the door and kept running for blocks. When Digby finally caught up to me, I was sitting on a bench, panting.

"So . . . that wasn't suspicious or anything," Digby said.

Reader, I hit him. Hard. In the gut.

"Okay . . . I deserved that. Although, thanks for not hitting me in the nads."

"You realize Schell's gonna call the cops on us," I said.

"That's a good punch . . . definitely useful," Digby said. "Schell's not calling the cops. He doesn't even know who we are. Besides . . ." Digby held up a little black square.

"What's that?"

"Electrical tape I peeled off the camera," Digby said. "It was covering the little green LED that lights up when the camera's on. He's filming patients without telling them, so I doubt he'll call the cops."

"That guy . . . Aldo? You paid him to do that?"

"You didn't really think the timing of that was a coincidence, did you, Princeton?" Digby spat out brown-red stuff.

"Is that blood?"

"Meatball marinara. You kinda rearranged my lunch when you hit me . . ." he said. "Nah . . . he won't call the cops. Question is, should *we*?"

"With what? All you have is a piece of tape which, *hello*, isn't even on the camera anymore," I said.

"Yeah . . . yeah . . . you're right. Of course we can't call them now, but I'll bet we can after I get into these encrypted files." He scribbled in his notebook. "We should definitely go back for another look."

This time, I did hit him in the nads.

FIVE

Obviously my mother couldn't go back to Schell. But Mom isn't big on confronting reality, not even when it's right in front of her face. For days, I worried about it, saddled with the whole burden of knowing.

This wasn't new for me. I'd had to do it before—with my father's cheating. I'd figured it out one day, when I was doing laundry and it just came to me, apropos of nothing, that my father was having an affair. It wasn't like any one particular thing had given him away, it was just a lot of little things. Once it occurred to me, I was sure divorce was inevitable, and for months, I had insomnia, waiting for them to tell me. Months later, when I realized that no divorce was coming, a new waiting game started. This time, I waited for my mother to catch up with me. But when more months passed, it finally dawned on me that Mom and Dad were both lying, and to the same person: Mom.

I couldn't believe it. I watched her go about her life, oblivious, until every mundane thing she did irked me. I mean, yes, Dad was a dirtbag. It wouldn't even surprise me if he'd been cheating *on* Shereene the whole time he'd been cheating *with* her. But he knew what he was about and I could respect that at least. Mom chose to ignore reality. She was a coward.

††††

The next day, I was raking leaves before school, mulling this over, when I saw Red Plaid from the diner exit the mansion across the street. Some boys in blue plaid followed him. As usual, girls in prairie dresses were in the driveway with buckets of disgusting-smelling cleaning fluids. None of the boys were scrubbing, I noticed.

"Typical," I said.

The boys piled black garbage bags into a van parked in the driveway. One hotshot kid swung his bag over his head before throwing it in. The loud crunch of glass got him boxed in the ear by Red Plaid. When he readjusted the bag, I saw it had a BIOHAZARD MEDICAL WASTE logo.

"That's weird," I said.

"*Totally* weird," Digby said.

I jumped and jerked the rake so hard, it threw a puff of leaves in the air. I hadn't heard him come up behind me.

"They're supposedly running an herbal tea business." Digby was eating one apple and holding a second. "Medical waste? Definitely weird."

"You scared me. What are you doing here?"

"I thought we'd walk to school together. What are you raking for? This is upstate New York. It'll rain leaves until November."

There was already a carpet of freshly fallen leaves where I'd just raked.

"You're crazy coming here. That guy's gonna kill you," I said.

Luckily, Red Plaid walked back into the mansion without seeing Digby.

"The Twelfth Tribe Tea Company. And you know what's really weird? There's no mortgage on that mansion," he said. "They blew into town four years ago and paid cash. This is America—who pays cash?"

"It's a cult. They probably confiscated their members' money. Anyway, how'd you find out about their mortgage?"

"It's online. All you need's a real estate agent's login."

"And you have one of those because . . . ?"

"It's a long story involving a box of donuts, a cup of coffee with a loose lid, and the rule that there's no such thing as a free lunch."

"I'm making a mental note to never use a computer around you."

I guess Red Plaid saw us from the window, because he stalked out of the mansion, doing the corny roll-up-the-sleeves-to-fight move. Except, because he was doing it to beat us up more effectively, it seemed a lot less corny.

Digby put his apples on my mailbox and took something—I couldn't see what—from his pocket that he gripped in his closed fist.

"Get that punch of yours ready," Digby said. "I don't think he wouldn't hit you just because you're a girl."

Red Plaid didn't bother with the usual opening threats. There was no pose-down. He just ran up and hit Digby in the face. Digby went down. Instead of getting back up, Digby waited for Red Plaid to come closer and kicked Red Plaid's shin. It was Red Plaid's turn to go down and as soon as he hit the ground, Digby straddled him. They did what sounded like mostly open-handed slap-fighting, but somewhere in there, Digby landed two hard punches on Red Plaid's face.

Red Plaid managed to kick Digby off him just as his gang of plaid shirts poured out of the mansion. I should've called 911, but I ran into the garage and got a tire iron instead. My ears buzzed with adrenaline, and, jacked up as I was, I seriously believed our two could take their six.

"Quit hiding behind your girlfriend and fight me like a real man," Red Plaid said.

"*Real man*? What, you learned English from a comic book?" Digby said. "And I'm not hiding. Come at me. See what happens."

I swung the tire iron from side to side, thinking, Do I even know how to fight? But I never found out because as the plaid shirts closed in, a huge amazon came out of the mansion. She was wearing a floor-length black dress and her thin black hair was pulled back in a tiny tight bun.

"*Ezekiel!*" she shouted.

All the fight instantly went out of Red Plaid, whose name was apparently Ezekiel. The amazon took her time crossing the street. Even though hostilities were clearly canceled, my grip on the tire iron tightened as she approached. We were all scared of her.

"Have you completed your chores? It's almost eight o'clock," she said.

She was taller than all of us, even Ezekiel, who was at least six feet. She made him look like a sulky preschooler when she grabbed his chin and looked at the shiner that was already coming in.

"Young man, I could call the police and have you charged with assault with a weapon," she said to Digby.

"I'd hardly call my lunch money a weapon." Digby revealed the roll of quarters his fist was wrapped around. "Good luck telling the story of how I got your boys to cross the street for me to assault them. I mean, they're dumb, but is anyone that dumb?"

The amazon stared. I was sure she was making some awful calculation about what size boxes she'd need to stash our bodies.

Digby resumed his apple consumption, reaching past the amazon to casually photograph the mansion's windows with his phone.

Then I noticed her. A crying girl wearing a prairie dress, peeking out of an upstairs window. She was there just a second. Digby got two shots before an arm yanked the girl out of sight. She was gone by the time the amazon turned to look.

"Back in the house. This instant," the amazon said.

As they were leaving, Mom came out of our house. "Zoe! Gotta go, babe! I gotta copy handouts for my class. Oh, hello . . . !"

My adrenaline was still pumping, but there wasn't so much of it that I wasn't embarrassed by her reaction to seeing Digby.

Mom asked, "Who's this?" What her expression said but her mouth didn't was: "Zoe likes a boy!" Luckily, though, Mom's from the MTV generation and has the attention span to prove it. "My tire iron! I thought I'd lost it in the move," Mom said.

Never mind the huge red welt on Digby's cheek or the leaves stuck all over his suit. Never mind that my trembling hands were still gripping the tire iron like a baseball bat.

Mom offered Digby a ride to school and I sat there, my adrenaline rush wearing off, listening to them chat about how great it was living in River Heights. "*Blah-blah-blah* great school system *blah-blah-blah* yoga at the community center."

I pondered almost getting killed on my own lawn and the fact that in addition to needing to tell Mom about Schell, I needed to tell her about our pissed-off neighbors who'll now probably murder us in our sleep.

I wished Mom would ask some nosy parent questions already so we could get it over with, but when we got to school she, oblivious as ever, just waved good-bye and drove off to work.

SIX

As far as I could figure, Mom's obliviousness was a defense mechanism that went into overdrive toward the end of her marriage, when Dad didn't even care enough to hide the fact that he and his assistant shared a room on business trips. That all ended, though, when Dad brought Shereene home not knowing Mom and I were in the basement. From the way Shereene banged around upstairs and complained about our still-broken espresso machine, it was clear she'd hung out at our place before. A lot.

When Dad and Shereene went up to the bedroom, Mom went upstairs and threw Dad out of the house. He moved out for real soon after. Mom had no choice. She couldn't pretend anymore because now she knew I knew she knew, if you get my drift.

You'd think after all that, Mom would've dropped the obliviousness act, but old habits die hard. Madam, your daughter seems to be getting into fistfights. Oh, really? Then I should tweet about gelato. Which is what Mom did that lunchtime.

And speaking of embarrassing me on social media, I realized I should create new accounts before friending people at River Heights. If anyone *did* friend me, that is. So far, all I had going was Digby.

Speaking of whom, here he was coming to sit with me. Digby's tray was piled high with two of everything the cafeteria served. "So, are you aware that fries count as a vegetable?"

"What? In *wonderful* River Heights with the *wonderful school system* and *wonderful clean sidewalks and community center*?" Listening to him kiss up to Mom had really annoyed me.

"I was just being nice to Liza, Princeton. Try it sometime."

"Don't assume I'm not nice to my mom. You don't know my life."

"No, but I do know your mom's scared you're lonely. This morning she was so happy to see you with a friend, she ignored the fact that we were mixing it up with the neighbors in the yard."

"You don't know what you're talking about. She didn't notice jack."

"Didn't you see how fast she snatched that tire iron out of your hands? In the car on the way here, she almost hit that guy on the bike because she was staring into the rearview mirror at the bruise on my face," he said. "And I saw her phone. She'd dialed 911 but just hadn't hit CALL yet. She noticed a lot more than you think."

Last thing I needed was this guy telling me about my own mother. I was silent. I noticed that the red welt on his face had darkened into a rosy bruise. It was brutish, which, strangely, made him look kind of . . . good?

"So, it's a boarding school?" he said, changing the subject.

"Prissy-priss academy? Sounds like a boarding school. Little Harry Potter gowns, hats, all that jazz . . ."

"Yeah, but I'll be a day girl and live at my dad's. He and his wife live close by."

"Bet your mom loves that."

"She wants me to get into a good college."

"What's the step situation? Step*mom* or step*mother*? They have kids? Is it a Cinderella situation?"

"No."

"Will they be having any?"

"Dunno. She's young and pretty. She won't want to get fat."

"Ah . . . the fairest of them all . . . potential Snow White situation," he said. "Sounds like a happy scene."

After sitting alone in the cafeteria for weeks, a fresh start anywhere but here sounded like freaking bliss.

"Anyway, yes, I knew they count fries as a vegetable," I said. "But did you know some school boards count ketchup as a vegetable too?"

"Wow, then I'm in luck." He opened a pack of ketchup and squeezed the entire thing straight onto his tongue. "I can get my five-a-day this way."

"That's vile. You don't even need someone to dare you to do that?"

"This kind of stunt's supposed to win friends. Try it some-time for, you know, better lunchtime conversation," he said. "Find the girl-world version, though. The popular girls here are stuck-up."

Digby pointed with his arm fully outstretched so the girls

would see he was talking about them. One girl said, disgusted, "Oh, my God."

"I don't see it working for you," I said.

"But you're new—they don't know what you are yet. There's hope for you," he said. "Me? I'm a known quantity. Kind of an untouchable. Doesn't matter what cool tricks I pull."

"Won't I turn into an untouchable too, if I hang around you?"

"This town's beef with me is pretty specific. I don't think it's contagious."

"Maybe it's the suit. You look like an undertaker."

"I'm sure it doesn't help."

"Seriously, what's with the suit? I mean, you wear it all the time. Is it the same suit every day?"

"It's a housekeeping thing."

"It doesn't fit."

"I like it roomy."

In the five minutes since sitting down, Digby had plowed through his meatloaf, which he stuck between Texas toast with handfuls of fries and, you guessed it, more ketchup. Then he ate two sad little fruit cups of brown-green grapes on half a canned peach.

"And what's the story with all the food? You're always eating, but you're so freaking skinny still," I said. "Do you run marathons on the weekends? Is there some kind of worm issue?"

Digby sucked down his juice box until it went supernova into a tiny cardboard ball. "It's a housekeeping thing."

"What does that even mean?"

"Heads up," Digby said.

Musgrave appeared. "Mr. Digby, Ms. Webster." He said the *Ms.* with a hard *Z* to make sure I knew he didn't like me either. "Working hard on your independent study?"

"You know, Harlan, I find working lunches distract me from the fine culinary offerings of our hardworking kitchen crew. I understand Jojo and Barb worked especially hard on reheating today's meatloaf." Digby folded an entire bear claw into his mouth and smiled.

"You call me *Mr. Musgrave.*" He slapped away the second pastry Digby was holding. "And *surprise,* smarty-mouth, your project needs *two* faculty members to grade it, and guess who just signed up to do it."

My stomach took a dive.

"Now, I don't know how you've conned your way this far into your academic career, but I can tell you that streak is over." Musgrave didn't care that people were staring. He pounded on our table, his neck-rolls bright red and bulging out of his collar. "That's right. December twenty-first, last day of the semester, I expect to see that report typed up on my desk or I personally get to add an F to your transcripts. See this?" Musgrave's index finger made a pressing motion over and over. "That's me hitting the F key on my keyboard."

An F on my transcript. I was going to vomit.

"Well, we'll try not to disappoint you, *Mr.* Musgrave." Digby gave him an extra-wide smile.

Musgrave swiped at the apple Digby was now holding but Digby saw him coming and pulled back so Musgrave's hand instead hit a carton of chocolate milk. One huge gush fell on my computer's keyboard and an arc of chocolate milk splashed across Musgrave's suit. Some kids slow-clapped. Musgrave grabbed some napkins from Digby's tray and ran out, cursing and wiping the front of his suit.

"Wait until he realizes there's a bunch of gravy some-where in those napkins," Digby said.

I tipped chocolate milk out of my keyboard. Maybe it would be fine.

"That's why I keep all my important stuff in this." Digby waved his little black notebook. "Any idea how many times I've spilled chocolate milk on this?"

"Teachers can't pick on students. That's harassment," I said. "Or assault . . . he hit you."

"Bet he rehearsed that whole shakedown in the mirror."

"Why does he hate you so much?"

"Told you. People in this town have a beef with me."

"I don't get that. You're the victim."

I froze. I couldn't believe I'd said that.

He'd frozen too.

"Digby, I'm so sorry . . . I was googling and . . ."

"You know what? Don't even worry about it. Small town, big story, you were bound to find out."

"I didn't mean to—"

"Bygones. Anyway, some FBI profiler told the media that in many disappearance cases, a family member's involved. The cops couldn't make that stick to any of us, so everyone here thinks we've gotten away with something," Digby said. "Musgrave was an actual cop back then. The night Sally disappeared, he was assigned to watch me. He took me to my parents' room, turned on the TV, gave me M&M'S, and went through the closets—illegal search, by the way. I was seven, but I knew that, so I told on him." Digby bit his apple as if that were the end of the story.

"Then what happened?"

"Well. To this day, I can't eat M&M'S without gagging . . . which is sad, because I used to love them," Digby said. "Speaking of shakedowns . . . check it out. Behind you."

Digby had completely moved on to the next thing. I turned. "I don't see anything."

"Beside the table of cheers."

Dominic Tucker and Felix Fong were the only people at the table by the cheerleaders. Dominic was a moron football player who shaved his number into his hair. He howled *"Aggro!"* (as in *aggressive*) after huddles and before every swirlie or atomic wedgie he gave some poor nerd. Felix Fong was one such nerd. Felix was the school genius whose parents thought they were doing him a favor by skipping him three grades. I heard he audited a college Electrodynamics course. I googled *electrodynamics* and ended up even more confused.

"Not exactly big news. Jock bullying nerd in cafeteria," I said.

"Except that's not what's happening," Digby said.

"What are you talking about? He's practically sitting on poor Felix Fong, who looks like he's crapped his pants."

"I mean that's not *all* that's happening. Bullies like an audience. This conversation's way too quiet."

Meanwhile, my computer screen went white, then black.

"Oh, *no*! I just got this," I said. "It's fried. What are the chances Musgrave will pay for this?"

Digby barely looked my way. He was watching Dominic and Felix. "Zero."

"What are the chances he'll give me an F if I complain to the principal?"

"Like, a hundred percent. But you might as well since he's gonna fail you anyway because you're partners with me."

"That's just great. So what about my computer?"

Dominic left Felix looking miserable.

"Yeah, this is definitely something else," Digby said. "Oh, and . . . I was about to tell you this morning, when the Children of the Corn jumped us. I read Schell's records. Guess what? Marina saw him right before she disappeared."

"Shouldn't you tell the police? You know . . . plus that stuff about blurry fingerprints?"

"Not yet. But we should get back in there to take another look."

"Whatever, dude. Told you. I'm not going back. He wants to do an exam on me and no way *that's* happening."

"We won't be going back during office hours this time."

"Yeah, right." Then I realized he was serious. "Hell, no."

Felix got up.

"Okay—gotta go." Digby grabbed his tray and got up.

"Where are you going?"

"Take care of some business. I'll pick you up at your place."

"I'm not going with you," I said.

"Okay, great, see you at eight," he said.

SEVEN

I admit it. I was a little happy that Digby was clearly unstoppable in his idiotic plan to break back into Schell's office. It left me no choice but to go to the one person who'd know how to talk him out of it. Henry.

True, I could've told Mom or even Please-Call-Me-Steve, who went around practically begging students to "share," but Mom would've just freaked and called the cops, and no one ever got good guidance from a guidance counselor.

And, yeah, I might've taken a little extra time getting dressed and I totally took three tries at my eyeliner before I went back to Olympio's, but what can I say? Digby was right about Henry bringing all the girls to the yard.

Henry was refilling salt and pepper shakers when I got there. It was empty except for two girls, who were giggling and pretending to read the menu but were actually flirting with Henry. I recognized them from civics. The blonde was Sloane Bloom.

I later found out from Digby that Sloane's family was practically county royalty. Her parents were pillars-of-the-community rich and her father's a real estate developer who stuck a picture of himself on every building he owned or managed. Digby said it was back-door publicity for his congressional campaign.

Sloane herself was a big deal in school because she'd modeled in New York City and had actually booked a zit cream advertorial in *Seventeen*. She and her posse were the kind of girls who "practiced" their cheerleading cartwheels in the mall and then complained when boys stared at their asses when their uniforms rode up. See what I mean? They were easy to hate.

That day in Olympio's, she looked murderous when Henry stopped what he was doing to talk to me. She and I were in hate at first sight.

"Let me guess. He's gotten you in trouble," Henry said.

"Not yet, but I'm pretty sure what he's planning for tonight will," I said.

"Nah, it's too late: You care. You're on Planet Digby now. You're already in trouble."

"If I tell you something, promise not to tell anyone?"

"See? Secrets. Trouble." Henry held up his hands. "I shouldn't get involved."

"I just need advice."

Henry sat down in a booth with me. "I don't think Digby would appreciate it if he found out you were talking to me about him. We have some history, you know."

"He said."

"But did he tell you what happened?"

"About his sister? Sort of . . . plus, I read some stuff online. Is that what you mean?"

"That and a whole lot else," he said. "The police tore that family apart. Before his parents finally split, the three of them sat around at breakfast, wondering if one of the others did something to Sally. Digby basically lived at my house."

"So what happened with you two?"

Henry got up for some pie. I tried to act cool when he brought over one plate and two forks.

"They interviewed everyone. Digby had told me stuff about his mom that the police used against her. Digby assumed I was the one who told the police."

"And you weren't."

"Of course not. I knew what that'd do. You met his mom?"

"No."

"Val's . . . well, Val's cool, but when she goes off her meds . . . anyway, I think Digby's therapist was the one who told the police."

"Why didn't you just tell him that?"

"This therapist was pretty much the only adult Digby would talk to. If I'd told him she was selling him out . . . anyway, she ended up recommending to the court that Digby move to Texas with his dad . . . which is exactly wrong. Maybe I should've spoken up. By the time that happened, though, Digby wasn't talking to me anymore."

"What's wrong with Digby's dad?"

I glanced at Sloane watching me share the slice of pie with Henry. She was livid. It was the most delicious slice of pie I'd ever had in my life.

"He was a recovering alcoholic but he started drinking again when Sally disappeared. Maybe Digby never told his therapist that, but everybody could see."

"And telling Digby now that you didn't tell wouldn't help?"

"Digby's just spent five years in Texas with his angry alcoholic dad. What do *you* think?"

His jaw muscle clenching and unclenching was hypnotic.

"What's happening tonight?" he said.

"He wants to break into a gynecologist's office. He's convinced the guy had something to do with the girl who disappeared this summer."

"You mean Marina Miller? Digby knows something about Marina?"

Henry's phone rang. It was adorable he was embarrassed that "Can You Tell Me How to Get to Sesame Street?" was his ringtone. "My little sister picked it."

He read the message, gasped at the screen, and laughed. He turned to look at Sloane, who was giggling as she took her phone out from under her shirt. Henry got another message.

"I'm sorry, these girls are crazy." He actually blushed. "I'll delete these because you know, I don't need to be on some sex offender registry because I got sexted at."

"Heeeeeenry. It's your turn," Sloane said.

Henry shook his head, but he definitely looked interested.

Sloane and her friend started throwing fries at him.

"I gotta deal with this." He walked toward Sloane, picking up the trail of fries she'd thrown as he went.

"Wait! What do I do about tonight? He's picking me up at eight," I said.

"Where?"

"My house. One fifty-two Ashton."

"Henry! We're out of fries, so we might have to start throwing our burgers," Sloane said.

"I'll think of something," Henry said to me. Then to Sloane and her friend, he said, "Guys, stop throwing food around. I'm the one who's gonna have to clean up."

"Oh, boo, you're no fun." Sloane waited until Henry wasn't looking and flipped me the bird.

"That's classy," I said. It was a taste of things to come.

EIGHT

I tried not to act suspicious at dinner, but I was squirrely. I was becoming obsessed with the idea of Schell and his camera. I waited until my mom poured herself a glass of wine.

"So, um . . . I wanted to talk about Dr. Schell." There. I'd said it.

"Dr. Schell? My gynecologist?" she said. "Wait. Is this about that boy who picked you up before school today? Is he why you're so nervous?"

"Digby. Yeah, actually, it is kind of about Digby."

"Is he . . . pressuring you?"

"What?"

"You know, Zo, you shouldn't let people pressure you. Especially someone you've just met. Sometimes I worry you're too trusting. They say it's something I should look out for because children of divorce . . . and you know, you're the new girl . . . and you've never really been that confident . . ."

What the hell was she talking about? I'd lost control of

the conversation. "Mom. Shut up and listen to me."

Mom took a big drink of wine. "Sweetie, if you need to see Dr. Schell, I'm okay with it, but we should talk more before we go see him. Together. All three of us. Because it's important that, as your partner, Digby understands he has responsibilities too."

The idea of me and Digby. The idea of Mom imagining me and Digby. The idea of going to Dr. Schell with Mom. God. Classic Mom. She was trying so hard to confront reality that she was confronting the wrong reality. I shut the conversation down. We ate the rest of dinner in silence.

++++

Later that night, I sat on the steps outside my house. I'd gotten off the porch, gone back inside, and come back out twice already. The second time I came out wearing all black and a hoodie. By 8:15, it felt like I was daring myself to stay out on that porch for some reason I couldn't really name.

But I did really like my outfit.

++++

At 8:30, a crappy white Chevy Something stopped outside my house. I watched the driver grind the gears and do a sucky parallel parking job for a few minutes before I realized that, in fact, it was Digby driving. When he finally gave up, one front wheel was on the sidewalk and the butt of the car was sticking way out into the street. Digby got out and walked to my porch.

"No way. There's no way I'm getting in that car with you behind the wheel," I said.

"What?"

"What d'you mean, 'what'? Your driving is ridiculous. Even the car looks embarrassed."

"Do you suggest we take the bus home after breaking in?"

"I'm suggesting we don't break in at all."

"Let me show you something." He took a piece of paper from his pocket. "This was on Schell's computer. A list of his patients—some with numbers by their names. Including Marina Miller."

"Credit card numbers? Or something to do with their prescriptions . . ."

"Your mother's name has numbers next to it."

I grabbed the paper from him.

"It's not her Social Security number . . . and there aren't enough numbers for them to be credit cards," I said.

"We really need to get back in there."

"Or we could tell the police."

"You know if we did, it'll suddenly become about us— how'd you get this, are you aware that's a crime, *blah-blah-blah*. We should just go and—"

"This list probably doesn't mean anything. He's, like, one of two gynecologists in this dinky town. It's probably just a coincidence that my mom and Marina were both patients—"

"Digby!"

Digby and I both jumped when Henry emerged from behind some bushes, sweaty and panting.

"Oh, heeeey . . . Henry, I didn't know you were coming," Digby said.

"Of course you did—that's why you tried to run me over on Chestnut," Henry said.

"Oh, I'm sorry. I didn't know that was you," Digby said.

"I could hear you laughing in your car, bro."

"You can't stop me, Henry."

"What's this doctor got to do with Marina?" Henry took the list from me. "Marina's on this list . . . so's your mom. You think because Val's on this, he has something to do with Sally?"

"*Digby's* mom's on the list too?" I said.

"Stay out of this, Zoe. This has nothing to do with you," Henry said.

"Oh, but wait a second . . . this has something to do with you?" Digby said. "Why are you here, Henry? I know it's not because of me . . ."

Henry looked uncomfortable.

"It's not because of her." Digby pointed at me. "She's not your type. No offense, Princeton."

I hate when people use phrases like "no offense" right after they say the crappiest things to you.

"Oh, buuuuut . . . Marina's *exactly* your type. Senior girl. Niiiiice," Digby said. "Although, super-bleached-out hair, heavy eye makeup, push-up bra on picture day . . . minus ten points. Insecure girls are easy pickings."

"D'you mind? A little respect," Henry said. "Yeah, we went out. Just for a month. We broke up at the beginning of summer."

"What, she found out you still had a curfew?" Digby said.

"Something like that," Henry said. "Anyway, she went psycho on me. Texting, turning up at the diner. Then I get this crazy text from her telling me to suck it because she's hooked up with some guy with lots of money. She kept calling him a 'real man,' whatever that means. Kinda gave the impression the dude was older. She disappeared a month later."

"Whoa, you think it was Schell?" I remembered Schell's pink bald head. "Ewwww . . . he was so shiny and gross."

"You told the police?" Digby said.

"Sure. They said Marina's friends and family never heard of any rich guy. They said she probably made him up to get back at me. But I don't think that's true," Henry said. "Look, I'll come along. But leave Zoe out of it."

"Let her make up her own mind," Digby said.

"Yeah, I can make up my own mind," I said.

"So, you *are* coming?" Digby said.

"No. But not because of what Henry said," I said.

"Doesn't matter why. You should just stay home tonight," Henry said.

"Stop telling me what to do," I said.

"Yeah, you gonna let him tell you what to do?" Digby said.

"And can you stop being on my side, please?" I said.

"You don't need her to come. I'm coming," Henry said.

"If I let you come, you're not allowed to lecture me," Digby said.

"If you don't want me to lecture you, let me do the driving," Henry said.

"I don't get it. Suddenly, everyone's got a problem with my driving?" Digby said.

"After you jumped the curb and you tried—but failed—to run me over, you turned on your left turn signal and made a right," Henry said.

"What? That there was some good Texas driving," Digby said.

"Dude, seriously, you'd drive better if you were *actually* drunk," Henry said.

"Getting your mom to let you back the van into the loading dock doesn't make you a driving expert," Digby said.

"Got my license last month," Henry said. "Only way I'm going, Digby, is if I drive."

This was an argument Digby was only half interested in winning. He threw the keys to Henry.

"Fine. But I call shotgun," Digby said, pointing at me.

"Take it. I'm not coming," I said.

"She's not coming," Henry said.

"Of course she is," Digby said.

They walked to the car.

"She's coming." Digby held up his hand in Henry's face, fingers splayed. "I'm putting five on it."

Watching my parents squabble after Dad moved out, it annoyed me that they couldn't admit they missed each other. They fought about me, but really, I could've been a dog and the arguments would've been no different. Just kiss already, I used to think when I watched them. I thought the same thing watching Digby and Henry bickering on their way to the car. Just admit you've missed each other and kiss already. Sure, part of me wanted to go ride around town with them, but their bickering was seriously causing flashbacks. I'd heard enough bickering to last me a lifetime. *Nothing* could get me in that car.

Inside the house, Mom yelled, thinking I was still in my room, "Zoe! Wanna come to the Scrabble mixer with me?"

Except maybe *that*.

"Sorry, Mom, my friends are here!" I ran off the porch.

They were already pulling away when I opened the door and jumped in the car. Henry really hadn't thought I was coming and he slammed on the brakes, surprised.

"Welcome to the party, Princeton." Digby handed me a stick of gum and made a greedy gimme-gimme-gimme gesture in Henry's face until he slapped five bucks in Digby's hand.

NINE

The parking lot outside Schell's clinic was deserted.

"Stop here." Digby pointed at a chiropractor's office next door. "There's a camera behind that glass door. When it sweeps around, it captures everything from the parking spot next to us all the way to the entrance of Schell's office."

"So what are we supposed to do now?" Henry said.

"Princeton's gonna spray the chiropractor's camera." Digby held up a can of snow spray, the aerosol kind you use to decorate windows for Christmas. "It'll block out the camera's view."

"What? *Me?* Why me?" I said.

"You're the only one dressed for it." Digby flicked my top's hood.

"Uh . . . I'm not doing it. Let's go to Plan B," I said.

"There's no Plan B," Digby said.

"What were you gonna do if I didn't come?" I said.

"You were always gonna come," Digby said.

"This again," Henry said.

"There's no way you could've known I'd wear something that would hide my face," I said. "Do what you were gonna do if I hadn't."

"Sure I knew. Good girls like you hide when they do bad things," Digby said. "By the way, personal theory—you're not hiding your face from the world because you're afraid you'll get caught doing something bad. You're hiding your face from the world because you don't want the shame of anyone seeing how much you like it. Tell me I'm wrong."

"I'm not doing it. Think of another way," I said.

"It took hours to come up with this plan," Digby said.

"Shut up, you just came up with it right now. Rummage around that insane brain of yours and come up with another one," I said.

Digby pulled out his little black notebook and flipped to a flowchart titled: "Plans for Break-in." The first box in the chart had my name in it with an arrow to another box containing the words *spray fake snow on chiropractor door.* Written over the arrow were the words *good girl in disguise* and a little doodle of my face covered up with a Batman mask. He'd drawn a halo over my head.

"If it were raining I'd ask you for an umbrella, and if I'd cut myself I'd ask you for a Band-Aid," Digby said.

What could I say? I always kept a folding umbrella in my backpack. It was right by my first aid kit.

So I grabbed the snow spray from him.

"So you really just wear those diamond earrings every-where? What, did your dad tell you to?"

"Do you want me to do this or not?" I pulled up my hood and got out of the car.

++++

I was terrified. My heart raced and my feet felt like they were a thousand miles away from my brain. In fact, it took me a second to realize I'd tripped on the curb in front of the chiropractor's door and was lying facedown on the ground. I heard laughing coming from the car.

The snow spray rolled out of my hand and I barely stopped it from disappearing under a parked car. Of course, my first worry was that the security camera had filmed my face and I almost got whiplash stopping myself from reflexively looking up straight into the lens to make sure it hadn't. I stared at the ground and crawled to the door instead.

I heard the *pssht* of a soda popping open. I turned to see Digby offering Henry something from a little cooler. Who brings a picnic to a break-in? This fricking guy.

I pointed the can in the general direction of the camera and held down the nozzle. Digby hadn't said how much to put on, so I sprayed until the can sputtered out. Little flecks of the stuff went up my nostrils.

"Whoa . . . did I mention there were two cameras we needed to spray with that can?" Digby said.

"*No,* you sure didn't. The hell?" I'd used the whole can. Half of it had run down my arm.

"Kidding. You did good. You know, I actually thought it was gonna take a lot longer to convince you to go. I didn't think you had it in you," Digby said. "Maybe we can be bunk buddies in juvie."

"Yeah, great, so I can strangle you in your sleep." I wedged the can into one of my hoodie pockets.

"You can't recycle that," Digby said. "Just leave it."

"That's littering," I said.

"Uh, let's see . . . blocking a security camera before breaking and entering. Obstruction of justice? Tampering with evidence . . . Plus the actual breaking and entering, Juvie. You know, I think Juvie is catchier than Princeton."

"I probably shouldn't add littering to my rap sheet, then," I said.

"You realize good girls don't really go to heaven, right?" Digby said.

"Just let her keep it and let's go in before someone sees us. By the way, Digby, you couldn't have bought black spray paint? This is so . . ." Henry gestured at the clumps of snow spray on the door. "I mean, it's September, dude."

"Yeah, I guess black paint would've been less suspicious." Digby smiled. Clearly, the ridiculousness had been part of the plan.

"Yeah, ha-ha, you're funny. Come on. Let's get going," Henry said.

Digby tugged at Schell's door handle. Of course it was locked.

"Hey, you never know." Digby pointed at the sticker for the security company on the door. "Guy spends twelve grand on a state-of-the-art security system but puts a fifteen-dollar lock on the door. Total security theater."

Digby inserted a screwdriver's blade into the keyhole of

the lock assembly at the base of the door, hit the screwdriver with a small hammer, and punched out the lock barrel. Then he used the screwdriver to slide out the bolt, and the door swung open. As soon as he did that, though, a loud beeping started.

"Well, he's probably pretty confident no one would be dumb enough to break in. You know, seeing as how he has a twelve-thousand-dollar system," Henry said.

We stepped in and Digby closed the door behind us.

"Seriously, Digby, now what do we do?" Henry looked freaked out. I would've been freaked out too, if I hadn't watched Digby memorize the security code.

Digby punched in 1-2-1-3-1, then stopped, short the last digit. The beeping continued.

"So, why'd you break up with her?" Digby said.

"What?" Henry said.

"Marina didn't break up with you. She went crazy when you broke up with her. Why'd you break up with her?" Digby said.

"We didn't get along. Just put in the code. *Please*." Henry was trying to sound calm, but he was obviously panicking. Digby was loving it.

"Why not? She's exactly your type. She even looks like she enjoys those craptastic school dances you like so much. How'd you meet her, anyway?" Digby said.

Henry took a break from panicking and looked embarrassed. "She asked me to the Sadie Hawkins dance."

"Exactly," Digby said. "And why'd you break up with her at the beginning of the summer? You like your summer romances.

73

Fourth-grade summer, Laura Prescott. Fifth-grade summer, Beth Daniels. Sixth-grade, Jane Parker—"

"I wasn't ready to get serious," Henry said.

"What does that mean?" Digby said.

The beeps of the alarm had been getting louder and closer together the whole time Digby interrogated Henry. Now even I was freaking out, so I shoved Digby aside, pushed the last digit of the code, and hit ENTER.

"It means she wanted to have sex and he didn't. *God,*" I said. Henry looked shocked. "We're about to break into her gynecologist's office. What else could 'serious' mean? Now, can we do this already?"

"I wanted to hear him say it," Digby said.

We went to the exam room and Digby turned on a flashlight to scan Schell's desk. He flipped pages on the notepad, turned over the stapler, and did general thief-in-the-night stuff.

"It'd be faster if you told us what to look for," Henry said.

"We need his password to open those encrypted files I cloned," Digby said. "He's gotta have it analog-style somewhere . . . the guy's totally two-thousand-and-late."

"That's it?!" I was whisper-screaming, he made me so mad. "You made me break in here for a lousy password? We could've used decryption software from anywhere. I'm gonna kill you . . ."

Henry was already hunting around. "Doesn't matter. We're here. Let's just find it and get the hell out."

I started helping. "Put the stuff back the way you found it so it's not obvious someone's messed with his desk."

Digby's phone rang, but I was surprised when he answered a

phone I'd never seen before and, in a clipped voice said, "Yes, sir. Yes, sir . . ."

When I caught Henry's eye, he mouthed *His dad*.

Digby said, "Yes, sir, I read you five-by-five." When he noticed me gawping, he ducked out to finish the call.

"Five-by-five?" I said.

"His dad was air force . . ." Henry said. "You know, I wasn't, like . . . scared or anything. With Marina, I mean. We did other stuff. You know."

"Uh . . . *no*, I don't know," I said. "But that's okay. Don't feel like you have to describe it or anything."

He was quiet, but I could hear the little hamster running on the squeaky wheel in his brain as he relived the moment he just-said-no to Marina. The truth was, I was curious how far they'd gotten before Henry chickened out. *Stuff* sounded like something around third base, but before? Or after? Plus, there were a lot of stops between third and home . . .

Great. Now *my* hamster's on his wheel, I thought.

"What?" Henry said.

Or I thought I'd thought it. I guess I'd said it aloud.

"I just wanted it to be special. You know. My first time," Henry said.

I willed myself not to melt at how amazingly well he pulled off that sensitivity. "Uhhh . . . hey, look." I flipped over a statuette of Buddha holding a pointy staff. A strip of paper was taped to the base.

"X65*$$ . . . what's this?" Henry said. "Is this his password?"

I photographed it. "Who knows if it's *the* password, but it's *a* password."

"Why would you ever write down your password?" Henry said.

"That's what happens when you have too many secrets," I said.

My father had gotten careless too, when he was cheating. He'd left a pizza delivery receipt to a Jersey Turnpike motel in a sweater he knew I liked to borrow. When Mom found a tube of lipstick in the car, I had to let him tell her it was mine. It was a nasty orangey red that was worn to a point in the middle, like the person had applied it by sucking on it. Gross. The worst part of the whole cheating thing was how it forced my father to say and do the most weasely things. It was all so far beneath him.

"Maybe he has backup security," I said.

"Like what?" Henry said.

Tchak-tchak.

There's something about the sound of a shotgun racking that's so familiar even if you've never heard it in real life. It's like a rattlesnake rattle. True, that's something else I've never heard in real life, but my point stands. You just know to be scared. My butt puckered.

"Turn around. Don't try anything. I have a gun."

The lights came on. Schell was in the door holding a shotgun. We all just stared at one another in the stunning brightness for a long while before the next thing happened. When it happened, though, it happened fast.

First, Schell recognized me. "You! You're the kid with—"

76

Second, Henry threw the Buddha statue at him. It's never a good thing when a quarterback throws something at your face. Blood flowed right away.

Schell screamed. "You little bastard!"

Henry rushed at him but it was a long space, so Schell had time to step back out of the room and slam the door shut.

"I'll shoot through the door!" Schell said.

Henry and I froze and, before we could decide whether he actually would, Schell locked the door. We heard him call someone.

"Hey, it's me . . . I'm at work . . . some kids broke in," Schell said. "*Look.* They didn't just walk in, they had the alarm code . . . I don't know if *she* sent them, but the timing's interesting, don'tcha think? Just get your ass here and help me get rid of them. I can't do it alone, I'm hurt . . ."

Another long pause.

"Whatcha think I mean? *Get rid of them,*" Schell said.

Even I knew what he meant. Henry tried to call 911 on the office phone.

"I cut the phones, you punk-asses," Schell said.

I dialed my cell, but I'd forgotten he had a cell signal blocker.

"I got you, you little bastards," Schell said.

"Where's Digby?" Henry said. "You don't think . . ."

"We would've heard a shot," I said. "He left us."

It frightened me that Henry looked freaked out.

"Wow. I'm hurt," Digby said.

We couldn't find where his voice was coming from. It took a second to realize Digby was in the drop ceiling, looking

77

down from a gap he'd made by moving a ceiling tile aside.

"I'm hurt, *hurt,* that you'd even *think* I could bail on you," Digby said.

"Where were you? This guy's got a shotgun. He's on the phone talking about getting rid of us," Henry said. "Dude, I think he means he's gonna kill us."

"Oh, ya think?" I said. "Digby, he's blocking the phones."

"Yeah, but he didn't spring for the full spectrum one . . . Wi-Fi's still on. Like I said, the guy's so two-thousand-and-late." Digby dialed. "Hello, I need to report a break-in at twenty-five twenty-seven Pine. Three intruders are being held at gunpoint. . . . What? No, we're the *intruders.* Better hurry—I'm pretty sure he's pissed off enough to kill us."

Digby held out his hand and Henry gave me a boost. He climbed up after me and Digby replaced the ceiling tile. Then we heard a horrible metallic groan. The ceiling was buckling.

"Spread out!" Digby said.

We scrambled like roaches, arms and legs spread to distribute our weight across the tiles. The creaking stopped.

We heard Schell reopen the door.

"What the hell?! *What the hell?!*" Schell's voice was high and hysterical.

He ripped apart his office. The wheeled office chair crashed around. He opened the coat closet and knocked hangers to the floor. He was so confused, he checked for us in desk drawers. Then, silence.

We froze in our wounded soldier crawl poses. I prayed Schell would leave, but instead, a ceiling tile right by me rose. Schell was using his shotgun barrel to push it up. A second later, Schell's shotgun barrel pushed up another tile even closer to me.

I panicked. I got up on my hands and knees. My body just wanted to run. There was a loud creak, then a huge *SNAP*. There was total horror on Digby's and Henry's faces. Then a split second later, the ceiling collapsed and I crashed into the office below.

Schell and I both screamed. My chin was on fire when I landed and when I touched it, my hands came away covered in blood.

"Where's your friend?" Schell randomly stabbed ceiling tiles with his shotgun. Another section of the ceiling collapsed and there was Henry, sprawled on the floor in front of me.

"Get over there," Schell said.

Sitting on the floor with a shotgun pointing at me, I imagined a crime show with some cop looking at my blown-off face saying, "Gentlemen, looks like for this kid"—puts on sunglasses— "school's out forever." Then credits rolling and some '70s rock song about not getting fooled again starting with a scream.

After a second, I realized the screaming was no imagined rock song and that, in fact, the screaming was coming from me. Later, Digby told me I sounded like his grandmother's cockatoo when its wing accidentally got caught in the vacuum.

"Shut up! Shut up!" Schell said.

But I couldn't stop. I wasn't even pausing for breath. I just screamed.

Then Digby exploded through the ceiling and landed on

Schell's back. Henry grabbed the shotgun, and the three of them twirled around, crashing into furniture. It felt like they went on like that forever until *KA-BAM*, the shotgun went off. Plaster from the wall behind me puffed up into a dust cloud.

After that, I couldn't hear myself scream anymore. All I heard was a loud ringing. I watched them crash around on mute. Then, as Digby just about pried the shotgun away from Schell, two people ran in holding handguns. They must have told them to freeze, because Digby, Henry, and Schell stopped struggling. Schell slowly dropped his shotgun.

One of the new arrivals was a tall lady with bright red lipstick who immediately ran to me. I couldn't hear her clearly but I think she yelled to the chubby guy who I guessed was her partner, "Call it in, she's been shot!"

I thought, Oh, God, I've been shot? before I passed out.

TEN

When I came to, Conan O'Brien was standing over me holding a giant needle. Weirdly, he was dressed as a paramedic.

"Sir, are you sure you're allowed to do this?" Henry said. "Shouldn't we go to the hospital?"

"Relax, kid. I'm certified," Conan O'Brien said.

It was then that I saw the needle in Conan's hand was attached to black thread coming out of my chin. I realized Conan O'Brien was sewing me up with a huge needle.

"Yup," Digby said. "There she goes again."

Everything went white.

++++

When I came to again, I was lying on the couch in Schell's office. Digby, Henry, Lady Cop, and Chubby Cop were in the middle of an argument. No one noticed I'd woken up.

"Lemme see those badges again," Digby said.

"You've seen them," Lady Cop said.

"I wanna write down your badge numbers," Digby said.

Chubby Cop looked exasperated, but he and his partner handed their badges to Digby. "You three are in serious trouble . . . breaking and entering's a felony," he said. "Me, I wanna bring you down to the station and book you, but my partner thinks we should give you a chance to explain what you're doing here tonight."

Lady Cop moved oddly close to Digby and used a gentle voice. "Look, kids, maybe there's a perfectly reasonable explanation. We're willing to listen . . ."

"You've got five minutes. Then I slap on some cuffs." Chubby Cop pointed at Digby. "You look like the instigator. Start talking."

Digby noticed I was awake and watching.

"Hey. She's up. Her chin's bleeding," Digby said. "Maybe you should get her some water?"

"Sure, sure . . . let's talk a little and we'll get her water in a minute," Lady Cop said.

Digby barked "Ha!" and crossed his arms. "A real good cop would've gotten her water." Digby pointed at the pudgy cop. "And Officer Cooper? A real bad cop never would've winced at the blood."

The cops' faces fell, confirming Digby had seen through their acts.

"I get it, though, because Officer Holloway even looks like the nice lady cop on that show," Digby said. "But you gotta smize. You know, smile *with* your eyes—"

"Okay," Holloway said. "That's enough. The conditions are the same. Talk or we'll take you to the station."

"You know, it's interesting that we're not at the station now. In fact, it's interesting that you patched her up here instead of taking her to the ER," Digby said.

The two cops looked distinctly uncomfortable.

"Maybe we oughta go to the station. Maybe we should call our parents. Or our lawyers," Digby said.

"Okay, Stella, shouldn't we—" Cooper said.

"You don't need lawyers," Officer Holloway said to us. "Schell isn't pressing charges. He claims it was a misunderstanding and that you two are his patients." She pointed at Digby and me. "If you corroborate his story, we'll let everybody go."

"Which you don't wanna do," Digby said.

"No," Holloway said.

"But you don't want us. It's him you want," Digby said.

Holloway was silent. Cooper stared at his shoes.

"When my sister was abducted, the cops took eighteen minutes to come," Digby said. "You two were here three minutes after I called."

"We were across the street. We watched you break in," Holloway said. "This . . . isn't exactly our case."

"What's going on?" Henry said.

"I'll bet they need what we have on Schell, but they have to get it from us legally or they can't use it," Digby said. "You let us break in because we would've been a reason to search the office."

"Good guess, kid," Holloway said.

"You're not detectives and you're not in uniform . . ." Digby said.

"We're off the clock," Holloway said. "This is our side project."

"Side project? Like . . . vigilante?" Digby said.

"Like budget cuts eliminated proactive investigations," Cooper said. "Even when we have solid leads about a doctor writing illegal prescriptions that can be directly tied to two fatal ODs."

"Can't you get him on a weapons charge? He shot at us," Digby said.

"Legit permit," Cooper said. "And, technically, it sounds like the weapon discharged accidentally."

"Okay . . . what if there's another way?" Digby said.

"We're listening," Holloway said.

"What if someone else pressed charges? Say, a chiropractor whose storefront was vandalized?" Digby said. "Then maybe you'd have to take us in? Check our pockets?"

"Where we find . . ." Holloway said.

"A list of names and numbers . . . and maybe those numbers are URL addresses to a members-only porn site that shows him playing doctor with patients," Digby said. "Except the patients don't know they're playing."

"Wait. That means you knew what those numbers were the whole time? We didn't need to come here at all? What was this stupid break-in for, then?" I said.

"And maybe if you found another file one of us was holding, you'd let him keep it since it has nothing to do with your case against Schell," Digby said.

"Sorry, kid, that's stolen property," Holloway said.

"Yeah, but since technically, this"—Digby held up Schell's files—"is tainted evidence, and I think if we dropped all the *maybe*'s from this conversation, we'd be in a conspiracy . . ."

"Christ, kid, you get all that from watching TV?" Holloway said.

"I only need one file. Check the name—it's my mother's. Let me keep it and we'll cooperate," Digby said.

"Cooperate?" I said. "What does *that* mean, exactly?"

"Deal?" Digby said.

Holloway stared at Cooper, pleading.

"I'm sure this is not only illegal, but it's probably also a violation of his constitutional rights too," Cooper said. Finally, looking pained, he closed his eyes and nodded.

"Okay, great. You get twenty minutes. Read it here before we take you in," Holloway said. "Best we can do."

"I take photos," Digby said.

"No," Holloway said.

"Notes?" Digby said.

"Fine. But you're struck with amnesia about how you got them," Holloway said.

"Deal," Digby said.

"In fact, all three of you get struck with amnesia about what's happening here," Holloway said.

"I'm not even sure I know what's going on," Henry said.

"Don't we all have to agree? I can't have this on my permanent record," I said.

"Uh . . . me neither," Henry said. "Football scholarships require a clean record."

"Wow. I never thought the whole permanent record thing would blow up in our faces," Cooper said.

"There's no such thing as a permanent record," Holloway said.

"Stella, don't tell them that," Cooper said. "Yeah, kids, *there is* such a thing as a permanent record."

"Your partner really *is* the good cop, isn't he?" Digby said.

"You have no idea," Holloway said. "He's vegan and he won't even put honey in his tea because he refuses to exploit bees."

I couldn't help it. I thought, He's vegan? and immediately my eyes gravitated to his belly hanging over his belt. I guess we were all doing it and he noticed.

Cooper pulled his jacket over his stomach. "Carbs are vegan."

"Don't most college applications ask you to list just felonies?" Digby said.

"That sounds right," Henry said.

"What's vandalism?" Digby said.

"In this state, a misdemeanor offense," Holloway said.

Digby turned back to Henry and me. "He was filming patients and posting it online. This guy *seriously* deserves prison time. Besides, the misdemeanor will come off our records when we're eighteen. In a way, it's a good deal. We're not even getting busted for the crime we did commit."

"I know that in your head, that totally made sense, but now that you've said it, you do realize it's actually totally insane, right?" I said.

"Come on, guys, let's do the right thing," Digby said.

"You don't care about doing the right thing. You just want to read your mom's file," I said.

"That's true. But *you* care. It's your civic duty," he said.

"Civic duty? I hate this town," I said.

"*I* don't hate this town," Henry said.

"Two against one, Princeton." When I shook my head and stood fast, Digby said, "Don't be a Squidward."

Squidward? I gave Holloway and Cooper the nod.

"Now we have to bust you for vandalism in a way the DA will believe," Holloway said. "It would've been better if we'd found incriminating evidence in plain sight. But I guess that'd be too good to be true."

"Hm . . . plain sight, you say?" Digby whacked my hoodie. The can of snow spray flew out of the pocket and rolled up to Holloway's toes. "Plain enough?"

::::

Mom came straight from singles Scrabble and turned up at the police station wearing what she calls her Minnie-Mouse-knows-what-Victoria's-Secret-is dress. When Officers Holloway and Cooper brought us in to booking, Mom was sitting on a bench with some women who were handcuffed.

"What's all this?" Holloway asked a uniformed officer.

"Brothel raid on William. These lovely ladies are waiting to get booked," the uniformed officer said.

These women weren't in the normal uniform of plastic platform heels, short shorts, and bad makeup. They looked like normal women who'd put on special red lipstick for a night out. Kinda like Mom. Which is probably why Holloway turned tough-cop again when Mom got up and walked to me.

"Step back." Alarmingly, Holloway put one hand on her holster. "*Yo*, why isn't this suspect restrained?"

"Whoa, wait. She's my mom," I said. But that just deepened the misunderstanding.

"Your mom's a—" Cooper said.

"What? No! I just sat down on that bench," Mom said. "Never mind. I got a call about my daughter, but no one told me what the problem was."

To his credit, Cooper looked uncomfortable with the lie we were about to tell. Holloway put on her bossy face and made herself taller to tell it.

"We found a defaced chiropractor's office and a can of snow spray in your daughter's possession and brought her in for misdemeanor vandalism," Holloway said.

"Vandalism? Zoe? I don't believe that," Mom said.

"Believe it," Holloway said.

"I don't appreciate your tone," Mom said.

Cooper inserted himself. "Please. Excuse my partner. It's been a long night. What she meant to say is—"

"Don't apologize for me, Cooper," Holloway said.

"I'm not apologizing for you," Cooper said.

"You're not apologizing? Because someone should," Mom said.

Cooper caught Digby's eye.

"Go on. I wanna see how you get out of this," Digby said.

The station doors burst open. A lady holding a sleeping baby ran straight for Henry, screaming so loud and fast, it took me a while to figure out she wasn't speaking English. She jammed her finger in Henry's face and ended her rant with a smack to the upside of his head.

"*Signomi*, Mama," Henry said.

"Hello, Hestia, long time no see," Digby said.

She smacked Digby on the upside too. "You call me *Thia* Hestia." She pointed at Holloway. "What are you saying these boys do?"

"They vandalized a chiropractor's office," Holloway said.

"You have proof? I want to see proof. You show me proof. This is America."

"We found a can of spray snow in her possession—"

"So *she* do it. My son has no can so why you arrested him?" Mrs. Petropoulos said. "These are good boys! Maybe this one, she is bad influence."

"Hey! I guarantee this wasn't my daughter's idea," Mom said.

"They're not under arrest, technically. We're writing citations. They have to appear in court, but until then, we're releasing them to a parent or guardian," Holloway said.

"Filipos, is that Val coming?" Mrs. Petropoulos asked Digby.

"Well, Val's redoing the fireplaces at our country house . . ." Digby said.

"That mother of yours." She handed a well-worn piece of paper to Holloway and pointed at Digby. "I take care of this one also."

"Power of attorney. Old but it still works," Holloway said.

"We go now." Mrs. Petropoulos grabbed the power of attorney from Holloway, the citations from Cooper, and Henry by the collar even though he was a head taller than her.

"Want me to drive, Hestia?" Digby said.

"You shut up, Filipos. Tonight, you sleep on sofa. Tomorrow, we talk. You in big trouble now." Then Mrs. Petropoulos got a tragic look on her face. She released Henry and stroked Digby on the cheek. "You poor, broken little boy." Then they walked out with her shouting all the way to the car.

"I can't believe that baby slept through all that," Cooper said.

"So what we were hearing was her *inside* voice?" Holloway said.

Mom snatched my citation from Cooper's hand. "You know, these kids are innocent until you can prove them guilty. Which I don't think you can. Tell me, do you sit around with the rest of the George Bush Nostalgia Society perfecting intimidation tactics?"

"Ma'am, I'm a lifelong Democrat," Cooper said.

"Ma'am? *Ma'am?!*" Mom said.

"Um, Stella . . ." Cooper said.

"But you're doing so well," Holloway said.

"I want your badge number. And hers too. I'm writing my congressman," Mom said.

Cooper sighed and gestured for Mom to follow him to the desk.

"I thought you said she wouldn't care," Holloway said to me.

"Yeah . . . this is kind of a surprise for me too."

"She seems pretty worked up, in fact. Which is a problem because this plan depends on her being as oblivious as you said she was," Holloway said.

We watched Mom argue with Cooper.

"I have a bad feeling about this," Holloway said.

I did too.

ELEVEN

Mom gripped the wheel in silence on the tense ride home from the station and sent me to bed without a lecture. Part of me hoped it'd become just another thing we didn't talk about. This was the same part of me that got hopeful when I scratched off supermarket Instant Win tickets that gave away, like, one TV for every million customers.

The silent treatment continued the next morning. After breakfast, she said, "This isn't working."

"What isn't?" I said.

"None of it is." Then she went to do the laundry.

The local paper reported that they'd arrested Schell the night before. As Holloway said, because we were minors, the press hadn't contacted us. That was good because I wouldn't have known what to say.

That night at dinner, Mom turned off the TV. Uh-oh, trouble, I thought. But then she busted out fancy napkins and made pork chops. Mixed message. Chops were not trouble food. Especially not with fancy napkins.

"The police called," she said.

I did that cartoon thing where my fork froze in midair.

"So . . . turns out, my gynecologist was filming his patients," Mom said. "Apparently, I was one of the lucky ones. He didn't care enough to do anything more than give me my Pap smear. I shouldn't be offended, right?"

I put my fork down.

"You expect me to believe it was a coincidence you three broke into *that* office? After you tried to talk to me about him earlier that night? How did you know?" Mom asked. "Can we talk about what happened, Zo?"

Great. The one time she actually wanted to talk, I couldn't say anything at all. I couldn't keep straight all the things Digby and Holloway told me to say and not to say. I focused on cutting my chop into smaller and smaller pieces.

"You know, when you were little, I was just glad that your dad was interested in you. He was totally different from the other dads who were just . . . not there for their kids. But then, it became this strange dynamic in our house with you and him . . ." she said. "I just felt . . ."

Left out. She'd felt left out. I knew because I remember leaving her out. It wasn't exactly on purpose, but I'd known Dad and I were doing it.

"And then during the divorce, my therapist told me not to crowd you with my problems. He told me to give you space . . .

let you mourn your own way. I'm beginning to wonder if that was a mistake."

"You're *beginning* to wonder?"

"Okay, yes, clearly it was a mistake. But I'm listening now."

"Ugh, Mom, stop."

"I just bailed you out of jail, Zoe. I think we're past the small talk."

"That's a pretty dramatic interpretation of what happened."

"Maybe this is a chance for us to make a new start." Then, just before it turned into a pathetic PSA-style "moment," featuring hugs and promises, Mom said, "For now, though, I need us to talk about what we're telling your father."

"Do I have to tell him anything?"

"I can't afford the lawyer, Zo. We'll have to tell him," she said. "He's probably going to think this is me sabotaging this little Prentiss plan you two have. He isn't going to take this well."

No. He was not.

++++

The Monday after I became a criminal (Mom's word, which isn't accurate because we only got charged with violations, although, yeah, we sort of got arrested), girls were eyeing me in the bathroom mirror. I considered this progress, because the week before, these same girls didn't know I was alive.

When someone cut in front of me at the lunch line, someone else pulled him back and said, "Careful . . . she'll shank you in the yard." The next day, Henry told me a rumor was going around that we'd formed a vigilante group and that we had a list of people we were going to "punish."

In Wednesday's PE class, I got picked second out of forty girls for volleyball, which was fishy, because the week before, I'd tripped on my shoelaces and almost broken both arms when I'd gotten them tangled in the net on my way down to the ground. The janitor had had to cut me out. While waiting for our turn to play, two girls asked me about the whole thing.

"Is it true you got shot?" Volleyball Girl #1 said.

"Last Friday? Five days ago?" My implication was that if I'd gotten shot on Friday, wasn't it hugely unlikely I'd be playing fricking volleyball on Wednesday? But the two girls took it to mean something else entirely.

"You mean you got shot another time too?" Volleyball Girl #2 said.

++++

By the following Monday, I decided to embrace the dark side. I wore the outfit from the break-in. There was still my blood on the hoodie's front, snow spray up one sleeve, and plaster across the back. I looked bad-ass dirty. By Thursday, I realized I wasn't attracting the right kind of attention. I got "Hey, gangsta"–style comments, but I wasn't getting into any meaningful conversations.

So I wore my usual dress and boots on Friday. Mom actually sighed in relief when she saw my outfit at breakfast.

For two weeks after our break-in, I didn't see Digby in school except for once in the parking lot. I was about to call out to him, but he ducked behind some bushes as Dominic Tucker got off the football team's bus. After a bit, Digby hopped out of the bushes and ran onto the empty bus. I didn't want to know what new insanity he was up to, though, so I kept walking. I had all the notoriety I needed for a while.

TWELVE

I was doing the recycling one day when I saw Digby on my neighbor's lawn, scribbling in his notebook. I knew better, but I walked over anyway.

"Dumb question, but why haven't you been coming to school?" I said.

"Looking for me, huh? I've been around. I'm there even when you don't see me. And you won't see me unless I want you to."

"Unless you want me to? Did you want me to see you sneak onto the football team's bus? I'm pretty sure those guys would've pounded you if they'd seen."

"You saw that? Hmm . . . that's not good."

"It's really not."

"I had to look before they unloaded their bags. You know what those guys're doing? They—"

"*Please* don't tell me. I don't wanna know."

"But they—"

"I don't. Last time you told me something that was none of my business, I ended up nearly getting arrested," I said. "And, by the way, Mom's driving me crazy, trying to weasel out of me what happened."

"So tell her already."

"Mom thinks your influence turned me into a criminal. She calls me Scarface now." I pointed at the scar on my chin.

"How *is* Liza?" he said.

"Oh, great . . . just great. All she ever wants to do now is talk. How was school? Are you meeting people? She ends our gab sessions with 'good talk, honey' and pats my head."

"What's with the hostility? That sounds nice."

"That sounds nice to you?"

"I thought you were mad before because she was oblivious. Well, now she's interested."

"But she won't stop asking questions now. She's still broken, just the other way," I said. "Seriously, though, why are you here?"

Digby pointed at the window of the house we were in front of. A tiny old lady was walking around her living room.

"Do you know Mrs. Preston?" Digby said.

"Um . . . no," I said. "Why do *you* know Mrs. Preston?"

"I was taking a walk and got in a conversation with Mrs. Preston." Digby read from his notebook. "Apparently, while she was watching *Magnum P.I.,* she noticed the Dumpster in the alley behind her house was on fire. Again. Apparently, it happens a lot. She called the police, but they didn't do anything."

"I refuse to believe you're interested in Dumpster arson," I said.

Mrs. Preston paced back and forth in her living room.

"Why is she wandering around in there?" I said.

"She's looking for her notes. She wrote down a description of the arsonists," Digby said.

In the window, Mrs. Preston waved a piece of paper at Digby.

"Oh, she found it. Let's hope she doesn't stroke out from the excitement." Digby shouted toward the house, "Take it easy, Mrs. Preston."

Mrs. Preston shuffled out to us. "Here it is! I knew I'd written it down." She read from the paper. "Two men, both tall, one of them rode a bicycle."

We waited for her to go on, but then we realized that, in fact, that was all she'd written. I saw the title on the page was "For the Police!!" Yes, two exclamation points.

"Thanks, Mrs. Preston, I'll make sure the neighborhood watch looks out for these guys," Digby said.

Neighborhood watch? I studied Digby's face. Not even a twitch when he lied.

"Good evening, Mrs. Preston." It was the amazon from the mansion, calling out as she crossed the street. Her black bell-shaped skirt completely covered her feet, so she appeared to be levitating. Mrs. Preston pulled her cardigan closed as the amazon got nearer.

"Children." The amazon talked like a strict Victorian nanny in a black-and-white movie.

She loomed over Mrs. Preston and didn't try to hide that she was reading Mrs. Preston's notes.

"The police? Oh, dear, Mrs. Preston, more problems in our neighborhood?" The amazon stared at me when she said "problems."

"Boys are setting fires in the Dumpsters behind my shed," Mrs. Preston said.

"And you're sure they weren't girls? The way some girls dress nowadays, you can hardly tell." The amazon gave me another sharp look.

"Are you saying I don't know a boy from a girl? I got a perfect score on the DMV eye test, you know," Mrs. Preston said.

"Not at all, Mrs. Preston," the amazon said.

"It's a fire hazard. The police won't do anything, but now the neighborhood watch will patrol." Mrs. Preston pointed at Digby.

The amazon's eyes narrowed. "The neighborhood watch? Do you have any literature? That's something my boys should be involved with."

"We're still printing them up. I'll drop some off when they're ready," Digby said.

"They're not . . ." My voice came out high and squeaky. "They're not all *your* boys, are they?"

"They are not my offspring, no," the amazon said.

"So you're . . ." I said.

"I am their keeper," the amazon said. "They are my flock."

I mean, really, what can you say to that? But poor Mrs. Preston tried anyway.

"Mealtimes must be interesting in your house. So many to feed," Mrs. Preston said.

"Quite. Very much like feeding a small army every day," the amazon said.

"A small private standing army. A militia, even," Digby said.

The amazon's lips pulled over her teeth in a snarl she tried to cover with a smile.

"Please. Bring the information about the neighborhood watch when you can. I will be sure to tell my boys about it," the amazon said.

She floated footlessly across the street and into the mansion.

Mrs. Preston sniffed. "I don't care for that woman's outfit."

"Me neither, Mrs. Preston," Digby said.

"And those boys of hers are no kind of Christians I've ever seen. I saw one of them kick the Haggertys' cat," Mrs. Preston said. "Now, that stupid cat eats my tulips and throws them back up on my driveway, but that doesn't mean it deserves to get kicked."

"Could you tell me which one?" Digby said.

"The yellow ones mainly, but sometimes the orange ones too," she said.

"Not which tulips, Mrs. Preston. Which boy did the kicking?" Digby said.

"The tall one." Mrs. Preston stared at Digby and me with the expectation we'd know who that cat-kicker might be based on her description. It occurred to me then that because Mrs. Preston was tiny, everyone looked tall to her.

"Okay, Mrs. Preston. We'll look out for these guys," Digby said. "And the boy who kicked the cat too."

"Good. This was a nice neighborhood when me and my

Sid, God rest, moved in. I hate seeing it go downhill. I heard the new people who moved in"—Mrs. Preston lowered her voice—"*divorce*."

So Mom and I were the talk of the block. I hate this town.

Mrs. Preston said, "That's how it starts." She looked at her watch and jumped. "Oh! I have to go. My program's on. I don't even listen. I just watch that delicious Anderson Cooper's lips move."

We watched her go back in.

"You know she's not totally there, right?" I said.

"Doesn't mean her Dumpster isn't being set on fire," Digby said. "You going in to dinner?"

We walked back toward my house. "Yeah . . . sorry I can't invite you in."

"Your window looks out on that alley, yeah?"

"Um, so I'm supposed to . . . what? Watch out my window all night every night? You know people are saying we're some kind of crime-fighting posse."

"Which reminds me. I have something for you." Digby pulled out a black mask. "It's more Hamburglar than Batman, but you get the idea."

The mask was satin and, actually, very pretty. I tied it on and hit some kung-fu poses.

"Too fun. I'm keeping this." Of course, when I turned around, Mom was on the front lawn of our house with a betrayed expression on her face.

"Looks like mealtime will be interesting at your house tonight," Digby said.

"I told her I wasn't talking to you anymore. I should go."

"If she gets on you, remember—there's at least one other person in your life who she hates even more than she hates me."

"No, there isn't." As I walked away, I thought he said something else about tonight, but I was focused on Mom's rarely seen but greatly feared throbbing forehead vein. "Yeah . . . okay . . . see you later."

++++

"What was that about?" Mom was playing it cool.

"Just . . . neighborhood stuff. Someone's vandalizing Dumpsters," I said.

"I see you met Zillah."

"Who?"

"The high priestess of our neighborhood cult. Her name's Zillah. Wanna hear something weird? I mean, beyond the obvious?" Mom said. "I've been watching them clean and so far, I've seen a dozen different girls."

"Yeah, but I don't think they're being trafficked or anything. They, like, play in the yard and stuff," I said. "Although . . . Digby pointed out they could have Stockholm syndrome."

"Digby. That boy's trouble, Zoe. Trust me, I know trouble. I married trouble," Mom said.

Digby's comment suddenly made sense. There *was* one other person in my life who bothered Mom more than Digby.

"So, speaking of . . . when should I tell Dad?"

"You still haven't told him you got arrested?"

"I'm gonna tell him when he calls on Sunday."

103

"And since we're talking about your father, he e-mailed me about Christmas. He and Shereene are taking you to her parents' in Aspen. Do you have skis and boots, he wanted to know. I told him yes but we left them in our Switzerland house because we're tired of flying that stuff back and forth every weekend," Mom said.

"I don't even really know *her* and now I have to hang out with her parents?"

"I bet he'll make you sit for a group portrait. Remember those? How he used to make us sit for those tacky Christmas notes?"

"How excited do you think they'll be when they realize I'm now officially in the system?" I said. "In the system and in their Christmas photos."

"Oh, Zo, thank you. The bright side. But, seriously, will you be okay?"

I hadn't really thought about it much, and now, horrifyingly, my eyes started to tear up. "Yeah, whatever . . . I don't even listen to Shereene half the time."

"No?"

"No. I zone out and make up shipper fanfic stuff. I just say uh-huh every few minutes."

"Really?"

"Easy Bella/Harry Potter stuff when I'm feeling lazy or some Bella/Hermione when I need a challenge," I said. "What will *you* be doing this Christmas?"

"About that." Mom sipped her wine and avoided eye contact. "So, yes . . . about that . . ."

"Just say it, Mom."

"I'm seeing someone. And . . . I want us all to go out some-time but it's early and I don't want to jinx it but he's a good man and I don't want it to be weird for you . . ."

"Mom. Please. Don't ask my permission to date. That's even weirder. Look, I don't need to meet anyone until you decide he's gonna be my new daddy."

"I didn't just screw you up, did I, Zo?"

"Ugh, Mom . . ."

"Because I don't know what to tell you and what not to. I like us talking, but if I tell you everything . . . I don't want to make you cynical."

Make me cynical? Typical Mom. Always late to the party.

THIRTEEN

That night, I dreamt it was Water Safety Day. The girls lined up on one side of the pool and boys along the other. When the whistle blew, we were supposed to jump in and tread water. But suddenly, everyone was staring at me, mocking me. My swimsuit was totally see-through. Digby was there, wearing his usual black suit. His were the only words I could make out. He pointed at my privates, shaking his head, and said, "That's the ugliest thing I ever saw."

I woke up, feeling sick. I thought I heard a noise, but it stopped. I rolled over to go back to sleep.

A voice cut through the dark. "Whoa . . . until I saw *this*."

I tweaked my back sitting up so fast. How I controlled myself from screaming, I don't know. I was terrified. My toes buzzed with adrenaline. I turned on the light and there was Digby, standing with a huge pile of my stuff on the floor in front of him. He had my five-fingered running shoes in his hand.

"What the yuck are these?" he said.

"Uh . . . I was briefly into running . . . What are you doing here?" I said.

"And ugliness propelled you down the track?"

"Shut up."

"And what's this?"

"My ewer?"

"Oh, so when pitchers are super fug, they're called ewers? Why do you have this thing?"

"I made it. I had a pottery phase—"

"Anyway. You're not a jock." He threw my shoes and hit a deflated basketball sitting on the pile, a relic of the brief moment when I was the tallest girl in seventh grade. "You're not an artist . . ." He carelessly threw the ewer so it broke on top of the pile of my stuff. "You're not an emo philosophy nerd." He opened a Kierkegaard reader and loudly cracked the spine for the first time. He picked up a whip and leopard fur handcuffs. "And you're *definitely* not—"

"Those were a gift . . . a joke," I said. "And they were locked away."

"Behind a four-pin padlock. Those look tough but only take, like, ten seconds to pick," Digby said. "The one on your locker at school too."

I said, "What are you doing here? I know you have boundary issues, but this is stalker creepy."

"What are you talking about? I told you I was coming. You said, and I quote, 'Yeah, okay, see you later.'"

Oh. I guess that's what he'd said on the lawn this afternoon.

"I'm pretty sure I didn't say you could go through my stuff. Which is so freaking rude, by the way."

"I'm getting to know you."

"Most people do that with conversation."

"This is so much quicker."

"Instead of snooping around, why don't you just ask?"

"Ask."

"Yeah, ask."

He picked up a pair of silicone bra inserts. "Do you use these every day or just on special occasions?"

"O . . . kay . . ."

He held up my athlete's foot cream. "This is why you should be glad you aren't a jock."

"Digby, this is not a conversation."

"What we should really talk about is this." He held up a clipping from the local paper profiling Henry and his college prospects. "Because *this* is not going to happen. Sloane would kill you dead first of all."

"Wait. That was in my diary. You read my diary?"

"I didn't read it . . ." His weasel tone didn't sell his denial. ". . . much. I skimmed it. You know, you're way ahead of the game. Most people don't have their identity crisis until their forties. You're wrong, by the way," he said, and he quoted: "'Medium-length brown hair, brown eyes, medium height. All I see in the mirror is a medium brown blur.'"

I lunged at him.

"You don't really think that, do you, Princeton? Because that makes me wanna cry. And also . . . Henry gets 'hero

108

handsome' and all I get is 'Jehovah's Witness'?"

I jumped at him and this time, after elbowing him in the gut, I got my diary back.

There was rustling in the tree outside my window and Henry's head popped into my room. I checked my breath. Still minty.

"Hey, Zoe." Henry climbed in and knocked over a pile of my books. The three of us shushing each other was louder than the books hitting the floor.

"*Twilight? Princess Diaries? The It Girl?*" Digby looked through the books on my desk. "That explains 'hero handsome.'"

"Shut up," I said.

"Sorry I'm late, guys. The baby wouldn't go down, so I couldn't leave . . . then my bike got a flat . . ." Henry said.

"Seriously, you sound like a middle-aged accountant with your problems," Digby said.

"What are you doing here?" I said.

"Digby told me to come," Henry said. "Hey, people in school are calling us the Enforcers."

"And my room's the clubhouse?" I said.

Digby rifled through my drawers.

"Hello? Can I help you find something?" I said.

"I'm starving. Whoa, what's this?" Digby pulled something out of my drawer and traded nasty-boy looks with Henry.

"Morons. It's a flashlight. It's Swedish, so it's all design-y." I flicked it on and off to put an end to that idea. "Check the bottom drawer."

"By the way, Digby, nice move eating my baby sister's Mum-mums. She was teething last night and Mom melted down when she realized you ate the entire box," Henry said.

"I was starving. You know, for a family that runs a restaurant, your kitchen at home's pathetic," Digby said.

"But what was really excellent, though, dude, was how you put the empty box back on the shelf so the people who went to the store didn't know they needed to buy more. I learned a whole new level of Greek cursing," Henry said. "So, what? Val's cooking still crappy?"

"Yeah, still crappy . . ." Digby pulled more stuff from my drawers. "Wasabi peas. Digestive cookies. Plain. Candied ginger. Bottle of soda water. Princeton, you eat like my great-aunt Ruth. Only thing missing is denture cream and . . . oh, wait! This is close enough to dentures. A retainer . . . with a dust bunny and paper clip stuck to it."

"I never wear that thing," I said.

"You gotta keep that up or your teeth will move back," Digby said.

"Now *you* sound like *my* great-aunt Ruth," I said.

Digby opened the packages and dumped the peas, biscuits, and candied ginger on my duvet. I instantly felt crumbs stabbing my legs.

"Do you mind?" I said.

Digby sipped the soda water. "Tastes like sweaty bubbles."

The two of them ate off my duvet, trying different combinations. Peas and cookie, cookie dipped in soda water, peas in the water, peas with cookies while gargling soda water, and finally, the winner: a mouthful of peas chewed with candied ginger, washed down with soda water. Watching them picnicking on my bed reminded me of a Discovery Channel show where chimpanzees broke into the cameraman's supplies and ate his lunch.

"You guys going to the winter dance?" I said.

"Dances? We don't need no stinking dances," Digby said. "Besides, what's a big-city gal like yourself going to a small-town shindig for?"

"You're not going?" Henry said.

"Not unless I'm guaranteed an actual pig-blood prom queen sideshow," Digby said. "Are you going? What am I talking about? Of course you are. No way Sloane's passing up the chance to sashay . . . especially when her parents are paying for the party."

"They *are*?" I said.

"After the homecoming dance got canceled, the Blooms volunteered to arrange a winter formal for the juniors and seniors of the two schools in its place," Henry said.

"Who're you going with, Princeton?" Digby said.

"I thought I'd just go and see what's up," I said.

"What, alone?" Henry said.

"That's a bold statement. Sure you want to make it?" Digby said.

"The poster said it was a chance to meet people from Chester, so I thought maybe I'd meet people there," I said.

Chester B. Arthur was the school on the other side of River Heights. Our schools held joint dances from time to time, supposedly to help us to socialize, but from what I could tell, what the dances really did was make rivalries personal.

"You believe everything you read on posters, Princeton?" Digby said.

"Seriously, Zoe, River Heights is like Noah's Ark. People come in pairs," Henry said.

"Or what?" I said.

"Dunno . . . spend the dance alone?" Henry said.

"What's the difference between being alone at home and being alone at the dance?" Of course there was a huge difference. I just didn't want to admit it to these guys. "Anyway, it's, like, two months from now, so who knows."

"It's six weeks from now and Sloane has her dress already. Girls, am I right? Whatcha gonna do?" Henry said, looking straight at me, like we played on the same team.

"Nothing. I don't have to do anything. Because I *am* a girl." It felt dumb saying it, but seriously, it didn't look like that fact registered with either Digby or Henry even when I *did* say it. To make sure, I added, "Who likes boys."

An awkward second passed, then Digby pulled something out of his pocket.

"Look at this for me, guys," Digby said.

"Guess we're done talking about the dance," I said.

He passed us a picture of a blond girl whose face looked like it was carved from wax. The bottom caption explained: "This photo was produced by Computer Age Progression by the National Center for Missing and Exploited Children."

"I think this girl"—Digby handed me a printout of the photo he took of the girl in the mansion's window—"is Holly Marie Taylor. Went missing four years ago in Ithaca."

"How can you tell? This window shot's basically just blond hair," I said.

"Her bone structure's right," Digby said.

"Bone structure? This could be a fuzzy Sasquatch photo, bro," Henry said.

"Can I see those selfies you take, Princeton?" Digby asked.

I found them on my computer. Digby zoomed in on the girls cleaning outside the mansion in the background.

"I smell their chemicals all the time, but when they're out there cleaning, my eyes actually burn," I said.

"No one complains?" Digby said.

"Mom tried, but Zillah gave her a 'next to godliness' lecture."

"That woman's name is *Zillah*?" Digby said.

"You didn't ask me to come here just to show me this, did you?" Henry said.

"No, we're here to watch the Dumpsters burn," Digby said. "The show's starting in a few minutes."

"How do you know that?" I said. "Please don't tell me you're lighting the fire yourself."

"Mrs. Preston was watching *Magnum P.I.* at the time," Digby said. "No way she pays ten extra bucks for a rerun channel, and *Magnum P.I.* only reruns once a week on basic. On Thursdays. Now-ish. So, if I'm right about Mrs. Preston's cheapness, and the fact that these fires aren't random, we should be getting something in . . ."

A bicycle creaked down the street and turned into the alley below my window.

"D'you hear that?" Digby said.

"That bike?" Henry said.

"No, from the other side," Digby said.

Windows wrap around my room, so I could see both the alley behind my house and part of the mansion's front, but the sound Digby heard came from the part you couldn't see. Before I could stop him, he'd opened the door and run to the window on the landing. Henry and I followed.

"Get back in my room, Digby." Funny how panic-whispering is actually louder than just normal low-talking.

"Look," Digby said.

"I don't see anything," Henry said.

"Above those bushes."

It was Ezekiel hanging from an upstairs window. He dropped onto the lawn and jogged toward the back of my house. We ran back into my bedroom.

Digby lowered the blinds and turned off my bedside lamp. We peeped through the slats at the alley.

Here's what we saw. Bicycle Guy was nervous, smoking and jigging in place. He flicked open his Zippo, struck it, and shut it over and over.

Ezekiel pounded out a greeting with Bicycle Guy and took a brick-sized package from under his shirt. They got to work. It looked like they were opening paper packets and collecting whatever was in them into a Tupperware. When Bicycle Guy stooped, the butt of a gun flashed from his pants' waistband.

"Gun!" I said.

"Let's get a closer look," Digby said.

Henry grabbed Digby's arm. "They aren't messing around, dude. They *will* shoot us."

"They won't see us . . . c'mon, Princeton. You don't wanna

see what these people are doing in your neighborhood?"

"Wow, easy question—*no*. Not even a little," I said.

"We'll go to your back fence and listen. They won't even know we're there," Digby said.

Digby left. We had no choice but to follow.

The backyard was freezing and I shivered in my pajamas. I didn't realize I was being loud until Digby jammed a finger between my chattering teeth and shushed me. He removed his jacket and slipped it around my shoulders. The pockets were packed with stuff. I flapped the jacket, feeling its weight.

"It's full of junk."

"Batman has a utility belt . . ."

We snuck behind Mom's car and looked out the fence into the alleyway. Bicycle Guy tucked the Tupperware into his backpack and handed Ezekiel a big roll of bills. They were talking, but all I heard were them repeating the words *used whore*. Gross. Bicycle Guy picked up the empty paper packets, sprayed them with lighter fluid, and lit them with his lighter. He tossed the flaming bouquet into the Dumpster. As had probably happened before, the garbage in the Dumpster caught fire too. Bicycle Guy whooped and gave the trash a squirt of fuel that made the flames dance higher. They shared a dudely hug/back-pat combo and split up.

They were barely out of the alley when Digby threw the gate open. "I need to get into that Dumpster."

I think we actually did have the whole "It's on fire, are you crazy?/I need to see what they set on fire" argument telepathically. I lost.

"Wait!" I ran into our shed to retrieve the mini fire extinguisher Mom was planning to install in the kitchen.

Digby was already running down the alley when I got back. Henry grabbed the fire extinguisher and sprinted after him. Digby leaped from a trash can straight into the burning Dumpster. Henry followed, spraying the extinguisher from the moment he got air. When they finally climbed out, they were covered in white extinguisher dust. The Dumpster was fizzling.

"Dude, I hope that was worth it. My new jeans are wrecked," Henry said.

"Check it out." Digby showed us a shred of brown paper with a sticker of a skateboarding banana with an Afro wearing sparkly gloves and an eye patch. "Does this look familiar?"

We stared at the sticker in the half darkness.

"Let's go inside . . . I'm freezing." I led them back through the house.

Digby somehow managed to snag the fruit basket on his way up and was eating the plums Mom was saving for her lunch. Henry noticed me noticing and patted my back.

"Dude, get used to it. Just so you know, putting 'do not eat' notes on your food won't help," Henry said.

So annoying that he called me dude.

"It looks familiar. Like a tattoo or a T-shirt I've seen . . ." Digby said.

"Zoe?" Mom was groggily calling to me from bed.

"Party's over," Digby said.

Henry climbed out the window. I gave Digby his jacket and he handed me the basket and last half-eaten plum.

116

"By the way, Princeton, I'd describe you as a classic wide-eyed American girl next door with a nice-to-meet-you vibe who's hiding behind a disappointed divorce-kid downer persona," Digby said.

"Zo? Are you watching TV?" I heard Mom getting out of bed.

"Go," I said.

"And looks-wise, I'd say a young Anne Hathaway." Digby stepped out onto the tree. But, just in case that left me feeling too good about myself, he ducked back in for an encore. "Except horsier. Seriously, Princeton, wear your retainer."

He disappeared just as Mom came in and flicked on the light. She saw me holding the half-eaten plum.

"You ate all my plums?" she said. "And what's that smell? Barbecue?"

FOURTEEN

Even though it was my twentieth-something day in River Heights High and I was getting used to eating solo (heck, doing everything solo), I was glad when Digby came over with his tray the next day.

"That skateboarding banana haunted my dreams last night," Digby said.

"At least you *could* dream. I was wide awake after you guys left," I said. "I was so stressed about getting the fire extinguisher back in the shed before Mom noticed."

"You put the fire extinguisher back into the shed?" Digby said.

"Yeah."

"Um . . . so when there's a real fire and your mom goes for the extinguisher, it's actually totally empty . . . ?"

"Oh, God . . ."

"Yup."

"So, I gotta sneak it back out . . ."

"Yup."

"Buy a new one just like it . . ."

"Yup."

"And then sneak that one back in . . ."

"Yup."

"Being friends with you's more stressful and expensive than getting mugged," I said. "Which happened to me for real, by the way, so I know what I'm talking about."

"Gun? Knife?"

"Screwdriver. Hey, you know what's funny? I'm getting more screwed hanging out with you than when I was getting mugged by a guy who had an actual screwdriver."

"Um-hm, um-hm . . . I get it. Wordplay."

Henry came and sat down with a tired sigh. "So, this morning, Mom found my jeans . . . you know, with the ashes and food scraps and fire extinguisher crap all over them. She assumed it was from a kitchen fire at the diner. She called Jorge and, of course, he denied it like I denied it and so she thinks we're all hiding some fire from her," he said. "Now Jorge's in trouble. Jorge doesn't need the aggravation. So, how do I tell her that I was in a totally different fire somewhere totally else without getting in more trouble?"

"Henry, man, there's something about your problems . . ." Digby said. "Maybe it's this weird thing you have with Hestia or maybe it's the way you talk about them . . . you always sound like a middle-aged accountant."

"Whatever. Digby, you owe me an explanation for a pair of slightly burned pants covered in food and fire extinguisher powder," Henry said.

"Oh, it's harder than that. You need an explanation that at the same time completely excuses you for lying to her this morning," Digby said. "You need the lie to work retroactively too. Challenge accepted."

"Wow," I said.

"And I need it before my shift today," Henry said.

"Don't sweat it. I do my best work after lunch," Digby said.

"Hit me with a text," Henry said.

"'Hit you'? Seriously? You know, it's that other crowd you're running around with. Don't think I haven't noticed," Digby said.

"Not everyone can do the lone wolf thing like you and Zoe. I'm a team player," Henry said.

Great. Now I was officially a lone wolf too?

"Speaking of teams. The lawyer that Coach hooked me up with wants to talk to your lawyers before our desk appearance for the vandalism." Henry held out two copies of his lawyer's business card.

I was relieved that Digby's face looked blank too.

"I have to ask my dad for a lawyer . . . I'll do it soon." I took the business card. It was on thick ivory paper embossed with DEIRDRE KLEIN-ESSINK, ATTORNEY-AT-LAW.

"You haven't told him yet?" Digby said.

"Have you told *your* dad?" I said.

"Nah . . . it'll probably be legal aid for me," Digby said. "It's not even a misdemeanor. I'll save the legal dream teams for my future felonies."

"Ugh . . . did you say 'felony'?" It was Sloane, wearing her dance leotard and tights under denim short shorts. She was so pretty, it was ridiculous.

"'EES.' I said 'felon-ees.' Plural," Digby said.

"Whatever. Just better not drag Henry into it," Sloane said.

"Worried about your plan to become prom king and queen?" Digby said. "But, Sloane, when you rule the school, isn't every day prom?"

"I quote myself: 'Whatever,'" Sloane said. "Henry, let's go."

Henry pushed spaghetti down his throat really fast.

"Ew. Stop eating that crap." Sloane took the fork from Henry and smacked away his hand when he tried to reach back for it. She returned to her table and immediately started bossing around the girls sitting there.

"Aw, hell, no. If someone took the food out of my mouth like that . . ." Digby said.

"Yeah, we all know how excited you get about your food, but I gotta go. Seriously, she hates your guts," Henry said. "She doesn't want me being friends with you anymore."

"Speaking of . . . did I miss something?" I said. "You two don't talk for years, then suddenly you're breaking into places together, you're sleeping at his house . . . what's up?"

"Do you mean did we kiss? And make up?" Digby said.

Henry and Digby hugged and made moany and kissy noises to each other to mock me.

"Oh, Henry, it's not wrong to feel."

"Aw, Digby, my pal, how I've missed you."

"Guys are weird," I said.

"*Girls* are weird. Not everything's gotta be a big drama, you know," Digby said.

"Yo. Big drama looking this way right now." Henry pointed with his chin.

Musgrave was in line with a salad and a bottle of water, glaring at us.

"Check it out. He's amping himself up," Digby said.

From across the cafeteria, I could see Musgrave's face getting redder and puffier as he stared at us.

"He's dying to come over here." Digby waved at Musgrave. "Look at him fighting it. He's so crabby. I bet it's the diet. Just have a hot dog and chill, Musgrave."

"Cool it, dude. He's one of my assistant coaches," Henry said.

"Think he'll give me a break, then?" Digby said.

"Doubt it. He and Coach gave me the whole 'bad influence' talk the other day and I couldn't really defend you, seeing as how I'd just asked for the name of a good criminal defense lawyer," Henry said.

Musgrave paid and approached our table, clearly about to start another cafeteria fight with us.

"Here we go," Digby said.

"Mr. Petropoulos, I see you didn't understand the thrust of our last conversation," Musgrave said.

"Uh . . . no, sir, I got it," Henry said.

"Henry!" Sloane, back at her table, was tapping her foot, waiting for Henry to heel.

"May I be excused?" Henry said.

"I think you'd better go," Musgrave said.

"Hey, good thinking with the fire extinguisher." Henry thumped me on the back so hard, I burped. Having established me firmly in bro territory, Henry jogged off to Sloane.

"Something about you ain't right," Musgrave said to Digby. "I can spot a criminal in the making a mile away. I see you, kid. I see you. And you . . ." He turned to me. "How's that independent study coming?"

"We're working on it right now." I was getting better at lying. Maybe Mom was right: Digby *was* turning me into a juvenile delinquent.

"Oh, yeah? Let me hear what you've done so far," Musgrave said.

I'd congratulated myself too soon. I had nothing.

"Wouldn't want to ruin the surprise." Digby's extra-polite grin looked even ruder than if he just sat there flipping Musgrave off.

Worryingly, Musgrave smiled. "Those are nice bright teeth, Mr. Digby. They show off that green gum in your mouth nicely. Of course, you know chewing gum's a Level I violation of the school's code of conduct. Three lunchtime detentions. Starting today. Follow me." Musgrave wiggled his finger at Digby.

"That'll have to wait." It was Officer Holloway. Officer Cooper was with her, hanging back a little. They were in street clothes with neck-badges on. "C'mon, kids. We need to talk."

"Oh, yeah? You have permission to be on school grounds?" Musgrave said.

"Who are you?" Holloway said.

"I'm the school resources officer." Musgrave must've heard

himself, though, because he immediately relented. "Fine. Three detentions starting tomorrow." Musgrave lunged at Digby's face. Impressively, Digby didn't flinch.

Holloway didn't like the way Musgrave was bullying Digby, though. "Detention? What for?"

"Chewing gum on school grounds," Musgrave said.

"Gum? Open your mouth, Philip," Holloway said.

Digby did. Of course the gum was gone, long since swallowed.

"I don't see any gum. And I don't like how you physically interacted with this student." Holloway asked Digby, "Do we need to talk about harassment charges?"

Digby took his time. "Nah . . . Harlan's just old-school. Right, Harlan? Good-bye, Harlan. . . ."

To his credit, Musgrave knew when he was beaten. He slunk off.

"Okay, that was cool. Like in *Jurassic Park* when the velociraptor's about to get them but the T-Rex jumps in and chomps the velociraptor in half," Digby said.

"Every time I see you, kid, you're getting cornered. What're you gonna do when I take a day off?" Holloway said.

"Like that would ever happen," Cooper said. "How are you, Zoe?"

"Fine," I said.

"Good, good." Cooper smiled like we shared a private joke. If we did, I didn't get it.

Holloway had us follow her. With Cooper taking up the rear, it looked like we were being perp-walked out of the cafeteria. Everyone watched and whispered. I felt new rumors forming.

We went into an empty classroom.

"So, your friend Henry's lawyer called the DA, and the DA, in his infinite wisdom, decided this isn't going to work," Holloway said. "The video evidence against Schell got excluded. The whole case folded."

"What does that mean?" I said.

"The vandalism violation's been voided. Your record's clean," Holloway said.

"Should we worry about Schell coming after us?" I said.

"He thinks you were in there stealing meds," Holloway said.

"But you're not letting him go back to work, are you?" Digby said.

"We filed a complaint with the medical board and they issued an emergency restriction on his clinical privileges pending an inquiry," Cooper said.

"That's it? No charges?" Digby said. "This same DA stalked my family for no reason at all."

"That's not true. The evidence against your parents was legit," Holloway said.

"All circumstantial. Nothing like a video of someone actually committing a crime," Digby said. "Wow. Nice to know I have nothing whatsoever to fear from the justice system if I decide to use my powers for evil."

It was weird to see Digby genuinely upset, because I'd mostly only seen him either mocking someone (usually me) or taking them for a ride (again, usually me). We all jumped when he kicked the trash can across the room.

"Calm down, please," Holloway said.

Digby swept books off shelves and tore apart some poor social studies student's diorama. It was heartbreaking watching him throw a tantrum. Finally, Digby sank onto a chair with his fists balled up on his lap.

"I'm starving," Digby said.

"I have sunflower seeds you could have," Cooper said.

Digby shivered. "Bird food. No, thanks."

"They're great for your skin."

"Do not even."

I checked that the Red Delicious sitting on the desk wasn't wax and gave it to Digby. We watched him mechanically eat it. When he was done, he asked, "Did you check his prints?"

"We ran them. Nothing," Holloway said.

"But you were able to take his fingerprints?" Digby said.

"Sure. When we arrested him. Why?" Holloway said.

"Just a dumb idea I had about the smudges in Marina Miller's room," Digby said. "Did you see she was a patient of Schell's?"

"Look, the search for Marina's stalled. If you know something more about it, you should tell us now," Holloway said.

"Are you saying you need my help?" Digby said.

"I'm saying you want something from us too," Holloway said. "Maybe we could help each other out."

"Sounds like you're out of ideas. You go first if you wanna trade," Digby said. "Well?"

Holloway and Cooper were silent.

"We're gonna be late for . . . Spanish?" Digby looked at me for confirmation.

"Language arts. You're kidding. Are you telling me you're in that class with me? I've *never* seen you," I said.

"So, what about it, policepersons?" Digby said. Still nothing. "Look, I'm not gonna blink first. I have all the time in the world."

"All right. I'm afraid to ask. What do you want?" Holloway said.

"My sister's case files," Digby said.

"File a Freedom of Information request," Holloway said.

"I did. They gave me stuff they released to the media. I want the investigating officers' notes. Full transcripts of the interviews," Digby said.

"I can't do that," Holloway said. "That case isn't closed."

"Good luck with Marina, then. Put her file next to my sister's on your special shelf for missing girls who stay missing," Digby said.

"Okay, okay," Holloway said. "We'll see what we can do."

"Don't 'we'll see' me. I'm not some eight-year-old kid asking to go to Chuck E. Cheese," Digby said.

"No, you're a sixteen-year-old kid asking me to steal confidential police files, so be realistic and let me see what I can do. In the meantime, stop playing games and tell me something worth committing larceny for."

"I got the prescription number from Marina's file and called her pharmacy. A week before she disappeared, she got eight months' worth of birth control," Digby said. "Were there seven and a half unused packs of pills when you searched her room?"

"I'll check the log at the precinct." Holloway paused.

"Thank you, Philip. That seems relevant to the case."

"You're welcome. Even if that was a little condescending," Digby said.

"Gimme a break, kid. You just schooled me, okay?" Holloway said. "But do me a favor. No more breaking into places?"

Cooper smiled and patted me on the head before they walked out the door.

"*That* was weird," I said.

"Those are some hugely inappropriate cops," he said. "Maybe that means there's a chance I'll get those files after all."

"Are you coming? We really *are* gonna be late now."

"Late? For what?"

"For language arts. Hello?"

"You go. I have to see about this skateboarding banana. It's driving me crazy."

"You're skipping again? Do you at least want me to make up an excuse for you?"

"Nah . . . it'll just confuse the teacher. Don't even mention it. He probably doesn't know I exist."

"Um . . . the teacher's a *she,* and she'll probably figure out that you do exist when she starts writing your report card and realizes she's never even seen you."

"Well, let's hope it doesn't come to that," he said, and left.

I didn't know how it *wouldn't* come to that, since in my experience of school, report cards were kind of impossible to avoid. But like I said, that was *my* experience of school, and this was Digby we were talking about.

FIFTEEN

That night, I googled Digby's family some more. By the time I looked up, I'd spent two hours in the Church of Search.

An interview with one detective fascinated me. Her name first of all: Rosetta Pickles. Who wouldn't follow that down the Google hole? And the weird mole on her lip looked like it'd pop whenever she said words with an *O* sound like *lost* and *home*.

Then I noticed something. I rewound the interview to make sure.

"She was the sweetest little girl," Rosetta Pickles said.

Past tense. I remembered something about murderers using the past tense to talk about victims they couldn't know were dead.

I kept googling, but Rosetta Pickles dropped out of the story. The only thing I saw was a listing for an apartment bought by a Rosetta Pickles in Manhattan. River Heights to Central Park adjacent? Nah, it couldn't be the same person.

I had twenty-three tabs open when my phone rang.

"If you get down to the mall in the next twenty minutes, I'll show you something that'll blow your mind, I swear to God," Digby said.

"Can't. Busy," I said.

"Oh, come on . . . you can screen stalk anytime."

He was too close to the truth for my taste. I shut down some tabs.

"Nope. Busy."

"Pretty sure you can sit alone in your living room eating leftover rotisserie tomorrow night too," Digby said. "And next time, if you wanna pretend you're busy, don't answer on the first ring."

I threw down the chicken leg I'd been chewing on.

"Still can't."

"What's your excuse now?"

"I feel crappy."

"You were fine at school today . . . what, did you and Liza have a fight?"

"No. Well . . . maybe. She's annoying."

"She's there?"

"She's out. On a date."

"Oh," he said. "Oh, okay."

"No, you don't get it. She's wearing my dress, which is way tight on her, and these heels that give her cankles . . ." I said. "It's not what it sounds like."

"You mean like a little kid moping around at home, mad because Mommy's out on a date?"

Maybe it was exactly what it sounded like.

"Fine. But if I come to the mall, can we not talk about my personal stuff?"

"Sure. But hey, I'm starving, so bring ten bucks."

"I'm not just your ATM, you know."

"Oh, right. Then bring twenty. No fun watching you watching me eat anyway."

††††

I still found the whole one-stop mall shopping thing weird. I liked going to three different places when I wanted three different things. Like, I got my shoes fixed in the subway station on Henry and Clark. I'd get croissants at a bakery on Montague, and Mom bought flowers at the bodega down the street because they always lasted three days longer than flowers from anywhere else.

In River Heights, though, you got your shoes repaired and bought your cakes and flowers at the mall. And in River Heights, going to the mall meant going to Promenade Plaza, which, except for a couple of dusty strips of depressing businesses like DVD rentals and inkjet cartridge refill places, was the only real mall for miles.

The food court was packed. The jocks were in a food fight in one corner. The pretty, popular girls were sitting on their boyfriends' laps uploading mall-haul videos. A big group of guys eating KFC were playing an RPG and taking directions from this one kid wearing a cape and giant plastic ears. The emo kids caught me looking in their direction and glared. They didn't have to consult each other. They just did it all together and at the same time. One girl snarled.

Henry and Digby were right. There was a huge difference between being alone at home and being alone in a crowd. I was lonely sitting home alone. At the mall, I was terrified.

I needed to get out of there and was halfway across the food court when someone wearing a full-body costume of a brown girl teddy bear in a tutu and ballet slippers stepped in my way. The leotard had SUZIE BEAR written across it. I moved to the left. The bear moved to block me.

"Hey," Suzie Bear said.

I moved to the right, and Suzie Bear moved to block me again.

"Hey," Suzie Bear said. "Gimme ten bucks."

I wondered if people were going to let me get mugged by a teddy bear in the middle of the food court.

"Don't tell me you forgot to bring the money, Princeton. I'm desperate. I just ate what I thought was a Skittle covered in lint," Suzie Bear said. "It wasn't a Skittle."

I finally realized it was Digby. My hand made a hollow *donk* when I slapped the head of his costume. "You scared the crap out of me. Will you take that thing off?"

"My boss won't like that," he said.

"Boss? This is your job?" I said.

"Would you feel better if I said this was my hobby? Yeah, this is my job. Not everyone's on the double-dip divorce allowance money train."

"I can't even fight with you right now. This place is too much. I don't feel good." I didn't. My head was swimming. In that moment, I realized how important it was for me to get out of River Heights if I didn't want to spend the next two years as a social outcast.

"Your lips are white. You gonna pass out?" Digby took off his costume's head. Underneath, he was still wearing his suit. He took my hand in his paw, dragged me into a Ye Olde Tea and Crumpets Shoppe kind of place, and sat me down at a little wrought iron table.

"Can I get you guys something to drink?" The cashier's name tag said: HELLO, I'M CHAD.

"Not me. You, Princeton?" Digby said.

"I don't drink tea," I said.

"Nothing for us," Digby said. "We're just gonna sit awhile."

"Dude." Chad threw up his hands in a give-me-a-break way. To which Digby replied with a wave around the totally empty store. "Dude. Seriously?"

Chad thought about it, gave up thinking about it, and pulled out his phone. "Whatever, dude." Chad walked into the back.

"So, what's the matter with you?" Digby took a dish of cut-up scone samples from the counter and started plowing through them.

"Even the food court's so . . ." I said. ". . . cliquey."

"Look, you don't even want to hang out with these people. I mean, if there were a show about the average River Heights life, it'd come on between *16 and Pregnant* and *Extreme Hoarders*. Be glad you don't belong here."

"So where *do* I belong? Because it wasn't easy making friends at my last school. It's a dumb metaphor, but I'm sick of being the weirdo book channel show only serial killers watch."

133

"No, Princeton, you're HBO all the way. Most people think it's depressing and pretentious, but the fans are *real* fans. They pay ten extra bucks a month for the original programming. Also the sex."

"Sex? That's Cinemax. Or, as Mom calls it, Skinemax."

"Right. Sloane is Cinemax," Digby said. "Bless her."

"It's weird to hear you say that while you're wearing a tutu."

"I'm not wearing the tutu. The bear is. I'm wearing the bear."

"As usual, the logic is bulletproof. What's the deal with the costume anyway?"

"I get minimum wage handing out flyers for the Make-Ur-Bear place, but this costume is awesome. It's basically an invisibility cloak."

"What do you need an invisibility cloak for?"

"Watch." Digby dropped the teddy bear head back on and worked the costume. He clumsy tippy-toe danced from the tea shop back into the food court. He pirouetted a guy's soda off his tray. He threw flyers up in the air. He was incredibly disruptive.

I didn't understand what he meant by the invisibility cloak comment, because everyone totally noticed him. Kids threw food at him and fries dangled off his fur.

Then I saw who was sitting at the table he was bothering.

Digby was doing pelvic thrusts for Ezekiel, who was sitting with Schell. Digby was right about the teddy bear outfit being an invisibility cloak. They had no idea.

Unfortunately, I didn't have a teddy bear costume and I'd

have to pass Ezekiel and Schell's table if I wanted to leave the mall. Living across the street had been stressful enough, and the only reason I was even sleeping at night was that his Amazonian overlord seemed to have him under control. But now, seeing him sharing a basket of fries with the guy who shot at me . . .

It didn't occur to me at the time that I could've waited them out and that they probably wouldn't murder me in the middle of the mall. I just wanted to get the hell out of there.

"Is there a back door?"

Chad gave me a dimwitted stare. "Well . . . yeah . . . but . . ."

That's all I needed to hear. I ran past him into the back. I didn't care that the door was clearly labeled NOT AN EXIT. I didn't care it said ALARM WILL SOUND. I went through it and ran until I caught the bus two stops past the mall. I heard the mall's screaming alarm for blocks.

On the bus, I was so paranoid, I didn't realize I was staring at some random old dude sitting near me until he said, "Please stop that. You're making me nervous."

Whatever. He looked like he had something to hide.

I felt like someone was hiding behind every bush on the way home, waiting to jump me. I was never this scared in the city.

I got home and collapsed into bed. At eleven-something that night, my phone woke me up.

"Hey, where'd you go?" Digby said.

"You ass. What if they saw me? Unlike you, my face wasn't hidden," I said. "I went out the back."

135

"You're the one who set off the alarm?" Digby laughed. "Then stay away from the tea place for a while. They got fined a thousand bucks for that false alarm."

"It's not funny. Did you know that psycho living across the street knew Schell?"

"Well, yeah."

"Don't you think you should've told me that before you made me piss them both off? And I'll kill you if you tell me that you just did tell me. You drag me around town getting me in trouble . . . Why do you call me to go on these things? Why do I take these calls? I'm done. I don't care if I have no friends. This isn't worth it."

I hung up on him. I wondered if we were really done as friends. I sat in the dark, trying to decide if I was glad or if I regretted saying it.

Then, just when I got the sinking feeling that maybe I did regret it, Digby slid open my window. He sat on the windowsill, holding takeout Chinese food.

"I'm sick of following you around, not knowing what's going on," I said.

"I've watched Schell and Ezekiel have dinner at the mall every Friday night since September. Usually they just talk, but today Schell gave Ezekiel some keys. I don't tell you things because you freak out. I keep calling you, Princeton, because you're good to have around during an emergency. Plus . . . you're cool." He mumbled the last bit. He held out the Chinese food to me. "The ladies running Wok Palace had extra when they closed. Kung Pao shrimp."

It was pathetic how good it felt to hear him call me cool. I took the food.

"From now on, you tell me what's going on. Deal?"

"Deal. So tomorrow, eleven o'clock at the Big Field? It's Saturday practice and Henry's QBing."

"Okay." It sounded kinda nice. I could bring some smoothies . . .

"Great. And since we're doing the whole full disclosure thing . . . we're also gonna score from the dealer who hangs around during practice, so maybe bring a twenty."

"There's a dealer who hangs around practice?"

"Yeah, you know . . . lots of people, but not *too many* people . . ."

"I'm not asking about her marketing strategy, I'm more curious how the police don't know."

"Oh, they know . . . but they leave dealers like her alone. This one mostly just sells pot . . . 'shrooms . . . hash . . . hippie stuff," he said. "River Heights, Princeton. This is the town that drugs built. During Prohibition, Canadian rum-runner trucks pit-stopped here and the *cops* used to help change out flats. River Heights has a hierarchy, and pot dealers don't rate."

"Okay . . . that's fascinating civic history and all, but you can't snow me. I'm not buying drugs with you."

"Just relax . . . it's not like we're gonna *do* the drugs we buy. We'll flush them right after we ask a few questions."

"Can't we just ask questions without giving my twenty bucks for drugs we don't want?"

"Drug dealers don't chat, and I don't think they'd be excited about talking to some looky-loos."

"Oh, so to be *safe*, we'll pretend to buy a bunch of drugs? Because that's the safe thing to do?"

"No, no . . . we're *actually* gonna buy the drugs. We're *pretending* we're going to use them. Come on, Princeton, don't get it twisted."

SIXTEEN

Mom got in really late that night and was still in bed when I left the next morning. She barely reacted when I told her I was borrowing her aviators. Part of me wanted to wear something cool like a short skirt/long jacket/ankle boots outfit, but I considered myself warned by Digby, so I wore jeans and motorcycle boots in case I had to run across mud or climb over barbed wire. I also threw water and PowerBars in my backpack. Preparing to survive a typical day of being Digby's friend wasn't that different from preparing to survive the apocalypse.

The Big Field was the midpoint between River Heights High and Chester B. Arthur High. It had a full-sized track, and both schools played their football, soccer, and baseball games there. It was the town's ground zero of teen heart-throbbing.

That day, our football team, the Buccaneers, was sharing the field with the Chester cheerleading squad. Neither team could keep their minds on their own tasks. The football players watched the cheerleaders in between plays and the cheerleaders lingered over water breaks, showing off for the footballers.

One cheerleader who was clearly the queen bee of that school pranced in front of her phalanx of pom-pommed Spartans. She did a coy cheerleader point at Henry and yelled into her mini-megaphone, "Hey, number thirteen, why doncha come over here and sack me?"

Okay, so, I've only seen random bits and pieces of football games on TV (plus *Varsity Blues* twice), but even I knew what she said didn't make sense. Her cheerleaders laughed and clapped supportively anyway.

Some of Sloane's blond posse was sitting near us. One girl said, "Oh, he dead," and started texting furiously when Henry jogged over to the Chester cheerleaders.

Digby arrived and climbed the bleachers toward me. "See Sloane's spies watching Henry for her? They follow him around town to make sure he isn't hooking up with other girls."

"Why doesn't she just come and see for herself?" I said.

"Sloane would never do anything that desperate."

"Right, because this is not at all desperate."

"You know, if you keep questioning the rules of their games, these girls aren't ever gonna invite you to play with them."

"I'll try to get over my disappointment," I said. "These girls are out of control."

"You think the girls in private school are gonna be any different?"

"Stop trying to make me feel bad about Prentiss. I might not even be able to go now anyway, thanks to you."

"You know, Princeton, one day, you'll figure out that where you go to school doesn't determine what you actually learn."

"No offense . . . I think you're, like, life smart and everything, but I don't think I should be taking academic advice from you," I said. "Being that you're generally not pro-school."

"I'm a straight-A student," Digby said.

"*How?* You never go."

"Look. A miserable senior year to *maybe* get into Princeton? It's not a fair trade. Your father's only asking you to make that trade because *he* was miserable when he was your age. He thinks misery's normal."

"Well, it paid off, because he went to Princeton and now he's a success machine," I said. "'Success machine' . . . his words, not mine."

"You can become the kind of person who says stuff like 'success machine' if that's really your life goal," he said. "Even if you start in regular old public school. There's more than one way to make that duck quack."

"Please-Call-Me-Steve better update his résumé, because you'd make an outstanding guidance counselor," I said.

"Me, a guidance counselor? Yuck . . . *No.* Can't stand kids. Why d'you think I skip school so much?"

"Uh, yeah . . . *sarcasm.*"

Henry ran up the bleachers to us.

"You two are, like, two overheard anti-social comments away from having all ten warning signs for school violence." Henry pointed at my all-black clothes and Digby's usual black suit. "You're supposed to wear school colors. It's kind of tradition."

Oh, yeah. Everyone else was wearing purple and gold. "I don't get it. It's just practice."

"We are true to our school in this town," Henry said. "So why are you here? You like sports now?"

"We're gonna score some stuff," Digby said.

Near the boys' locker rooms, a steady stream of smoke escaped from a small window in the equipment shed.

"Dude. Be careful. Someone got stabbed in there this summer," Henry said.

"Yeah, I heard. Could get hectic. That's why you're coming with us," Digby said.

"What difference can I make?" Henry said.

"Two people are whatever, but three's basically a gang. Plus . . . *football*." Digby flexed his biceps.

"Coach is on us about representing the school. We're not even supposed to *jaywalk* in our uniforms. He'd cut me from the team if I got caught with drugs."

"Yeah . . . let's clarify that." I got nervous. "This isn't like with the break-in, where we're gonna accidentally on purpose get caught with heroin down my pants, is it? Because if it is, then I'm out."

"Nice, Petropolous. You see how negativity is contagious? No one's getting caught. We're getting rid of the drugs right away," Digby said. "And, Henry, I watched the backup QB take a marker and write a giant *L* on his left hand and an *R* on his right hand to keep them straight. You're not getting cut from the team any time soon. But if the uniform bothers you, take off your jersey and wear my jacket instead."

"Dude. I don't think I could even get my arm in that," Henry said.

"Nah, you'll fit." Digby took off his jacket. "It's like the traveling pants. It fits everyone with a pure heart. Isn't that how it works, Princeton?"

I rolled my eyes, but yeah, I'd read that book. No, the pants didn't work that way. I mean, they fit Effie, and she was a brat.

++++

"You should've just worn your jersey inside out. You look ridiculous," I said.

He did. Even shirtless, he couldn't button the jacket. The sleeves ended above his wrists and the jacket's hem was above his shorts' waistband.

"I like it. I look like the Hulk," Henry said.

"You look like a stripper. Not the expensive kind, either." I also thought, Who knew a sixteen-year-old boy who wasn't a werewolf fighting sparkly vampires could have a six-pack of abs?

"What would you know about strippers, Princeton?" Digby said.

"Tell me you're seeing this," I said.

"I like it. It's seriously like the traveling pants," Digby said.

We got to the door of the equipment shed.

"Okay, now what?" Henry said.

"First, Princeton will give me twenty bucks." I slapped a twenty into Digby's hand even though I knew it was a Bad

Idea. "Then we'll go in and buy the stuff. While we're there, I'll just ask about the banana sticker."

"Just ask?" I said.

"It'll come up," Digby said.

"It'll come up? How exactly?" I said.

"I don't know exactly. I'll bring it up. Casually," Digby said.

"Casually bring it up? That's the plan? That's not a good plan. That's not even really a plan," I said. "That's like a day-dream of how you want this to go."

"She's right. That's not a good plan," Henry said.

"See, this is the problem with democracy. Everyone thinks they have a better way to do everything," Digby said.

"What if they think the police sent us?" I said.

"We'll tell them we aren't with the cops. They know it'd be entrapment if we were and lied about it," Digby said.

"Even I know that's a myth. It's right up there with not get-ting pregnant if you do it standing up," I said.

"That's a *myth*?!" Henry said.

"Somebody needs to have The Talk with you. Like, *immedi-ately*. Yeah, it's a myth," I said. "To clarify, she *can* get pregnant even if you're standing up."

"On the bright side," Digby said, "now you can take a load off."

"Not to change the subject or anything, but, Digby," I said, "is this the first time you've done this?"

"Listen to you. Don't tell me *you've* scored drugs before," Digby said.

"Of course not, but we lived by the park and I've at least seen deals before. In person. Not just on TV," I said. "From what I remember, there wasn't much talking and, now I'm thinking about it, the whole thing was over fast. When exactly would you ask your questions?"

Digby was stumped.

We'd been standing by the door, arguing, this entire time. The door opened, sucking air into the shed in a whoosh. The outward gust of smoky air from inside that followed was a punch to the lungs. Only Henry was uncool enough to cough and fan his hand in front of his face. It's the kind of gesture that's only acceptable when you're a handsome QB.

"You kids in or out?" A super-tiny Asian woman was at the door. She was wearing a pink T-shirt with KITTEN written in glitter across the front. It was as likely to have come from the kids' section as a stripper's closet.

Kitten pointed to a huge gorilla-looking guy with a tiny head and giant Hellboy arms except he had two, not just one, Hands of Doom. "You're making Alistair nervous."

"You're making me nervous," Alistair said.

"Well? In or out?" Kitten said.

"Definitely in." Digby stepped into the shed.

We walked to the back while Alistair took up his post by the door.

"So?" Kitten stared at us, smoking a joint.

"So, uh, we'd like to buy some . . ." Digby said.

"Some . . . ?" she said.

"Uh . . . what would you recommend?" Digby said.

Kitten blew out a stream of smoke in a laugh. "You're either the saddest noobs I've ever seen or the River Heights Police Department's sunk to an all-time low. This ain't no Jump Street, is it?"

"Jump Street? No," Digby said.

"Because if you were . . ." Kitten gestured at Alistair. "I don't keep him around for his pretty face, you know."

"We're not," Digby said.

Kitten looked at us hard and decided to take a chance. She offered us a bong.

Now *that* we didn't expect. We stood there like dummies.

"Now?" Digby said.

"After that Atlanta bar raid thing, my lawyer advised me to always use with new clients. Just to make sure," Kitten said.

A couple of uncomfortable moments went by. Kitten hardened with suspicion again. Finally, Digby took the bong. As I watched him about to take a hit, every crazy story I'd ever heard flashed through my head.

What Andy Recton's brother thought was BC bud was actually Mexican schwag laced with so much PCP, he scratched the skin off his neck because he hallucinated bedbugs running around underneath.

Sharon Thomas ate magic mushrooms at a party she went to while visiting her cousin in college in Madison, and ground her teeth until three snapped and broke off.

Nate Remedios smoked purple-y leaves from Thailand some girl gave his friend, and ended up in the hospital because his blood stopped absorbing oxygen.

The moral of these stories was the same. Never do drugs if

you don't know exactly where they came from and if you don't totally trust the person giving them to you. Point being, I didn't know where this bong weed came from and I didn't trust the lady giving it to us.

Digby's lips were already on the bong when I yelled, "Stop!"

Everything froze. Alistair leaned forward. For a second, while suspicion built in his mind, he actually looked intelligent.

"We have a desk appearance. In two weeks. My lawyer said there'd be a urine test," I said.

At the mention of "my lawyer," Kitten relaxed. She had a lawyer, I had a lawyer: We were in the same club. Alistair backed down.

"Desk appearance, huh? So what're you doing here, then?" she said.

I realized I hadn't thought it through.

"Party after," Digby said. "To celebrate."

"You don't mind if I . . ." Kitten made a pat-down motion. While she searched Henry, she said, "Okay, big boy . . . you call me in a few years." She found a bottle of pills on Digby. "What are these?"

"Adderall, Lexapro, Paxil, Effexor . . . there's Valium in there somewhere too," Digby said.

"Look, I'll sound like I'm full of crap considering I do what I do and we're about to do what we're about to do, but . . . be careful with this stuff. These are the real deal. Personally, I don't sell this to kids, but you scamps always find a way," she said. "Wait a minute . . . are you the kids they caught breaking into that pervert's office?"

"Uh . . . yeah," Digby said.

Kitten laughed and shook the pill bottle. "Is this from his stash?"

"Um, no, I got those . . . somewhere else," he said.

Scary thing was, he probably got them from a pharmacy with legit prescriptions.

"Hey, Alistair, these are the kids who got Schell busted. You should thank them for your new ride," she said. "When you put Schell out of business, some of his customers decided to switch to all-natural. Alistair bought himself a new Vespa with his bonus."

Alistair's high-pitched giggle ran up and down like a little girl's. "It's red."

I imagined he looked like a circus bear riding a unicycle.

"Just curious . . . was this Schell's?" Digby showed her the sticker of the banana on the skateboard he'd pasted to a page of his notebook.

"Bananaman? No . . . Bananaman's . . . *bigger*," Kitten said.

"Like how much bigger?" Digby said.

"Schell was a pill mill. Fake scrips, selling samples. Bananaman's higher up in the food chain. He's a producer. Millions of bucks of synthetics made right here, in sunny River Heights," she said.

"Synthetics? Meth?" Digby said.

"Plus a bunch of other stuff. But the thing about Bananaman is that for the past three years, his stuff was export only. No selling in town."

"But now?" Digby said.

"Something's changed. His stuff's been showing up local," she said.

"So, it'll probably only be a matter of time before the cops get interested . . . and maybe even responsible businessmen like yourself will feel the hurt," Digby said. "You should remind him that people sharing a small patch like River Heights should be more neighborly when they're doing business."

"You're interesting . . . I never saw a kid with so many ideas."

"I think we should share," Digby said.

"Share? Share how?" she said.

"Like I tell you that at least some of the stuff getting sold around here's been *stolen* from Bananaman. He probably doesn't know it's happening," Digby said.

"Who's stealing from him?" she said.

Digby cocked his head. "You've never seen *Sesame Street*? Your turn. Share."

"No one knows who he is or how he runs his operation, but I checked and his stuff turns up in Philadelphia, Baltimore, and Toronto by Friday morning every week. So that means . . ."

"Thursday night," Digby said. "Every Thursday night, a ton of this stuff leaves River Heights and goes all up and down the East Coast without anyone noticing."

"Alistair and I checked out every roadhouse, outhouse, and henhouse, and we haven't found anything. A cook operation that big should be easy to find. Of course, you could just tell me who's been stealing and I could figure it out that way," she said. "Or maybe I could *make* you tell me."

She cackled. Digby laughed. Alistair laughed. I wanted to

laugh to fit in, but Kitten's dead eyes freaked me out, so I just stood there, my face twitching.

"I don't get what's funny," Henry said.

"I'll tell you who they are after we're done with them," Digby said.

"I don't know, kid. I'm not the patient type. I don't think I could stand the suspense."

"I'm confident you'll find a way," Digby said.

Kitten tapped her nails on the bench she was sitting on. "Fine. But don't make me wait too long."

"You'll be the first one I tell." Digby started to leave.

"Hey!"

We froze.

"Aren't you forgetting something?" She pointed to a digital scale and held out her hand to Digby. "Okay, noobs, you're supposed to give me a dollar bill to calibrate the scale. Don't let them use their own bill because I guarantee, it'll be a funky hollowed-out one. It won't matter much for when you're just buying weed, but if you're buying stuff sold by the gram . . ."

I produced a dollar when it became clear Digby didn't have one to give.

"A dollar bill weighs one gram exactly," she said. The scale agreed. "So, you want an onion? A cutie pie?"

"Uh . . ." Digby said. "What does twenty bucks buy?"

"Usually, not much. But for you . . . a dime of my finest. My thank-you-and-please-come-again rate." She took the twenty from Digby, weighed out a pile of shriveled leaves, and poured it into a Ziploc bag labeled BALONEY. She winked and said, "Recycle and reuse." She gave Digby her card. "They call me Mello Yello. For obvious reasons."

"Right," Digby said.

"Because I'm chill," she said. "Anyway, I'm shutting down my bricks-and-mortar operation. Call anytime."

On the way out, Alistair pointed at Henry wearing Digby's jacket. "My jackets fit like that too. My wrists get cold in the wintertime. I wear wristbands."

++++

The sun seemed brighter when we finally got out of that shed. My skin was buzzing. Maybe it was the relief of making it out alive. Or maybe I was high from breathing Mello Yello's smoke. I looked to see if Digby and Henry felt weird too.

"I'm starving," Digby said. The munchies? But then, Digby was always starving, so that might not have meant anything at all.

++++

At the diner, after we stuffed our faces and high-fived each other for surviving another one of Digby's idiotic dares, we pieced together what we knew.

Marina Miller: still missing. Her gynecologist: Schell, known pornographer and small-time drug dealer. Ezekiel: friends with Schell. There was a good chance Ezekiel was also stealing from a drug dealer named Bananaman. Bananaman: not small-time.

"Lemme guess, you're not telling the police any of this," Henry said.

"Not for free, anyway," Digby said.

151

"You mean in exchange for your sister's case files?" I said.

"For starters," Digby said.

The guns, the drugs, the missing girl: These were really happening to the three of us. But after we were done talking about all that, the conversation turned to the dance. Even at the time, I was aware it was ridiculous that the ideas of getting shot and turning up dateless at the dance caused me an equal amount of stress. They did, though.

SEVENTEEN

At school the next week, I was on my way to Spanish when I realized I really needed the bathroom. "No biggie, just go to the bathroom," you say? It's not that simple. Girls' bathrooms here are marked off and defended like gang turf. The bathroom I usually went to was clear across campus, though, and I was already late to class. Again.

The nearest one was the main bathroom by the cafeteria. I'd gone to it once at the beginning of the year and swore I'd never go back. This was the bathroom where the Big Girls on Campus (mostly seniors and a select group of junior girls who were either majorly ballsy or had been given the seniors' seal of approval) hang out and competitively primp. No one went in alone and no one's there to actually use the toilets. The place smelled like a salon.

But I really needed to pee, so I went in, hoping it was close enough to the start of classes that it might have emptied out. No joy: It was packed.

One group of girls shared a curling iron. "No, it's good when your hair steams. It's the frizz coming out," one girl said.

Another group huddled together passing around lipsticks.

At one of the stalls, two girls were using Sharpies to write a Hot or Not list of boys on the door.

"Ew, Darla . . . *no*. Nose grease," one said as she crossed off her friend's last entry. "Disqualified."

I felt a fireball of hate hit me in the chest. Sloane. She stared at me as I walked to the stalls. She and her backup blond girls were at the sinks nearest the windows, which was probably the most valuable bathroom real estate because they were beside the only full-length mirror and the hand blower with a nozzle that could be flipped up so it doubled as a hair dryer.

One blond backup pointed at me. "Hey, isn't that—"

"Yeah. Why's she here?" Sloane said.

I ducked into a stall and caught my breath.

Outside, Sloane said, "Okay, check this out. Who am I?" I peeked out of the crack by the stall door and watched Sloane do robot arms and mime falling forward stiffly over and over. "They had to cut the volleyball net," Sloane said to her laughing posse. "Loser."

I felt a wave of exhaustion. Two more years of this if I didn't get into Prentiss.

Then the laughter hushed up. It reminded me of a video I once saw where it went really still right before a tornado touched down and ripped up a town. I looked back through the crack but Sloane and her gang weren't by the window anymore.

Then, out of the corner of my eye, I saw Sloane's phone peeking over into my stall.

Now, in the old days, I probably would've done the normal thing: Scream, storm out of the bathroom, thank God they hadn't filmed me actually peeing, and then obsess about why Sloane was picking on me.

But these were new days. I had a scar on my chin. I was on a first-name basis with cops. For the past few nights, ever since the Dumpster fire, Digby had been coming over to hang out and eat, and I guess the sly tricks from the outrageous stories he'd been telling me had sunk in. I batted the phone out of Sloane's hand. I heard her gasp as she lost her grip on it. It clunked against the porcelain before slipping underwater in the bowl. That's the sound of eight hundred bucks going down the toilet, I thought. I wanted to cheer when the screen distorted, then shorted out and went black. I kept it together, though, and walked out of the stall.

Sloane confronted me at the sinks. "You owe me a phone." There were red spots on her cheeks.

"You mean the phone you were using to film me in the bathroom?" I said.

The red spots on her cheeks grew, but she backed off. "Whatever. It's fine. Plenty more where that came from."

"It's okay, Sloane, you can get it fixed," one blond backup said.

"Leave it," Sloane said.

But the blonde had fished the phone from the toilet and was holding it out to Sloane.

"I said *leave it*!" Sloane screamed. That's the problem with

155

needing a posse to represent: They represent, all right, and when they do something humiliating like dive into a toilet, they take you down with them.

Sloane ran out and the other groups of girls openly laughed at her.

"That was like that YouTube of the giraffe kicking the lion." One of the Sharpie vandals stuck her hand out for me to shake. "My name's Bill. This is Darla." Bill draped a toilet paper sash across my chest. "For your bravery, your bitchiness under pressure, and your service to all the girls of River Heights High . . . we thank you."

"Hi . . . Bill?" I wasn't sure I'd heard right.

"Well, it's really Isabel but *yuck,* right? Ever since that movie-that-must-not-be-named, Isabel, Isabella, Bella . . . *no.* Just *no,*" Bill said. "So, did you really get arrested?"

"Well, we were taken into custody, which isn't really the same thing."

"That guy Digby. What's up with him?" Bill said. "Are you two . . . ?"

"Digby? No." I said.

"I remember in grade school his sister was murdered. He was *messed up,*" Bill said. "I mean, he was never normal or anything. But now . . ."

"With the suit," Darla said.

"And the attitude," Bill said. "Hot."

"Hot," Darla said.

"He's number four," Bill said.

I read the list. "No Henry Petropolous?"

156

"Petro-puh-lease. He's so . . . pedestrian," Bill said.

"*So* pedestrian," Darla said.

"Saying you like him's like saying your favorite pizza topping is cheese. *Snore,*" Bill said.

It was like I'd stepped into some weird alternate universe. Where had these girls been the whole time?

Instead of jewelry, Bill had grocery lists and notes-to-self scribbled up and down her arm like a tattoo sleeve, new writing sitting on top of the old scribblings that hadn't washed off yet. Her clothes were a vintage-y, Grandma, biker mix and she wore makeup but not in a way that said she was doing it to look pretty, because that would be lame. Plus, she had a gravelly voice. Darla had the same vibe, but she was basically an echo. Darla was Bill Lite.

Then I remembered who they were. "Oh, wait. You guys got the homecoming formal canceled," I said.

"Everyone remembers that part but forgets that we got the budget for the formal donated to the Covenant House," Bill said. "Anyhow, all we did was start a petition. The people spoke."

"And it was basically only a moral victory because the Blooms just cut a big-ass check so their little Cinderella would still get to go to the ball," Darla said.

"Darla, we didn't do it to piss Sloane off. We did it for Covenant House," Bill said. "Your life's not a movie starring Sloane."

"Whoa. You're right. That's deep," Darla said.

See? Bill Lite.

"So. Digby," Bill said.

"Yeah, we want to know about Digby," Darla said.

"Among other things . . . like how you get your bangs so smooth." Bill held her phone out to me. "We need to hang."

I know I sound weird, but it was an instant friend crush. I wanted to be friends with Bill so much that, high from the first meaningful contact I'd made in that school besides my questionable friendships with Digby and Henry, I blurted out something I would regret horribly. "Yeah . . . we should hang out. Gimme a call and I'll call Digby." They wanted the Digby freak show? I'd give them the Digby freak show. I took her phone and entered my number.

My feet weren't touching the ground when I left. I saw it all so clearly: Bill, Darla, and me at the mall, the three of us eating lunch, the three of us not taking crap from Sloane. I was so busy daydreaming, I didn't notice the boys' bathroom door open until a hand shot out and dragged me in by the elbow.

++++

I found myself standing beside the urinals.

"Hey, Princeton, I was just gonna go looking for you," Digby said.

"What the hell?" I said.

A boy at a urinal turned and also yelled, "What the hell?" and then what-the-something-else when he realized he'd peed on his own shoes. Some boys coming in saw me and backed out of the bathroom.

One kid said, "Oh, man, I *heard* she was a guy."

"You realize that's gonna be the new rumor about me now, right?" I said.

"I like it. I might help spread that myself. Big-city transgender teen moves to small town to establish new identity, start new life. Calls herself Zoe," Digby said. "That TV movie writes itself. You'll be famous. All the girls will finally want to be your friend."

"Until they ask to see it and I'm suddenly some big fraud."

"Stuff a sock down your pants and don't date until college. Who's gonna know?"

"As always, excellent advice. So what am I doing in here? This place reeks."

"I remembered where I've seen that banana logo before."

"You couldn't come out of the bathroom and tell me that instead of dragging me in here?"

"No, look." Digby took me to a stall where, on the wall, someone had crudely drawn the skateboarding banana.

"Okay, so . . . now you wanna find who drew this?"

Digby pointed at writing under the drawing. "F2 1600."

"What does that mean?"

"I don't know, but look. The paint underneath . . . it's streaky. Like this spot's been wiped." Digby stuck his nose against the stall wall and sniffed.

"That's disgusting."

"Turpentine. This writing under the banana changes. I bet these are, like, instructions and they change all the time."

"Time. Like, sixteen hundred . . . military style? Four p.m.?"

"So F2 is . . . the place? Obviously the place. Drug dealer

telling customers the place and time. But what does F2 mean?"

We stood there in silence. The halls had gone silent too.

"Great. Class started. I'm late. *Again*. And I still haven't peed."

I went into a stall and tried to pee. Seconds passed. Then a minute.

"Hey, Digby, turn on a tap. I can't go."

"Would you feel better if I peed too?"

"Just do it, *please*. It's starting to hurt—"

"Hey, let me see your book."

Digby reached over the stall door, took my bag off the hook, and rummaged through it. My lip gloss rolled across the floor. Of the boys' bathroom. No way was I putting that on my lips again.

"Just tell me which book you need, I'll get it for you," I said.

"The Student Handbook. I *know* you carry yours around, Princeton."

The handbook had the school rules and regulations, pictures of the teachers, and the class schedules and room assignments. It was totally dorky, but I carried it around because I liked the homework planner in the back.

"The one with the blue cover. Would you not throw my stuff on the floor, please?"

I finally peed and came out of the stall. Digby was looking at the campus map in the handbook.

"F2's a storage room across from the labs," he said. "That's gotta be it. They'll be there at four. We should go."

"Because our last drug deal wasn't stupid enough."

"What are you talking about? That went well."

"Don't you think we're gonna eventually run out of luck? Plus, we go to school here. Whoever's selling will probably know we were the ones who broke into Schell's office," I said.

"Hm . . . you're right. We can't go."

"No. We can't."

Digby washed his hands, a vague expression on his face.

"Hello?" I said.

"Hey," he said.

"What?"

"I'm thinking." He balled up his paper towel.

"So, you agree? We can't go."

"Yeah. No. We can't go."

He three-pointed the paper towel and said, "Um, okay . . . see you at four." He walked out before I could remind him again that we couldn't go.

EIGHTEEN

I had after-school plans to group chat with friends from back home. I'd flaked on them the last few times without giving a reason and they thought I was just blowing them off. Truth was, I'd gotten caught up doing Digby stuff, which I couldn't explain to them because, frankly, I didn't know how to.

They used to get pissed when I bailed. I'd get angry messages and, like, a turd icon in my inbox. But the last time, they were just "whatever" when I skipped. My former closest friend, Cecily, never brought it up, but she had definitely been treating me differently. She'd chat but be really distant, then she'd include me when she sent group updates like, "Sex and the City+pizza=Woohoo!" to remind me I was missing out. Honestly, freezing me out for real would be less hurtful.

So, I was actually glad when I got Digby's message summoning me as I was packing up after school.

"G4 1550 Bring food."

I checked my handbook. Computer lab across the quad from

the storage room. I thought about refusing, but what was the point? I hit the vending machine and headed to the lab. Digby and Henry were already there.

"Oh, man, you're saving my life right now." Digby grabbed the food. I was barely able to snatch back some chips for myself.

"You know, it only takes, like, an extra second to type 'hi' when you send a message. I mean, 'G4 1550 Bring food'? That's rude. You can't just order me around."

"Probably doesn't help that you keep showing up anyway," Henry said.

"She knows she'd miss out if she didn't. C'mon, this is fun, right, Princeton?" Digby said.

"Big fun," I said.

"She loves it," Digby said. "She writes all about it in her diary."

"You let him read your diary?" Henry said.

"No, I didn't. He helped himself."

"Oh, *no,* dude. I did that to my sister once. Not good. She beat the tar out of me," Henry said.

"His sister Athena . . ." Digby did a closed-fisted double biceps downward flex and grunted.

"A big girl," Henry said.

"A truck," Digby said.

"She plays lacrosse," Henry said.

"She's big, but she's fast," Digby said. "And silent."

"For a truck," Henry said.

"Don't be such pigs. And you." I pointed at Henry. "She's your sister."

"Nah, she'll do well. Greek guys love big women. My grandfather told me I should marry a big woman so she can keep me warm in the winter and give me shade in the summer," Henry said.

"It's so inspiring to hear what really goes on in the mind of the average teenage boy," I said. "Anyway, what are we doing here? Are we waiting to see who the dealer is?"

"No, he turned up a while ago." Digby produced a Lenny the Binoculars from *Toy Story*.

"Interesting spy equipment," I said.

"It works. Look," Digby said.

We crossed the lab, ducked below the windowsill, and looked out across the courtyard at the windowless gray storage trailer. A uniformed janitor stood in the doorway.

"Our janitor's dealing?" I said.

"Look. In his hand," Digby said.

He was flicking his Zippo lighter, lighting and slapping it shut over and over.

"Bicycle Guy from the Dumpster fire's our janitor?" I said.

"That's *Floyd*. He's also my team's equipment manager. He drives the bus for away games," Henry said.

"You didn't recognize him before?" I said.

"From the back, in the dark? He was just another skinny dude wearing a hoodie," Henry said. "He's dealing?"

"We're about to find out." Digby's phone rang and he turned on the speaker. "We have audio. Here's our inside man now."

Through the binoculars, I watched Felix Fong walking toward Floyd. He looked so small but super-determined. His hands were balled into fists and his knees were stiff and hardly bent as he walked. He was wearing a ridiculous shirt that said:

"'Your girlfriend's in good hands'?" I read. "It's surprising a shirt that offensive comes in a size that small."

We heard Felix's thin voice say to Floyd, "Hey, um . . . you holding?"

"You sent him?" I said. "That guy had a gun, if you remember, and that kid's completely clueless."

"Don't worry. We did research. He knows what to say," Digby said.

"Whatcha want, kid?" Floyd didn't sound like he believed Felix was actually there to buy.

"Oh, you know . . . Adderall, Dexies, Bennies, uppers, speed, wake-ups . . ." Poor Felix was so nervous, he was uncontrollably reeling off every nickname he'd learned.

"Yup . . . and he's puking out research all over Floyd, dude," Henry said.

"He's gonna die and it'll be your fault," I said. "And mine too, because I'm right here . . . letting it happen."

"Okay, cool it, Felix," Digby muttered.

"You know what you're asking for?" Floyd said.

"Um . . . yeah," Felix said.

"What? You gonna party?" Floyd openly laughed at Felix.

"Um . . . sort of. I'm building a simulation? About black holes and entropy? I need to do two weeks' work in one?" Felix said.

"Good job, Felix," Digby said.

"Buy some Red Bull, kid. Get lost," Floyd said.

From Felix's body language, it was clear he was about to give up. He turned in our direction. For a second, I thought he'd wave at us to come rescue him.

"He's losing it. He's losing it." Digby took out a small mirror and caught the sun with it. The bright flash that momentarily shone across Felix's face was the reassurance he needed.

"I have thirty dollars and you're selling me something to help me concentrate," Felix said.

"Or what, kid?" Floyd said.

"Yeah . . . or what, Felix?" Digby said.

"Or . . . or . . . I have lots of friends who have lots of science projects," Felix said. "Maybe we'll find someone else."

"Nice," Digby said.

"You've turned the school genius into a narc. I hope you're proud of yourself," I said.

"All right. But don't do something crazy like OD or have a heart attack and die and get me busted, okay?" Floyd said.

"Okay," Felix said.

"I'm giving you one—*just one*—you take it, show me you don't lose your mind, and maybe I'll sell you more," Floyd said.

Three boys in football team jackets walked across the quad toward Floyd. One of them was Dominic Tucker, the boy who'd been tormenting Felix in the cafeteria.

"Oh, man, *no*." Henry turned around and closed his eyes.

"What's the matter with you?" I said.

"The team honor code," Henry said.

"He's gotta turn them in if he sees them doing substances . . . so he doesn't wanna see them." When I still didn't understand, Digby said, "If he doesn't physically *see* them, he doesn't have to report them."

166

"What? That's insane. Here they are buying drugs. You know they're doing it," I said.

"All I saw was a couple of guys walking," Henry said.

"I'm looking at them and I'm telling you, they're buying drugs," I said.

"Didn't see it for myself. Doesn't count," Henry said.

"That's not much of an honor code," I said.

"Welcome to team sports," Digby said.

"Hey, Floyd, you got some?" we heard Henry's teammate say through Digby's phone.

"Just finishing up. Be with you in a few," Floyd said.

Henry plugged his ears and walked away singing "Rubber Duckie."

"That's it? This little blue pill's five dollars?" Felix said.

"That's off-season pricing. It's eight bucks come finals," Floyd said.

Felix froze, the pill in his open palm.

"Um . . ." Felix said.

"What, kid?" Floyd said.

"Um . . . so if I need more, you can get it?" Felix said.

"I just said I could," Floyd said.

"Because, um . . . my friend . . . she told me you could get more . . . my friend Marina? You know, Marina Miller?" Felix said.

"You know Marina?" Floyd sounded more interested.

Felix looked our way again. Digby and I actually ducked.

"She's, um . . . she's a friend of a friend," Felix said.

"Get outta here, kid. I got business," Floyd said.

"Okay, Felix, it's obvious he knew her . . . that's all I needed. Now get out," Digby muttered.

The football players started pushing Felix, bouncing him around like a pinball.

"Hey, squirt, where's my paper at?" Dominic said.

"Uh, yeah . . . it's coming," Felix said.

"Better make it good, squirt. I need a C to pass," Dominic said.

Felix finally got away and jogged out of the quad. He couldn't resist flashing a thumbs-up in our direction on his way out.

Digby hung up his phone and threw a Dorito at the back of Henry's head. "Hey! You can stop singing now.

"So Ezekiel is getting drugs from Bananaman, Floyd is dealing them for Ezekiel, and he definitely knows Marina Miller," Digby said.

"Think she was a customer?" I said.

"Did she ever take anything in front of you, Henry? Act like she was on stuff?" Digby said.

"No, but she kinda kept a lot of secrets," Henry said.

"Did she keep a diary or . . ." Digby said. "You know what we should do?"

"I see where this is going. Pass. I'm out," I said.

"What?" Henry said.

"Come on, this again?" Digby said. "Is this our dance now?"

"What dance?" Henry said.

"She says no, I ask and ask her, and then she agrees like she was always going to in the first place," Digby said.

"No. I'm done breaking into places," I said.

"Where are we breaking into?" Henry said.

"Marina's house," I said.

"Look at you, Juvie," Digby said. "We don't have to break in. We're going in with the permission of Marina's mom. Legal and legit. All we have to do is pretend we're her classmates."

"Is it just me or are we in some weird place where lying to get into someone's house seems kinda all right? I mean, I actually feel relieved," I said. "It's *just* lying."

"Wanna go tonight?" Digby said.

"Can't. Working," Henry said.

"I'm hitting the mall with Mom to check out dresses for the dance," I said.

"Um . . . yeah, the dance. You got a date yet?" Digby said.

"No . . ." I said.

"You want one?" Digby said.

"Dude. Wow. Are you asking her to the dance?" Henry said.

My stomach did a weird up-down thing at the thought of going to the dance with Digby. I couldn't tell if that meant I wanted to or if I really, really didn't.

"No. Better than that. I suck at dancing." Digby tried a little too hard to look nonchalant. "Why don't you go with Felix?"

"Um, because he's ten and he comes up to my armpits," I said.

"Actually, he'll be thirteen soon, and if you shave your armpits, then it won't be an issue," Digby said.

"I'm not asking Felix to the dance. That would be even worse than going alone," I said.

"Oh, you wouldn't have to ask him. He'd ask you," Digby said.

"It's not who does the asking that's the problem. It's the whole turning up together at the dance that's the issue," I said.

"So you'd say no if he asked you?" Digby said.

"Yeah. I'd have to say no," I said.

"You can look in that sweet little kid's face and crush him if he asked you to the dance?" Digby said.

"That's cold," Henry said.

"I'd do it nicely, but yeah, I can look him in the face and tell him *nicely* that no, I can't go to the dance with someone who still can't get on the good rides in Six Flags," I said.

"Okay, you can't do that," Digby said.

"What do you mean?" I said.

"You kinda should say yes," Digby said.

"What? Why do I have to say yes?" I said. "Oh, God, he's not dying of cancer or something, is he?"

"*Cancer* . . . I should've said he had cancer. But no, he doesn't have cancer," Digby said. "You have to say yes because I sorta said you would so he'd agree to do this."

"You *what*?" I said.

"I offered all kinds of other stuff, but the heart wants what the heart wants," Digby said.

"But I'm not yours to give away," I said.

"Oh, hey . . . it's not like that. I didn't promise you'd go with him. I said you *probably* would and that I'd put in a good word," Digby said.

"I don't understand why you didn't just offer to get the bullies off his back, for example," I said.

"Yeah, I'm already working on *that*. He's doing something

else for me for that," Digby said. "Anyway. I guess you don't have to say yes. He's gonna ask you and of course you could say no. And if you said no, you'd go alone, Felix would stay home, and it'd pretty much be a lose-lose, but hey, you can totally say no."

"What if someone else asks me?" I said.

"If it ain't happened yet . . ." Digby said.

"Dude, *that's* cold," Henry said.

"Fine. I'll think about it," I said.

"That's all Felix and I are asking," Digby said.

"So when do you want to go to Marina's house?" Henry said. "I'm working after school all week."

"Saturday?" Digby said. "And, Princeton, wear something prissy."

"Prissy?"

"Yeah . . . you know, uptight."

"Uptight?"

"Like the sweater thing you wore on Tuesday," Digby said.

That outfit took me an hour to put together. And, no, uptight was *not* the look I was going for.

NINETEEN

So, when you're a minor and you get busted, the cops send notifications to both your parents, not just the one with custody. I was not aware of that.

I found this out from the all-caps hate-mail I got from Dad calling Mom a "LOUSY MOTHER INCAPABLE OF SETTING RULES." He signed off with "DON'T BE ONE OF THE PATHETIC SHEEPLE," and then, inexplicably, "MOO."

I'd gotten the e-mail on the way home and when I walked in the house, I heard Mom in the backyard, yelling into her phone. In many ways, it was like old times, with Mom sputtering and struggling to finish her sentences.

"Of course I've met—" she said. Pause. "You can't ground a six—" And then, "I know *you* would, but she's practically—"

He thought I should be grounded? It didn't bode well for our living arrangements if I were to get into Prentiss.

"Mom. Give it to me!" I didn't mean to yell, but I was feeling mean and I didn't want to lose any of the energy I'd built up by taking the time out to be polite to her. I took her phone. "Dad." I hated the quaver in my voice. I mashed the phone tighter against my ear and soldiered on. "It's me. Zoe."

"Zoe?" My father's enraged voice made my ear ring. "Is this true about you vandalizing a—"

"Dad."

"—an anti-social bottom feeder's crime—"

"Dad. Stop."

"Don't you interrupt me—"

"You asked me a question. Do you want me to answer it or not?"

What I then found out over the next five seconds was that Dad's silence was just as scary as his shouting.

"Well?" he said.

"It's true. I did it. Now I need a lawyer."

The ranting response that followed was ugly. I didn't say anything because I didn't want him to know that I'd started to cry sometime after he'd called me a "rude, spoiled little pig" and accused me of humiliating him. When he ended his sermon by screaming that he'd be coming down the following week to "straighten out the mess I'd made with my life," I didn't have the strength to say anything more than "Fine."

Mom and I just stood there, staring at each other in shock after I hung up. Then, finally, she climbed atop the back patio bench, reached around the top of the trellis, and retrieved a pack of cigarettes in a Ziploc bag from amongst the trumpet vines.

"I thought you quit those," I said.

"For emergency only. *That* was an emergency," Mom said.

"In fact, you want one? Just kidding. But really, that looked bad. Are you okay?"

"He's coming up next week . . . over Thanksgiving."

"Should I make a turkey?"

"Well, that'd show him. But if you really wanna punish him, make your hummus."

"This also came in the mail from him today." Mom took an envelope out of her sweater pocket. Inside was a stack of mall chain-store gift cards. They were worth hundreds and hundreds of dollars. "We should return them . . . it's probably not appropriate . . ."

"Or . . . we could spend them," I said. "Before he figures out how to cancel them."

"Revenge shopping? I know that game." Mom lit a cigarette. "I used to be an All-Star."

++++

"I can't." We were at the mall. I'd given up on finding a dress for the dance, and Mom was turning down a bite of my chili fries. "I watched this documentary about slaughterhouses and . . . I can't."

"Why would you watch a documentary about slaughter-houses?"

"For a date. Not that he made me or anything. It was show-ing and he wanted to see it, so I went with him. I'd feel like a hypocrite eating that."

"Well, he's not here right now." Then I realized I had no idea if that was true since I didn't know who the guy was. "Or is he?"

"Are you saying you're ready to meet him?"

174

"Are you saying you're ready to marry him?"

"Why are you being so sassy?"

"I don't know. Why are you being so defensive?"

"Geez, should I blame hormonal teen-angst or that boy Digby for your new verbal stylings?" Mom said. "What's going on with the two of you, anyway?"

"Nothing. Stop asking me that. Besides, we don't hang out as much anymore . . . I mean, since you told me not to."

"Right . . . because you don't do things I tell you not to do," she said. "Anyway, you mind eating alone? I'll meet up with you in a half hour? I threw all my makeup out. I need cruelty-free."

"Seriously?"

"One day you'll get it. It's unbelievable what you'd do for someone you like. In fact, the more unbelievable, the more you probably like them." Then she thought about what that sounded like. "Not in a codependent 'he beats me because he loves me' way, of course. Because that's certainly not love, honey. Love *never* hurts—"

"Okay, Mom! You're going down a weird road."

✝✝✝

After Mom left me to buy makeup, I didn't want to go back to the main part of the food court with the high school kids, so I sat in the kiddie area with the stroller moms. Halfway through my fries, I saw Digby dressed in his teddy-bear-in-a-tutu dancing toward me. I waved him off, but the kids around me were screaming for his character, Suzie Bear, to come over.

"Get out of here. I don't feel like getting into it with my mom again." I waved him away again. But he kept coming toward me.

"I'm not in the mood. Go away." I put a little something extra behind my whispering to send him the message that I was serious. I shooed him again, but he kept coming. He mocked me, cupping a paw behind the bear's ear.

"Oh, you can't hear me? Can you hear *this*?" I hit him over the ear. "Bet you heard that."

Suzie Bear pawed me on the shoulder. It was a shockingly hard hit, actually. Hard enough that my fork flicked fries out of the bowl because of it.

"Ow . . . what the hell?" I got up and pushed Suzie Bear away. "Seriously. Let's talk when you come over later."

But he kept coming at me and, somehow, we ended up locked in something I later found out wrestlers call a tie-up. By this point, the kids had gathered around. The future trouble-makers among them chanted, "Fight, fight, fight."

I floated out of my body and over the scene. I saw myself twirling around the tables with a giant teddy bear.

And then I saw Digby himself standing to the side, yelling, "Five bucks on Suzie Bear!" It took me another second to process the fact that if Digby was standing in the crowd, then I was tussling with a stranger.

Digby told me afterward that Suzie Bear was being worn that day by a hearing-impaired girl named Wendy. He also said that my agitated waving and whispering probably made Wendy think I had something to say to her.

I didn't find this out until later because security hauled me off to mall jail before there was any explaining. It took fifteen minutes solid of Digby's fast-talking about various fur-oriented phobias he claimed I had to convince the mall cops to let me go.

"Hey . . . your earrings are gone," he said.

I touched my earlobes. I'd been self-conscious when I'd removed them after getting off the phone with Dad. It wasn't like removing them was some grand gesture, because I knew, of course I knew, that even if Dad had been there physically watching me take them off, he wouldn't have cared whether or not I wore them beyond the fact that he thought I'd lose them if they weren't in my ears.

"It's good. They were a little . . . 'To-my-suburban-soccer-mom-wife-on-her-fortieth-birthday,'" Digby said.

"Thanks for the fashion advice but what the hell? Aren't *you* Suzie Bear?" I said.

"Not always. Sometimes I'm Angelo the Duck and I peel shrimp for Cajun Connection on Thursdays," he said.

"You have three jobs, you go to school, and you still have enough free time to get me in trouble."

"Hey, this was all you, Princeton. And I think I just got you *out* of trouble."

"Right . . . thanks for that. I don't need an assault charge on top of everything else. I owe you one."

I regretted it as soon as I said it, because of course I knew what Digby wanted from me at this point.

"Funny you say that," Digby said. "Felix will be wearing a red cummerbund, so stick to black, red, or white. Wait, not white . . . you might look like his nurse nanny or something."

And that's how my first date in River Heights (first date anywhere, actually) ended up being with an almost-thirteen-year-old.

⁜

Later that night, at 8:30, Mom was running late, still upstairs getting ready, when, usually, she would have been gone by then. Digby had been coming over basically every night since he realized on the night of the Dumpster fire that in my house, as he said, "There's food lying around everywhere."

I peeked out the glass in the front door and saw Digby jogging down the street toward our walk. I waved for him to stop. We had a frustrating pantomime exchange for a couple of seconds until he finally understood that I was telling him to wait by the side of the house.

I started clearing the dinner table to kill time until Mom left.

"Zoe, could you come upstairs, please?" Mom said.

I went up to her room. "Yeah, what's up, Mom?"

Mom was dithering over her collection of black boots. "I think black's too . . . middle-aged? Don't you have some dark brown ones? Can I borrow them?"

"Hang on." I went into my room and after rooting around on my closet floor, I found the boots. I got the scare of my life when I stood back up, though, because suddenly there Digby was, sitting on my bed. "*God*. You scared the crap out of me."

Digby caught the boot I threw at him. "What?"

"I meant *wait* by the tree, not climb it, you idiot—"

Digby lobbed the boot back to me and shushed me right as Mom said, "Zoe? What did you say?"

I heard her footsteps approaching, so I grabbed Digby and threw him in my closet. "Don't touch anything." I slid the closet door shut just in time.

"Oh, I meant the other brown boots. The ones with the stacked heel." Instead of leaving, Mom hovered in the doorway.

I couldn't think of a way to get her out of my room that wasn't shady, so I prayed Digby knew what a stacked heel was, cracked open the closet door, inserted just my arm, and flailed around. When I took my hand back out of the closet, I was shocked to see I was actually holding the right pair of boots. "Holy cow. These are the boots!" I checked my excitement. "Here. Have a great time."

"Okay. What?" Mom said.

"Nothing." Then, to underscore the fishiness of my response, there was a huge crash from inside my closet.

"What was that?"

"The tension bar in the closet must've given out again," I said.

"Tension is right . . . what are you so nervous about?"

"Nervous? I'm not nervous," I said. "When will you be home tonight?"

It was Mom's turn to be nervous. "I'm not sure. What time are you going to bed tonight?"

Game on. Mom had been sneaking her mystery man into our house late at night and sneaking him out super-early the next morning. I'd been letting them think they were fooling me because it was fun listening to her obviously big-boned boyfriend tiptoe on our creaky floors. Sometimes, to freak them out, I groaned and pretended to wake up.

"I don't know. I have a lot of homework. It could take hours. I could be up all night," I said.

Mom hesitated, pretending to take her time getting in the boots. I could see her trying to decide whether tonight was the night I'd meet the mystery man. Finally, she said, "Try to save the all-nighters for college."

I walked her downstairs. Just before she walked out, she said, "Would you put away the chicken, Zoe?"

"Um, yeah, I actually think I'm gonna eat a little more later," I said.

"Okay, but you're gonna leave me some for my lunch, right?"

"I'll try, but . . ." Who was I kidding? Digby was going to pick that bird clean. "But you know I like to eat while I study."

After Mom left, I got a pie plate from the kitchen and loaded it up with basically all the leftovers. Upstairs, I found my clothes dumped out onto my bed and Digby gouging away at the plaster of my closet wall with his pocket knife.

"What are you doing?" I said.

"I'm fixing your closet," he said. "You had this bar just kinda balancing on these pegs. How does this not collapse every time you reach for something, Princeton?" He pulled off a little plastic bag of spare parts that was taped to the bar.

"What are those?"

"These are wall anchors. I'm making pilot holes for them."

I remembered something Bill said about liking watching men using tools. I snorted.

"What?" Digby said.

"Nothing . . . just something my friend Bill Lowry said

about guys who are handy. She'd probably hyperventilate if she saw you right now. She already thinks you're sexy," I said.

Digby stopped what he was doing and turned to me. "Oh, so *Bill* thinks I'm sexy."

"Yeah. Bill's this girl in school—"

"I know who Bill is," he said.

"Anyway. Yeah. She likes you."

"Oh, yeah? Maybe I should check out that situation. I haven't seen her since middle school."

"She's nice. Really nice," I said. The insincerity in my voice surprised me.

"Okay, but is she really *really* nice?" Digby said. "You girls are all so political . . ."

"Ha-ha. Do you know what you're doing, by the way?" I said. "That doesn't look right."

"How would you know it doesn't look right? You didn't even know what an anchor was just now," he said. "Yeah, I know what I'm doing. You got a hammer?"

I didn't feel like admitting it to him, but I was sick of the closet bar collapsing every time I pulled out something from the back. When I got back with the hammer, Digby was holding up a blue oxford shirt with the Prentiss crest on the breast pocket.

"Dad got that for me . . . the rest of the uniform's in there too," I said. I put on the shirt to show him how ridiculous it looked.

"He's pretty confident you're going, isn't he?" Digby said. "So what would happen if you didn't get in?"

I didn't want to say it because I knew it'd sound melodramatic, but from my experience, people did what Dad expected of them or they just kind of stopped existing for him. I'd seen him tough-love a whole branch of his family into nonexistence this way.

"His way or no way, huh? I've heard that song before." Digby hammered an anchor into the pilot hole. Impressively, he sunk it in only three blows. I started to see Bill's point about guys who were handy around the house.

"I helped my father build a tree house I didn't want and a doghouse on the lawn for a poodle mix who hated getting mud on her paws just to get the guy to talk to me." He looked embarrassed. "Hey, I was twelve years old." Digby hammered in the other side. Something about the aggressive way he was working discouraged conversation. Finally, after he'd screwed in the supports and installed my closet bar, he said, "I finally spoke up about not really enjoying doing construction. That conversation turned out to be the last we'd ever have."

"So just because you don't have the same hobbies, what? He hates you now?" I said.

"Not like he hates me, exactly . . . more like he figures we have nothing further to discuss," Digby said. "I mostly just 'Yes, sir' him when he orders me around. Luckily, he drinks, so he forgets, like, two-thirds of what he tells me. After I figured out how to tell which third he'd remember, we were on easy street."

We hung my clothes back on the rod and, as had become our routine, I put on an episode of *Twin Peaks* for us to watch while Digby ate. It was awkward, though, when instead of sitting in his usual place at the desk, Digby plopped down on my bed.

He patted the spot on the bed beside him and said, "This plate looks awesome."

"It looks like something frightened villagers offered up to an angry volcano god," I said. I tried not to be weird when my bed sagged and pushed us up together.

I don't think Digby noticed. He plowed through the chicken and didn't stop until he was scraping sauce off the bottom of the pie plate with his dinner roll.

"Maybe tomorrow I should defrost a pizza too," I said.

"Uh, actually, I have plans tomorrow night," he said.

My heart immediately started to race. After years of watching Mom get played by Dad, I was used to looking for the real reason behind the excuse. "Working late" really meant a romantic dinner with someone else. "Urgent injunction application to be filed in the morning" really meant overnighters in a hotel. I couldn't help it. My mind started parsing the phrase "plans for tomorrow night" until I realized what I was doing. But it was too late. The emotional roller coaster had left the station. I felt close to tears. I hoped Digby didn't notice.

"I guess I could bring Felix here instead. Work on our thing here . . . the catering's good."

Why did I feel relieved to find out he was just hanging out with Felix?

Digby pointed at my blue Prentiss shirt. "But I don't know how focused he'll be on our work with all this hotness going on."

"Hotness? This ugly thing?"

"You know nothing about the way the male mind works," he said. "Are you blushing?"

"Of course not."

"When Sally disappeared, it was like a fog came down in my house. We walked around, bumping into each other, no one talking. I'd ask my mother a question and she'd just look right through me. I used to get so angry," Digby said. "Even at the time, I knew I was being selfish. I mean, obviously, they were just . . . wrapped up in what happened to Sally."

"But you were, what? Seven years old?" I said.

"Anyway, one of the few useful things I learned while I was getting my head shrunk is that when you get rejected a lot, you start to hear rejection all the time, everywhere, even when there hasn't been any rejection. And here's something else she told me that you need to remember . . . after rejection you feel shame," Digby said. "Rejection and shame. Those two always go together. The yin and yang of low self-esteem."

"So what are you saying I should do? How did you get over it?"

"I never said I did," Digby said. "But I also learned that just because my mother occasionally shows up in my wet dreams, it doesn't mean I'm a psycho. That part's less useful for you, though."

I was starting to recover and my heartbeat was coming back down to normal, but now my mind was post-gaming and just like Digby said I would, I felt embarrassed.

"It gets better, Princeton."

TWENTY

As planned, I borrowed Mom's pantsuit and met up with Digby and Henry the next day outside Marina's house, a huge mansion in a neighborhood called The Gates. Physically, it was behind my neighborhood, but spiritually, it was a universe away.

The Miller mansion was a big ivy-covered brick building that looked like something on a college campus. An expensive college that gave freshmen laptops.

"This is her house?" I said. "How many people live in it?"

"Her parents . . . her half sister. Live-in help," Henry said.

"What was she doing in public school?" I said.

"She got expelled from private school," Henry said.

"Besides, this is Marina's stepmother's pile. She's the rich one. Maybe she didn't like her stepdaughter enough to pay for tuition," Digby said before dialing on his phone and walking away, saying, "I need to place an order . . ."

"I heard Digby got you to go to the dance with Felix," Henry said.

"Did you hear why?" I said.

"Yeah . . . it's too bad. Wendy's nice," Henry said. "You know, back in the lab, I thought Digby was asking you to the dance."

"How weird would that have been? Me and Digby . . . posing for the formal photos . . ."

"Totally weird," Henry said. "Wait, does that mean you would've said yes?"

Strange. Thinking of Digby that way was . . . well, not exactly unpleasant, I guess. Definitely unsettling, though.

"I guess you're going with Sloane?" I knew he was. After all this time hanging out with Henry, I was surprised to find that I still minded.

"I'd invite you guys to dinner with us, but . . ." Henry said.

"She hates me?" I said.

"Not just you. Digby too."

"That's cool. It'd be weird anyway."

"*So* weird," Henry said.

Digby came back to the conversation. "What would be weird?"

"If we all went to the dance together," I said.

"Oh, no, Felix has something special planned. He sent me photos of the restaurant he's taking you to. He even highlighted the fire exits," Digby said.

"Wow . . . he's pretty excited. He probably thinks he's gonna get lucky or something," Henry said.

"But he's not her type. Princeton likes them . . ." Digby said. "Heroic? Is that the word?"

"Douche. That's a word too," I said.

186

"Okay, that's enough wordplay for today. We have a mission. Somewhere in that huge house is a clue to where Marina is," Digby said. "Maybe. Probably. Well, you never know until you try."

"Great," I said.

Digby took a camera out of his backpack and handed it to Henry. "You're Brandon Spano and you're taking photos for a special article in our school paper." To me, Digby said, "You're Brianna Wick and you're my editor. I'm Taylor Berry and I'm writing the article. Taylor, Brianna, and Brandon. Got it? I'll do the talking. Princeton, just hang back and put on your sourpuss face."

"Sourpuss face? What sourpuss face?" I said.

"That's perfect," Digby said.

"This is just my face," I said.

Digby rang the bell. It didn't faze me anymore listening to Digby spin his little webs. We were with the school paper? Sure. Writing an article? Why not?

The housekeeper showed us into the front sitting room.

Mrs. Miller appeared after twenty minutes. She was one of those women who wore uncomfortable outside shoes at home. Her heels click-clacked across the marble. She had on a full face of makeup and a head of pageant-perfect goddess curls. She gave us ten minutes of scripted motherly concern before her high-gloss shell cracked and things finally got interesting.

"The problem with Mari was . . ." Mrs. Miller pronounced it *Mah-ree*. "Well, frankly . . . she'd always been deeply troubled. Truly, I tried, but you can't fight genetics. My husband had her with his first wife, you see. We didn't emphasize that when

Mari went missing because we didn't want people thinking we were less than desperate to get her back, but now . . ."

I don't think she knew how to end that sentence.

"But now that everybody knows how upset you are, you can flesh out some details," Digby said.

"Yes, exactly. Now everyone knows I'm worried sick . . . well, I suppose the facts should be told," Mrs. Miller said. "But I'm not sure about photographing the house . . ."

"Mrs. Miller, to be honest, I overpromised these photos to my editor because I'm in trouble. Missed my deadline. She's a hard case." Digby nodded toward me.

Mrs. Miller looked at my face and softened. "Yes, I see."

"And what we really need's a picture of *you* . . . in her room. Maybe if someone who knows something saw how this was affecting Marina's family . . ." Digby said.

Mrs. Miller stood and checked her hair in the mirror above the mantel.

"I'm a mess, but I suppose it'll do. It's not HDTV or anything. The news crews came every day for weeks . . . *that* was a challenge." Mrs. Miller finished primping and snapped her fingers at us imperiously. "Come along."

There were no pictures of Marina on the walls we passed on the way up to her room. There were plenty of weird, posed glamour shots of Mrs. Miller, though. In one of them, she was naked on a fur blanket, cradling a newborn baby who I guessed was Marina's half sister.

"This is my Ursula." It was a picture of her on a yacht, hugging a teenaged girl.

Ursula was surprisingly unpretty. I'm always shocked when rich girls aren't pretty. How *could* you be unattractive if you had all the nicest clothes and makeup? It didn't compute. But I guess there really were some things money can't buy. Ursula was a hatchet-face. Even wearing a straw hat and a gingham bikini, she looked like she'd just murdered someone and was calculating how to dispose of the corpse.

"Here we are. Mari's room," Mrs. Miller said.

It was empty. Not like everything had been cleared out. That would've been less weird. This room still had a bed, a desk, a chest of drawers. There just wasn't much *stuff*. Hardly any books, no stuffed animals, no photos or posters on the walls. It looked like IKEA, except IKEA has fake cardboard stuff to make the rooms look fake lived-in.

"Was Marina always this . . . organized?" Digby said.

"I'm not sure. Mari kept the door locked." Mrs. Miller tapped on the sign on Marina's door. "Keep. Out. So I did." She positioned herself by the window. "How's this?"

Digby directed and Henry snapped away. Meanwhile, I glanced around, trying to figure out where in the empty room to look. Then, when it started to feel like we were lingering, the housekeeper came in.

"Mrs. Miller, the pizzas are here," the housekeeper said.

"What are you talking about?" Mrs. Miller said.

"You ordered ten pizzas for the party," the housekeeper said.

"Party? Don't you think I would've informed you if I were throwing a party? And *pizzas*?" Mrs. Miller said.

Off they went, bickering all the way.

"We have, like, three minutes to find something," Digby said.

"How do you search an empty room?" I said.

"It's not *totally* empty. This was on the closet floor." Digby held up a single CornNut and sniffed it. "Nacho."

"You wanna eat it, don't you?" I said.

"I'm seriously thinking about it," Digby said.

"That's disgusting. Anyway, other than that CornNut, this place is totally clean. We're not gonna find anything here," I said.

"No, you're *not* going to find anything." Marina's half sister, Ursula, was in the doorway.

We were so busted. Digby was in the closet, Henry had a desk drawer open, and I'd lifted Marina's mattress in case she kept her journal where I kept mine.

"The police took stuff away and Marina didn't have that much to begin with," she said.

"You're Ursula," Digby said.

"I am. And you're not who you told my mother you were," she said.

"Sure we are," Digby said.

"Brianna Wick is black, and Taylor Berry? Is a *girl*," Ursula said. "I've been to Marina's school."

Now we were fully busted.

"What are you trying to do?" Ursula said.

"What do you mean?" Digby said.

"Are you trying to bring her back?" she said.

"Isn't that what everyone's trying to do?" he said.

Ursula had a seriously evil smirk. "Su-ure."

"I get it. You don't like Marina. But do you hate her

enough to want to see her stay missing?" Digby said.

"Oh, no . . . I want her back now. It's not amusing anymore," Ursula said. "I mean, Marina's whiney and she dropped loser dust all over the place, but it's not as much fun as I thought it'd be without her around. It's kinda like the Joker told Batman: She completes me."

"It doesn't sound like she had it too good around here," Digby said.

"You met my mother," Ursula said.

"What's the age difference between you and Marina?" Digby said.

"I'm five months younger," Ursula said.

"Ah . . . doing that math makes your mother feel sleazy," Digby said. "So, Marina was, what? Cinderella?"

"Maybe in her mind. No, Marina was more, like, invisible. Gift cards for Christmas, that kind of thing," Ursula said. "Nothing crappy enough to write any fairy tales about."

"But you think it was crappy enough to make her run away," Digby said. "Because you don't think she was kidnapped."

"Neither do you," she said. "Why *don't* you?"

"She filled a prescription for eight months of birth control right before she disappeared and brought it with her," he said.

"Of course she did. She's so dumb," she said.

"Do the police know you don't believe she was abducted?" he said.

"You of all people should know what happens when people suspect you know something about a family member disappearing," Ursula said.

"You know who he is?" I said.

"He and his family were the most notorious people in River Heights for a year," Ursula said. "Of course I know who he is."

"But your mother didn't," I said.

"She only watches the news when she's on it or when someone she knows is getting indicted," Ursula said.

"Why do you think Marina took off?" Digby said.

"Dunno. Maybe she finally found her Prince Charming." She snapped her fingers and pointed at Henry. "Now I remember who *you* are. She was bummed out after you dumped her. Anyway, you probably wouldn't have been able to give her what she needed."

"Oh?" Digby said. "Marina told you Henry couldn't give her what she needed?"

"You're an idiot," I said. "Not everything's a sex thing." To Ursula, I said, "It wasn't a sex thing, was it?"

"More like a meal ticket thing," Ursula said. "Marina lived off my crumbs, but crumbs around here . . . still pretty sweet. She needed someone to keep her in the lifestyle to which she'd grown accustomed."

"She said she was going out with a rich guy," Digby said. "You couldn't save us a whole bunch of work and just tell us who he was, could you?"

"I don't know who he is. But I do know he gave her nasty habits." Ursula passed Digby a debit card. "She stole this from me and when I stole it back, I noticed a bunch of blue powder on it. Gross. She used it to snort her junk."

Digby ran his tongue along the line of blue powder.

"You don't even know what that is," I said.

"It's Adderall. Generic Adderall tastes like sherbet," Digby said.

"He also gave her a new phone," Ursula said.

"Don't tell me she took it with her," Digby said. "Because that would be really lame."

"No, the police have it," Ursula said. "But there's nothing in it. They told my mother the memory on the new phone was completely wiped. But . . ."

"The new phone was wiped . . . but her old phone," Digby said.

We followed Ursula down the hall to the upstairs sitting room.

"So . . . ?" Digby said.

Looking at Ursula's hatchet-face smile was like staring at the business end of a sharp blade. Chop, chop, chop.

Digby pointed at a phone sitting in a dock in the entertainment unit. "Is that her old phone?"

Ursula gave us a slow, elaborate shrug. "It's not mine."

"We're taking it," Digby said.

"Like I said, it's not mine," she said.

Digby pocketed it just as Mrs. Miller got back.

"Ursula, do you know anything about pizzas getting delivered? He threatened to call the police if I didn't pay. He was extremely rude," Mrs. Miller said.

"I don't know, Mother. Did you drunk-dial again?" Ursula said.

"Oh, Ursula. Don't tell those jokes in front of people we

hardly know. They might think you're being serious," Mrs. Miller said. "Anyway, did you get what you need for the article?"

"They sure did." Ursula handed Digby her card. "And I'm giving Brandon my contact information so he can call me if he has more questions."

"I thought your name was Taylor," Mrs. Miller said.

"That's what I said, Mother," Ursula said.

"I can smell the anchovies from up here." Mrs. Miller sighed dramatically. "Every single one has double anchovies on it. Based on that alone, they should have known it was a practical joke. What *are* we going to do with all those pizzas?"

++++

"Does she look like an iguana? Yes, she does. Do I find her attractive anyway? Kinda." Digby flicked the card Ursula had given him. "I think I'm gonna call her."

"Ursula? You're kidding," I said.

"No, I see it," Henry said. "For him, I mean. Not me."

"But she's so . . . she's . . ." I said.

"But that's exactly why, I bet," Henry said.

"Some people say the heart sees what's invisible to the eye. Other people say love means never having to say you're sorry," Digby said. "All I'm saying is, I see potential. I'm not apologizing for that."

"Love? Just like that? You're in love with her now? That's ridiculous," I said.

"You sound pissed, Princeton. What's it to you?" Digby said.

194

"Yeah, that was an eight on the tension scale," Henry said.

"It's disgusting," I said. "They treated Marina like she was some kind of second-class citizen in her own house. And their awful photos . . . rich people are just the worst . . ."

"Is it all rich people or just these rich people?" Digby said.

"Did you see the way she talked to her housekeeper?" I said. "She snapped her fingers at us!"

"Guess we've found another one of your hot-button issues." Digby dove back into the pizza box. "Last piece . . . you guys sure you don't want it?"

"I can't believe you ate that entire pizza," Henry said.

"The smell's making my stomach turn," I said.

"Yeah, I wasn't sure which one I'd end up with, so I got double anchovies on all ten," Digby said.

"I should've guessed that was you," I said.

"You thought ten pizzas just randomly came right when we needed to be alone in her room? See, what you do is order enough so the pizza place will refuse to take the pizzas back but not so many that the person with the credit card will put up a real fight with the delivery guy. When it works, you get privacy *and* a nice snack," Digby said. "Interesting fact: The perfect number of pizzas is double the number of cars in the driveway."

Digby scrolled through Marina's phone while he preached about his pizza con.

"Whoa . . . check this out." Digby passed the phone to Henry. "Things just got interesting."

TWENTY-ONE

"Sloane's number is in Marina's call log?" I said.

"Henry, call her and ask why," Digby said.

"She won't answer. She's doing a campaign thing at the mall for her dad," Henry said. "We could go see her, but, uh . . . Zoe, you don't have to come with us because . . . because . . ."

"Of course, it would be fun if you did," Digby said.

Digby got that look on his face and I just knew what was coming next. "Don't do it," I said. "It's so tacky . . ."

"Meeeeee-*yow* . . . catfight," Digby said.

"So degrading. For all of us," I said. "When guys fight, it's some macho tribal thing, but when girls fight, it's a big perverted joke. Makes no sense."

"Sure it does . . ." Digby said. "Girls don't fight. They kinda pull each other's hair, push each other around a little, then their clothes come off."

"Girls don't know how to fight," Henry said. "So it's funny when they try to."

"You realize girls have actually *killed* each other, right?" I said. "Girls in the Bronx smuggle razor blades into school in their cheeks."

"Are you smuggling a razor blade in your cheek, Princeton?" Digby said.

"What? No."

"Then . . . Meeeee-*yow*," Digby said.

"Seriously, you don't have to come," Henry said.

"I'm coming." The only fate worse than dealing with Sloane in person was to lose a game of chicken to her when she wasn't even physically around to play against me.

‡‡‡‡

Walking through the mall, I put all my hopes into "maybe she's gone home already." But, no. There she was, just like Henry said she'd be.

Sloane stood out from the dull-suited politico types in a pastel sweater-and-dress outfit that disguised her unfairly perfect boob-y ass-y figure. Her hair was in a little flip behind a pink headband and she was patiently pinning light-up badges on some kids' lapels.

Digby picked up a flyer. "The Bloom family's auctioning selected watercolors from their collection to replace the children's hospital ambulance," he said. "I guess it was stolen . . . which is weird."

"She looks . . . different." I felt crummy hating on her when she was clearly do-gooding.

Digby did not. "Puke." He balled up the flyer. "Sorry, Henry, no offense, but her dad's gonna run for Congress, so this whole thing's probably some campaign thing."

When Sloane spotted us, her serene smile dropped and her face tensed into her usual sneer.

"Ah . . . there's the Sloane we know and love," Digby said.

Sloane pushed past the kids and stalked over to us. "Henry? Why did you bring them here? Didn't you say you were working this afternoon?"

"So, Sloane, how do you know Marina Miller?" Digby said.

Sloane pointedly ignored him and kept talking to Henry. "Mother needs help at the booth." Mrs. Bloom waved at us.

"Look at her . . . she seriously thinks she's a Kennedy. It's so sad," Sloane said.

Henry hesitated, but Digby nodded. "Later."

"Later, dude." Henry jogged away.

Digby passed Marina's phone to Sloane.

"This call log shows you and Marina were talking around the same time she started dating Henry. The calls stopped when they broke up. Looks like Henry's not the only one who dumped her last summer. I guess you didn't need her if she didn't have Henry anymore," Digby said. "Pretty cold, Sloane."

"God. Boo-hoo-hoo," she said.

"But we're not here to judge. It's just interesting that you and Marina were so friendly," Digby said. "Tell me about it."

"What about you, Zoe? Do *you* find it interesting I knew Marina?" Sloane said.

"What?" I said.

"She's not interested," Sloane said. "If she were interested,

198

she'd ask me herself, wouldn't she? After she apologized for throwing my phone in the toilet, of course."

Digby was annoyed. "Sloane. These mind-games are—"

"Mind-games improve your memory. Without mind-games, I might not remember why Marina was calling me," Sloane said.

"Fine. Sloane, tell us about Marina," I said.

"Do it nicely. Please? With a cherry on top?" Sloane said. "The works."

Digby stepped between Sloane and me.

"I'd totally get it if you don't wanna do this," he said. "No one should talk to you like that."

"Is this important?" I said.

Digby hesitated.

"Screw it." In my most disrespectful voice, I said, "Sloane, I apologize for ruining your phone. Please, pretty please, tell us how you knew Marina. Cherry on top."

"Of course, Zoe. I would be happy to after that very nice apology," she said. "We were both on the equestrian team at the country club. Ursula too. Did you meet her? Ugh . . . Ursula. Such a pill. We get it. You're smart. Now go tweeze your eyebrows."

"Sloane. Marina?" Digby said.

"I let her borrow my car and driver," she said. "When she didn't want anyone to know where she was going."

"Where did she go?" Digby said.

"Mostly skanky places downtown. She got my driver in trouble because someone keyed the car at the 7-Eleven she used to go to," Sloane said. "That's the kind of thing she did. Get my driver to drive to some specific 7-Eleven in the ghetto."

Digby got excited and said, "Did she meet anyone? Did she buy stuff—"

"It's not like my driver and I have tea and chat," she said.

"Sloane . . . are these your friends?" said a guy wearing a three-piece suit. I noticed he carried three cell phones.

"This is my dad's campaign manager," Sloane said.

"Well, we haven't announced anything official, but James Patrick Bloom is exactly the kind of leader who'll lead this great state of New York into the bold, bright future." He spoke in a smooth, oily gush. "Hi, I'm Elliot Rosen. How do you know Sloane?"

"They're public school kids, Elliot. See what the Democratic Party's forcing me to deal with?" Sloane said. "I don't know what for. Not like Sasha and Malia ever saw the inside of a public school, and look where *their* dad ended up."

"Oh, Sloane. The presidency is such, *such* a long way in the future." Elliot laughed, but his eyes were worried. "Did I hear you mention Marina Miller? Is she . . . did someone find her?"

"I don't know. Did they?" Sloane asked Digby.

"Because if you knew something, *anything,* I'd appreciate a heads-up. I mean, is she de—" Elliot rephrased. "Is she alive? Because we'd need to get in front of this story. The Miller campaign's basically dead in the water, but even a dead cat can bounce if you throw it off a high enough ledge, know what I mean?"

Elliot offered us his card.

"Go away, Elliot," Sloane said.

"No, wait." Digby took the card. "Would this be a tit-for-tat situation?"

"You bet," Elliot said. "Wow. Sharp as a tack. Maybe I'll be working for you someday."

"Not unless you're a criminal defense attorney," Sloane said.

She and Elliot walked back toward the party. Digby and I started walking away.

"Oh, Zoe, you're welcome, by the way," Sloane said.

I couldn't help myself. I didn't turn around because I knew I'd chicken out. I just reached back, flipped Sloane the finger, and kept it up even after I heard the auction's audience gasping.

"Hey, Princeton, you know the local news is filming this, right?" Digby said.

No, I did not.

‡‡‡‡

Digby scored discarded, defective hard taco shells from the Mexican place, shook them up in a bag with salsa, and called it dinner. We walked to the parking lot.

"I don't get it. Marina's father's running too? Is everyone here running a political campaign?" I said.

"Just everyone rich. Look, Princeton, River Heights is lousy with old money . . . like, *old* before-George-Washington Dutch New York money . . . when it was Breukelen and Bronck, not Brooklyn and Bronx. Like Sloane's last name is actually van der Bloom. They dropped the *van der* part when Sloane's grandfather ran for senator. They didn't want people knowing how blue their blood was."

"Marina's family too?

"No, they're run-of-the-mill twentieth-century rich. They subcontract to the defense facilities."

"Ugh . . . these people run this country . . ."

"You know, Princeton, you were actually winning until the whole finger thing. It's only gonna get worse if you let her see she's getting to you."

"Why does she keep coming after me, anyway?"

"Well, number one, she goes after everyone. Mean-girling's her hobby. You're not that special. Well, except maybe, number two, she hates you because she can't get Henry to stop hanging around you. That makes her look bad," Digby said.

That made me feel good. "So what am I supposed to do?"

"Well, are you willing to curl up and die or get out of town? No? Then you'll just have to win a few and lose a few until she gets tired of you and moves on."

"That's some plan."

"By the way, not to burst your bubble or anything, but I should tell you that Henry isn't doing what you hope he's doing and what Sloane's *afraid* he's doing."

"Which is what?"

"I mean, you're probably thinking, Henry chooses me in some kissy-kissy *Beauty and the Beast* way."

"*Beauty and the Beast*? Am I supposed to be the Beast in this scenario? I don't understand your reference."

"*Beauty and the Beast.* Wasn't there a rose in that?"

"Um, yeah . . ."

"And he had to get a kiss from a rose by the grave?"

"Wow . . . the Seal song? Were we even born when that song came out?"

"And then he had to give the rose to the woman he picked,

202

which, in this case, you're hoping is you."

"Okay, now, *that* is *The Bachelor*," I said. "Seriously, you need to pick one channel and just watch something all the way through."

"The point is, that isn't what's going on here. This is more like bros before hos," he said.

"I hate that saying on so many levels."

"Because Henry's going out with Sloane."

"I know. I don't care."

"You don't care. You're not crying into your pillow at night?" he said.

"Shut up."

"Because if us three are gonna hang out—"

"Really." I hoped I was telling the truth, because he was right. There's nothing sadder than hanging out with someone who doesn't care you're dying of a crush on them the whole time.

"I want to believe you . . ." he said.

"Seriously. I'm over it," I said. "Can we move on now?"

Digby still looked dubious, so I moved on first.

"Now what?" I said.

In the parking lot were four limousines with drivers sitting in them.

"Those two are rentals," Digby said. "Leaving us those two . . ."

"May I contribute?" I said. "That driver's way too young and good-looking. No way Sloane's parents let that guy drive her around."

By process of elimination, we landed on the limo with the tired middle-aged driver reading the paper.

Digby dumped the taco bag on his way to the limo. I tried

to copy the confident swagger-y way he opened the door and slipped into the seat, still licking his fingers.

"Hi. Sloane said you'd take us home," Digby said. "She'll ride with Mrs. Bloom."

The driver snapped his paper shut and eyed us in the mirror.

"But Mrs. Bloom's going straight to the benefit and Miss Bloom specifically said she wasn't attending," the driver said. "She was very clear."

"That's what I said, but she told me to shut up and butt out," Digby said.

The driver put the car in gear. "Sounds like her . . ."

After we pulled out onto the interstate and relaxed into the drive, Digby started his spiel.

"I'm Digby. Sloane didn't tell us your name."

"Doubt she knows it. John."

"Nice to meet you, John," Digby said. "I hope this isn't rude, but I gotta ask. Is it weird working for a kid? 'Miss Bloom'? Seriously?"

John laughed. "Yeah, my daughter's just two years older than Miss Bloom. Ashley lives with her mom in Chicago."

"That's too bad," Digby said. "You must miss her."

"Yeah, she's a good kid. Works two part-time jobs and still finds time to volunteer at the shelter," John said. "I don't get to see her as much as I want, but me and her mom are putting away what we can for college."

"I feel you, John. Sloane drops five hundred bucks on lipstick, meanwhile your kid's smart enough to go to college, but she's being punished for not being born rich," Digby said.

"Sloane says she can choose between Wellesley, where her mom went, and Wharton, where her dad went, because she's guaranteed spots in both."

John's eyes narrowed at us in the mirror. He pulled over onto the shoulder of the road.

"Mrs. Bloom went to Vassar," John said.

"Great," I said.

"I drive these people around listening to them finesse each other all day long, so I know you're finessing me right now. What d'you want, kid?"

"Just a little information," Digby said.

John stepped out, opened my door, and said, "Get out."

We were in the middle of nowhere on the interstate. The cars were going so fast, the limo shook every time one passed us.

"Fix this, Digby," I said.

"I don't rat out the people I work for. The Blooms are very good to me," John said.

"No, no . . . we don't want anything on the Blooms. It's Marina Miller we need to know about," Digby said.

"Wh-what about her?" John said.

"You drove her around," Digby said.

"Miss Bloom told me to." John was instantly defensive.

"Relax. We're just curious where you took her. If she met up with anyone," Digby said.

John just stared.

"Listen. I know you're worried about the police, but no one's interested in that. Not us, not Sloane," Digby said. "By the way, was it Sloane's idea that you not come forward with this information?"

"Miss Bloom and I barely discussed the rides. And after Marina disappeared . . . well, it was never brought up again," John said. "But, th-there was one time, Marina got a nosebleed in the backseat . . ."

"Ohhh . . . there's blood evidence on the seats," Digby said. "You got nervous, you didn't say anything, then three weeks went by and it went from looking bad to looking like guilt . . ."

John folded. "She went to a 7-Eleven in the Js mainly. She was weird."

Digby explained later that the Js was a neighborhood in the old downtown core where crime was so bad, pizza places refused to deliver to it. The *Js*, by the way, stood for "the Jungle."

"She had me take her to a motel in the Js too. I didn't see who she met up with, but she never checked in at the desk or anything. Just went straight up into one of the rooms," John said. "I really had nothing to do with her disappearance."

"It's okay, John, we believe you," Digby said. "But we need you to show us where you took her."

John climbed back into the car. As he pulled away, Digby whispered, "See, Princeton? This is what it's like to be upstate political dynasty one-percenters. They tell their driver to take them wherever to do whatever and not only does he not ask questions, he protects their secrets." Digby checked his phone and said, "I was right, dammit. Mrs. Bloom *did* go to Wellesley. I shouldn't have flinched. I gotta learn to bluff better."

TWENTY-TWO

John took us on a tour of the sketchiest parts of River Heights, places I'd only seen on the local news, and pointed out stops he'd made with Marina. We went through a railroad crossing into a landscape of chain-link fences and bombed-out apartment buildings with garbage bags over smashed windows. It was literally the wrong side of the tracks.

"Funny there are abandoned shopping carts everywhere, because there aren't any actual supermarkets . . . just chips and beer for miles around. And, of course, the one-two punch that really socks it to 'em . . ." Digby pointed at a payday loan place and the liquor store beside it. "Location, location, location . . . people living here don't stand a chance."

I looked at the pedestrians. "It's like we're on a different planet. I never see these people anywhere else in town."

"Look at a bus map and count how many lines go from downtown to anywhere else in River Heights. Just a few in the daytime for maids and cleaners to get to and from their jobs," he said. I guess I made some kind of despairing sound, because Digby said, "Oh, this is nothing. Wait until you see how undocumented farm workers live outside town past the West Perimeter Highway."

++++

It was a relief when John dropped us off at my boring suburban house.

"You know, it's one thing for Marina to go slumming downtown twice a week, but . . . run away to do it full-time?" I said.

"I watched Nick Boskowitz drink an entire glass of OJ through a straw stuck up his nose, then burp the alphabet all the way to *W* before he threw the OJ back up on himself," Digby said. "*Never* underestimate the stupidity of the average teenager."

"Nick Boskowitz is my social studies partner. We're supposed to write a presentation on World War I chemical warfare. Man, I have the *worst* luck partnering up."

"That comment's really about me, right? Because we're partners on the project? Relax . . . we have *weeks*."

"To do a project we supposedly worked on for months."

"Chill. Seriously."

"Whenever you tell me to chill, my butt clenches tighter," I said. "What do we do now?"

"By now the police have checked out the birth control prescription and realized what we realized. They'll probably internally downgrade the case to a missing persons and take their foot off the gas."

"So you don't think the same thing happened to Marina and Sally . . ."

"Not unless my four-year-old sister ran away in the middle of the night to be a party girl."

"But you still wanna find Marina . . . why?"

"Princeton, I'm ready for Sally to not be the first thing people think of when they see me. Worse than the people who think I killed her are the people who pity me . . ." When I pretended not to understand, he said, "Oh, yeah, even *you* do. You wouldn't let me get away with half the stuff I say and do to you if you didn't feel sorry for me."

"Maybe I'm just bored," I said. "Maybe I just don't want to see you starve."

Just then, the front door burst open.

"Oh, *hey*, kids . . . come in. Stay for dinner, Philip. I haven't seen you in forever," Mom said. "I made spaghetti surprise." Mom was being weird. Not only because she was being nice to Digby, but also because she was talking super-fast and hardly breathing.

"Um . . . Mom? You okay?"

"I'd love to," Digby said. "I'm starving."

"After that entire pizza? The tacos?" I said.

"That was hours ago. Besides, on principle, I never turn down food," Digby said.

Zillah the amazon appeared at the doorway and loomed over Mom.

"God! Zillah!" Digby smirked at the annoyance his joke caused Zillah.

"Kids, Zillah has bad news. Zillah and her . . . family?" Mom said.

"We are all one in God's family, but we prefer to refer to ourselves as a household," Zillah said.

". . . are moving out. Such a shame to lose you from the neighborhood," Mom said.

"It *is* a shame. After four years here, I find the tone of life in River Heights changed. Unsavory elements have insinuated themselves. You only have to watch the evening news to see that." Zillah looked at me when she said that. "Now I should return to packing. So much to do before the movers come on Thanksgiving."

"Thanksgiving? How d'you get a moving company to work Thanksgiving?" Digby said.

"It isn't Thanksgiving in Canada, where my movers are from," Zillah said.

"They're moving to a farm just over the border," Mom said.

"Canada? Guess you're serious about getting away from the neighborhood," Digby said.

Zillah turned her back on Digby. "Good-bye, Liza. Let me know if you find out anything more about that other matter?"

"Of course, Zillah," Mom said. "So sorry to see you leave."

Mom pretty much slammed the door on Zillah's frowning face and leaned on the door like kids do to keep out monsters.

"There was one moment when I thought she was going to strangle me. She looks like a strangler. It's the hands. Like Molly in *Great Expectations*," Mom whispered. "Kid . . . your bad reputation came in handy."

"Anytime, Liza," Digby said.

"But don't push it," Mom said.

"So, what was the other matter you guys were talking about?" Digby said.

"Neighborhood thefts. She asked if I've seen anyone sneaking around at night," Mom said.

"Other than your boyfriend?" I don't know why I chose to say that right then. Maybe it was because Digby was around and I wanted it out there without creating a mother-daughter Hallmark moment.

Mom blushed. "You know?"

"It's not like you made it hard. He stomps around and there are weird seeds everywhere after he eats breakfast," I said.

Digby shivered. "Bird food."

"Sorry, Zoe . . . I didn't want to make you uncomfortable, but now I just look like I was trying to slip one past you," Mom said. "Maybe we could talk later."

"Can't wait," I said.

"So, Philip, would you like to eat dinner at the table, or would you rather wait until I leave and eat in Zoe's room?" Mom said.

"Ah," Digby said.

My turn to go red.

"Yeah . . . I'm not the only one sneaking around," Mom said.

"That's pretty detailed with you knowing the timing and the eating in her room," Digby said.

"You two leave the blinds up and Helen next door likes to talk on recycling night," Mom said.

"You're not freaking out?" I said.

"Tell you what: If the blinds ever went down, *then* we'd be having a different conversation," Mom said.

TWENTY-THREE

Right around Halloween, I started to feel like I was finally cracking the River Heights social scene.

"Join us," Bill said. She and Darla ran lunchtime surveys and posted the most interestingly worded responses on Bill's Facebook.

I read the header on the sheaf of paper Bill handed me.

93% of boys and 62% of girls are exposed to Internet porn before they turn 18, so we know what you've been up to. After the last time you saw porn, did you A) want to have sex, B) feel so grossed out, you had to shower, or C) no, really, I only use the Internet for homework. Add a comment.

I said, "People won't admit they've watched porn, will they? Doesn't this need to be anonymous?"

"People don't even want to be anonymous when I post their answers," Bill said. "Everyone wants to be a star."

There were a lot of names and answers on the booklet she'd

made. "You talk to a lot of people . . . from a lot of different cliques."

"You want to know how we did it, right? How we got in? It's all social networking and who people link to." From her notebook, Bill took out a folded piece of paper that looked like a celebrity who-dated-whom map. Arrows went back and forth between cut-out yearbook photos of students. Underneath the photos were lists of names of other students. Above the arrows were words like *is on the soccer team with* and *used to date*. "We skipped the Dropouts and the Felonious Punks because they don't have outside links. We started with the Dumb Geeks and then moved up to the Goody-Goodies. When the Wannabes started playing, it was basically like hitting the East Australian Current. We were in the mainstream. Everyone wanted to play."

"Isn't it genius? Ask how she came up with it," Darla said.

"It hit me when I watched a thing on terrorist cells. Terror cells stay separated because it's easier for them to resist penetration. *That's* what high school is. Cells that resist penetration, orbiting our leader . . . Sloane Bloom," Bill said. "She doesn't talk to us . . . she doesn't even acknowledge our existence, mostly . . . but we feel her presence everywhere and we arrange ourselves in order below her."

"And are you and Darla on this map?" I said.

"We float . . . like a virus." Darla looked pleased with her pronouncement until Bill's hard stare wore her down. "As Bill says."

"Not a vi-*rus*, Darla. That's negative. We're vi-*ral*. We started by invading weaker cells, knowing each one had at least one person who had a toehold in the social cell above it, and we just rode it all the way up through the school," Bill said. "The only person I can't place on this map is Digby. He only hangs with you and Henry. Once I saw him in the computer lab with Felix Fong . . ."

Ah, Digby. Here he was again. Bill mentioned him every couple of minutes. It was getting awkward. I knew she wanted me to produce him, but for some reason, I just didn't want to make it happen. At the time, I told myself it was a "worlds colliding" thing.

Despite the improvement in my friend situation, though, Digby's prediction was right. No one else invited me to the dance.

꞉꞉꞉꞉

The Thursday afternoon before the winter ball, Felix cornered me at the lockers at rush hour. Half the school was going on second-shift lunch, while the other half was coming off first-shift lunch. Basically, everyone was stopping off at their lockers and caught the show Felix put on. The kids standing close enough to hear what Felix said repeated his goofy speech for the kids in the back who couldn't hear.

"Zoe, you're a very special girl . . . um . . . lady? Woman?" Felix said. "Anyway. Would you do me the very big honor of letting me take you to the dance? Will you be my Doll?"

The "doll" thing will be clear in a second. People laughed, staring at us, waiting for my answer.

When I said yes, I tried to make it clear that I was agreeing only veeeery reluctantly. I put a lot of subtext behind my, "Um . . . yeah . . . fine . . . okay."

That paparazzi wannabe Derek Martino took a photo of Felix and me at that moment. I groaned because I could imagine exactly the caption, "The Moment," floating under our picture in "Memories of a Night to Remember," the ridiculously named thirty-dollar prom keepsake they were printing up. The worst thing, though, was that the photo memorialized yet another one of Felix's awful T-shirts. This one said: GREAT STORY, BABE. NOW MAKE ME A SANDWICH.

"Felix, what's with the T-shirts?" I said.

"Hilarious, right? Digby gets them for me from his work. Employee discount!" Felix said.

Employee discount? Probably not from shelling shrimp at the Cajun place. Probably not from wearing the mall mascot Angelo the Duck. That left . . .

"From the Make-Ur-Bear store? Are you wearing *teddy bear* T-shirts?" I said.

"They're from the Nasty Bear line for adults . . . the bears are bigger. They fit perfectly," he said.

"One condition, Felix, for us going to the dance together. No more rude T-shirts," I said. "Ever."

"Oh . . . okay," he said.

"No outfits from the Make-Ur-Bear for the dance, either." Boy, am I glad I made that clear, because his face fell and he made a disappointed "Ohhhhh" sound.

⁘

The dance itself sounded like it might be cool. When Sloane's mother had dropped off the check, she declared the theme to be "Guys and Dolls" and avoided the usual

Enchantment-Under-the-Sea cliché. People were confused at first, but after everyone googled it, the whole school was talking about gangsters and flapper dresses.

I found a pink dress that had a twenties-y shape at the Goodwill and glue-gunned tons of feathers to the bottom of it during a *Gilmore Girls* marathon that Saturday.

I made a headband using three of Mom's rhinestone necklaces and the lace from an old pair of tights and then joined together strings of plastic pearls to make one long knee-dusting necklace.

Mom took out a sequined clutch bag from a tissue-lined box. "I slept in on dibs-day after Grandma died, and this was the only nice thing I ended up inheriting. It'll look perfect with your outfit. And I've got the perfect shoes too."

She'd shined up an old pair of her pearly white tap shoes that were basically high-heeled Mary Janes.

"Are these loud?" I was worried because the metal taps on my soles click-clacked as I walked around.

"The music will block it out," Mom said.

"When did you tap dance, anyway?" I said.

"I was trying to lose weight, but I never tapped fast enough to burn any calories," Mom said.

++++

Speaking of failed attempts to exercise: It was November and out here, that meant cross-country season.

"You can win a race without coming in first," the gym teacher said. He and his assistant teacher were leading a small group of the sporty students in my gym class through a stretching routine.

The rest of us were in the back, doing halfhearted versions of their moves. Our class had been divided into two groups: the social runners and the competitive runners. They supposedly did that so the social runners wouldn't be pressured to run beyond their abilities. Really, though, it was so that they could use class time to drill runners who had after-school practice for other sports. They didn't need us slowing them down. I sometimes ran the course, but after tweaking my ankle on the uneven path through the woods, I began to fake-start the run and then circle back to do homework before I fake-crossed the line ten or so minutes after the fast runners finished. I had my Spanish homework folded up in my pocket and I had a grassy knoll all picked out.

The teacher's pep talk wasn't for me. "The intensity has to come from within," he said. "Attack the course. Push past the pain." And with a weird tribal screech, the fast pack were off.

There was a bunch of kids who, like me, skipped the runs. I looked at us, straggling off in different directions, and wondered why all the lonely people didn't just get it together and decide not to be lonely anymore. But I guess that's the problem with individualism.

Suddenly, I heard, "Hey, Princeton. Up here." There was Digby, looking down at me from the top of a rise leading to the dirt road beside the trail. "Come over here."

"That's super-steep. Why don't you come down here?"

His breathing was labored. "Can't. Just come up, okay?" And then he disappeared from my line of sight.

I expected to see him looking down, laughing at me as I struggled up the slope, but he didn't reappear. For every three feet I gained, I slid back down two. It was only by pulling myself up by the exposed tree roots that I finally managed to make progress. By the time I got close to the top, dirt was caked under my fingernails.

I said, "I don't understand why you couldn't have come down—" I stopped short when I summited and saw Digby lying flat on his back. "Oh, my God, Digby. What happened?"

Digby grunted but seemingly couldn't get the words out to answer me. I ran over and in a weird reflex, opened his jacket to take a look at his chest.

Digby was gasping. "Get . . . off . . . I haven't been . . . shot."

"Then what—"

"Can't . . . can't . . . I'm having an anxiety . . . attack . . ."

I rifled through his jacket pockets. "Is there a pill you take or something?"

Digby shook his head. "No . . . no . . . you gotta . . . you gotta sit . . . on my chest . . ."

"What? Digby, is this some kind of scam?"

"No . . . no . . . I gotta . . . gotta slow my breathing . . . please . . ."

I'd never seen that look on his face before. It was scary. He really was in trouble. I climbed over him and straddled his chest. At first, I was too scared to put my whole weight on him but gradually, I was fully sitting on his ribs.

Digby closed his eyes and sure enough, after a few minutes, his breathing slowed down. I started to wonder if he'd fallen asleep.

"Digby?"

He just sighed.

"Are you feeling better?" I said.

He nodded, blissed out.

"What are you doing now?" I said.

"Now I'm enjoying myself." Digby's eyes opened. "Strictly speaking medically, you could've just sat on me sidesaddle. Bump on a log style would've worked. This sexy cowgirl stuff's a nice bonus, though."

"You're gross." I climbed off. "What the hell was all that?"

"Oh . . . it's just an anxiety attack. I get them sometimes."

"Uh, 'just' an anxiety attack? Shouldn't you see a doctor?"

"I have. I'm supposed to take Paxil for it."

"Supposed to? Does that mean you don't?"

"I don't like them. They mess with my taste buds, my sleep . . . it seems crazy to take a pill every day to head off something that happens, like, once a month max."

"Wow. I don't think medicine works like that, Digby."

"Besides, I have these triggers, and if I avoid them, I'm all right. I slipped a little today. Looked at something I shouldn't have. My thoughts started cascading . . . that's all. It's nothing."

"Doesn't sound like nothing," I said. "What do you do when no one's around to sit on you?"

"I ride it out. Remind myself that it'll end," he said. "But the real trick, Princeton, is that after each one of these, I gotta pick myself up and not constantly dread it happening again, which of course it will, but you know . . . I gotta live."

"See, that whole thing you just said is basically the entire argument for staying on your medication," I said.

Digby stood up and dusted himself off.

"What are you doing here, anyway? Not going to classes, I know that much," I said.

"I went to see Steve."

Please-Call-Me-Steve, as the faculty advisor assigned to us, had been e-mailing me for the last week about meeting to talk about our project. Our fictional, nonexistent project. That was due in five weeks. I'd been avoiding him for a while, putting him off with a series of excuses that were escalating in their BS factor. I'd almost reached my limit and just the day before, he'd e-mailed me that he'd track me down in class if I didn't come to see him.

"Now it's my turn to have an anxiety attack. What did he say?" I said.

"He said my oral progress report was great. He's looking forward to reading it," Digby said.

"Reading what? We haven't written a single word. What are we going to turn in?"

"Oh, relax, Princeton. I'll take care of it. It's *weeks* from now."

I heard the gym teacher's whistle. "I gotta go finish my race. See you tonight?"

Digby nodded. "What's for dinner, honey?"

I kept up my end of the fifties housewife routine. "A roast with all the fixin's, dear."

Digby broke character in surprise. "Whoa. Really?"

"What? No, not really. More like chicken nuggets, tater tots, and bag salad."

"Sounds good to me."

I jogged off.

"Hey, Princeton. What would happen if I were just a normal guest tonight? Like, while Liza's there? I mean, I know she doesn't exactly love me, but she knows I come over and it's not like we're up to anything weird."

I stopped. I didn't have an answer for him.

"No, no . . . you're right. I'll wait until she leaves," he said.

He had a point, though. It had been almost a month since Mom told us she knew he was coming over, and I had no idea why we were still sneaking around.

++++

After school the next day, I got another one of Digby's abrupt summonses: "Mall in 20," it said. I messaged back about a dozen times and when he didn't answer, I considered myself warned. I suited up in a face-obscuring hoodie and baseball cap combo and took the bus.

When I got to the mall, I checked some of Digby's usual hangs: the shrimp place, the comic book bar at the record store, and the frozen yogurt shop where the makeup counter girls liked to take their breaks. No joy.

I was just paying for my yogurt when Digby sauntered in and laid a twenty on the counter.

"Whoa," I said. "Whaaaat is happening?"

"Yeah, that's right, Princeton. It's on *me* today," Digby said. He was dressed in his Suzie Bear tutu costume with the head removed and tucked under his arm.

"I just have to check. You didn't rob anyone, right?"

"What? Of course not. I got this money for legit work. Well, I guess technically, it's an advance on some legit work I'm gonna do," Digby said. "Well, if you wanna get really technical . . . the work is legit-ish. I mean, I wouldn't go chat with the police about it or anything."

"That's not why you called me here, is it? To help you with your legit-ish project that we can't tell the police about?" I said.

"No, I have that whole thing under control. Wait, is that why you dressed all Bangarang?"

"Don't act like I'm crazy for thinking something was up." I passed him my phone with his terse message pulled up.

"It's not my fault you assume there's always some catastrophe about to happen when I call you."

I tapped the scar on my chin and said, "You don't think it's your fault? Not even a little?"

"Oh, come on . . . bygones."

"So, what's going on anyway?"

"Nothing. I'm on my break and I wanted some company," he said.

It took a second for me to realize he meant he just wanted to hang out. "Uh . . . okay. Walk, I guess?"

We left the yogurt shop and were window-shopping and mocking the other mall shoppers until we got to the pet store. Digby just stared into the window where there was an open-topped glass case in which sat two furry rats with oversized ears.

"Those rats are gigantic," I said. "And they look like they stink."

"That doesn't even make any sense," Digby said. "And these little guys are chinchillas, not rats."

"I don't get it."

"Chinchillas. They're awesome."

"You like these things? You don't like anything." When he just stared at the chinchillas and ignored me, I shoved him and said, "Is it, like, some kind of weird fur-based fetish?"

"My sister asked for a chinchilla for her fourth birthday. My dad said no and made up an allergy as an excuse. Chinchillas live for fifteen years, you know? If we'd gotten her one like she'd asked for, we'd have a nine-year-old chinchilla named Mu. For Muhammad Ali. The Chinchilla from Manila," Digby said.

I felt awful. "Digby . . . I am so . . ." But then I realized he was laughing at me.

"The Chinchilla from Manila? You believed that junk?" he said. "Man. Making you cry is *too* easy."

"I'm not crying, you moron. And you can't tell a sob story and then make fun of the people who sob. That's entrapment." I flicked a spoonful of melted yogurt at him that landed on the arm of his Suzie Bear suit.

"Hey, watch the fur." Digby looked surprised and caught himself. He said, "Wow. I was just seriously annoyed you did that. You know . . . maybe I do have a little something weird going with fur."

"It's not funny," I said.

"What? My sister getting kidnapped? No, of course it's not.

It's the most horrible thing that's ever happened to me. But it's also not the only thing I think about. I can like a chinchilla without it being about my sister, Princeton."

"*You* brought her up."

"But you were thinking about her."

"Only after you brought her up."

"Semantics," Digby said. "Seriously, though. I need to change my life story. I'm done being the Boy Whose Sister Was Taken. I need to either find Sally or find out how she died."

It was shocking to hear it laid bare like that. I checked to see if he was smiling again, but he wasn't this time.

"She disappeared exactly nine years ago tonight," he said.

His anxiety attack from the day before made a new kind of sense to me. He put the Suzie Bear head back on. "Come on, Princeton. Let's go traumatize some kids."

‡‡‡‡

When the Friday of the dance rolled around, I woke up early, worried I'd caught some kind of small-town fever because I was totally excited to go to a school dance. I didn't know why I was. It wasn't because of the photo Felix sent me of the crazy stretch limo he'd rented. It definitely wasn't because we were going to Red Lobster, even though he was allergic to shellfish and had to demo his EpiPen for me "just in case."

Everyone at school was amped. The halls were decorated with WELCOME CHESTER B. ARTHUR STUDENTS posters (there was a mini-scolding over the PA because someone defaced a poster to read FArthur) and there was glitter on the floor. People peeked through gaps in the locked gym doors. Some popular tenth-grade girls were crying in the cafeteria, complaining it was unfair they couldn't go even though eleventh-grade boys had asked them.

The bathrooms were crazier than usual and teachers had to come in after the bell to yell at girls to go to class. Sloane and two of her blondes walked around with pins and curling papers in their bangs and I overheard Sloane insist a "real pin curl is soooo different" from one you make with gel and a curling iron.

In short, the dance was already a success. Everyone was obsessed.

By last period, our teachers had given up on getting us to concentrate. In English class, my teacher Miss Viv (who wore charms on her anklets and sexified literature to keep us interested) tried to squeeze value out of our excitement by talking about flapper sexual liberation. At one point, she jiggled and jangled, demonstrating the Charleston to the boys' gaping appreciation. We had more of that to look forward to, because she was going to be a faculty chaperone that night.

When the final bell rang, it was chaos. Clumps of kids choked up traffic in the halls with garment bags and slumber party luggage. Teachers patrolling added to the insanity by shouting useless instructions like, "Let's keep it moving, people" and making dramatic "these kids are crazy" gestures at each other. Within minutes, a swarm of school buses and SUVs vacuumed up the screaming kids and then the halls were quiet again.

I was unlocking my bike from the rack outside the faculty lounge windows when I heard Musgrave's signature scream-

and-swear combo when he spilled coffee on himself. Then he started talking to Principal Granger.

Now, instead of walking away like old me would've done, new me pressed up against the wall and listened. Just knowing Musgrave thought I was a criminal was enough to trigger criminal behavior in me. Whoa. Maybe I *did* understand what our nonexistent project, "Convicted in Absence," was about.

"Principal Granger, did you get my request for Philip Digby's attendance records?" Musgrave said.

"Look. It's like my secretary's been saying to you. You can't ask for attendance sheets without cause. It'd look like we were helping you single out and harass students. If a student's cutting school, the homeroom teacher lets my office know and *we* make the request to you for help," Principal Granger said.

"I *know* that kid's screwing around," Musgrave said.

"Well, obviously, he's attending classes. None of his teachers have raised a red flag," Principal Granger said.

"He's getting around them. I don't know how, but he is," Musgrave said.

"Keep it together, Harlan. I don't need a repeat of the Springfield scenario on my promotion year," Principal Granger said.

"That was a long time ago. I meditate now," Musgrave said. "Is his address on file?"

"If I won't give you his attendance sheet, what do you think the chances are I'd give you *that*?" Principal Granger said.

"Never mind . . . I'll call my buddy down at the PD. That punk's gotta be in the system," Musgrave said. "I'm gonna pay his parents a visit."

"You do that. Just don't make any claims about representing me, any of the faculty, or this school when you do," Principal Granger said.

"Yeah . . . wouldn't wanna infringe on the little sociopath's human rights," Musgrave said. "God bless America."

As soon as they left, I dialed Digby. No answer. All the way home, I called his number over and over. When I called the Make-Ur-Bear, they told me he'd taken the night off to go to the dance. After I processed the shock from finding out Digby was actually going to the dance he'd been mocking for weeks, I decided to head over to his place. Then I realized I didn't know where he lived.

Mom was waiting at home, excited to dress me. "I got industrial-strength gel and a tiny little curling iron. And look! Fake eyelashes," she said.

I tried to look excited, but my brain was vibrating, thinking about how I could warn Digby. He wasn't answering my texts, either.

"Are you nervous? Oh, you're cute . . . it's normal to be nervous on your first date, honey."

"Not a date, Mom. Felix is technically my date, but it's not a *date* date."

"Is there a difference?"

"A crucial one. Seriously."

When Mom went to shine the tap shoes again, I called Henry and told him what I'd overheard.

"I can't get him on the phone and I don't know where he lives. His address isn't listed," I said.

"Yeah . . . during the thing with his sister, a million weirdos showed up at their house. I know where he lives, but Mom's driving me to Sloane's and I don't think she'd be into making extra stops," Henry said.

"Wait. I have an idea. Will you be ready in an hour?"

"Yeah. Why?"

"I'll pick you up. What's your address?"

Then I called Felix with half a plan. "Felix? Can we make a stop before we go to dinner?"

"I don't know, Zoe, I sort of have this coordinated perfectly and messing with the itinerary might—" Felix said.

"Listen. Do you remember when Digby got you to buy those drugs but Floyd wouldn't sell them to you and you had to just make it up? Do you remember how fun improvising was?" I said.

"Yes, but . . ."

"Well, now Digby's in trouble and we need to—"

"Digby's in trouble? This is for Digby?" Felix said. "Why didn't you say so? Of course we'll help him."

"Really?" That was weirdly easy.

"Yeah, I owe our whole date to Digby. Besides, this'll make the story we tell our kids even funnier," Felix said.

"Our *kids*?"

"Ha-ha. Just kidding. We shouldn't even *think* of having kids until after I've won my first Nobel Prize," he said. "Okay, see you soon."

Click.

++++

While I worried about what would happen if we didn't get to Digby's place before Musgrave did, Mom gave me Cleopatra eyeliner and blow-dried my skirt's feathers so they puffed up like a tutu.

"You look perfect!" she said.

"Uh-oh . . . I'm shedding." A feather fluttered to the floor. "Should I be worried?"

"Redundancy, Zoe. I mean, you have eight pounds of feathers glued on there. You can afford to lose a few." Mom randomly stuffed the feather back into the nest of my skirt. "But . . . maybe don't slide your butt across the seat when you get in and out of the car."

Even through my Digby-induced worry haze, I could see Mom had done a great job. I figured I owed her a few minutes of normal mother-daughter post-makeover afterglow. We hugged, I agreed with her that yes, I did look very "fetch," and she put on big band music and danced me around the living room. But then I got sweaty under my headband and more feathers detached from my skirt, so we quit. We started posting photos online instead.

Finally, Felix's limo pulled up. I wish I'd had my camera when little Felix hopped out and Mom saw him for the first time. Her jaw actually dropped. It wasn't just that she realized Felix was a tiny twelve-year-old boy. It was also that he was wearing high-water pants and for some reason, his too-tight tux had a black cape attached under the collar. It was sewn on. First thing I checked.

"Felix. You promised . . . no teddy bear outfits," I said.

"No, I wear this to perform magic tricks," he said.

"Aren't real magicians supposed to call them 'illusions'?" Mom said.

"I will after I move up from novice to apprentice," Felix said. "Then I get a cape with a *gold* lining."

"Well, it's nice to meet you, Felix. Would you like to come in for refreshments?" Mom said.

"No, thanks. We have to make some stops and if we're late, we'll lose our reservation," Felix said.

I almost burst out laughing when Felix's dad stepped out of the limo's backseat. He was Felix's maxi-me.

"Hello, I'm Timothy Fong, Felix's father," Mr. Fong said.

"Liza. Nice to meet you," Mom said. "Are you . . . going to the dance with the kids?"

"Yes, but I'm staying in the car. I've brought work to keep me occupied," Mr. Fong said. "Don't worry, we'll get Zoe back safe and sound after the dance."

I pulled Felix aside while Mom and Mr. Fong exchanged numbers.

"How do we pick up Henry and Digby without your father figuring out something's up?" I said.

"It's okay. I told him we were picking up my wingmen," Felix said.

The kid really was full of surprises.

TWENTY-FOUR

We had one of those limos with facing seats that I've always wondered about because why is it classy to smash knees every time the driver hits a pothole, I wanted to know. Mr. Fong muttered, "Carsick," and he and Felix took the forward-facing seats. After a few minutes of watching houses whizz past backward, I understood what they meant. I was queasy.

Mr. Fong commented on my "plumage" and the "mating rituals of American adolescents," cracked himself up, then dived into his stack of files. The titles of the things he was reading were at least twenty words long, involving things with names like XKV357. The binders were marked PERSES ANALYTICS and had a stylized sword logo. He noticed me looking.

"These materials are classified, young lady. I'd better not catch you reading them or I'll have to kill you." He looked totally serious. "No, I'm just kidding." He laughed. "Security guys at work take care of that stuff." That time he didn't laugh.

Henry was on his porch holding a bouquet of roses when we pulled up.

"Fresh flowers! Dad, we forgot to get fresh flowers for Zoe," Felix said.

"Felix, it's okay," I said.

"Maybe we can stop at the mall," Mr. Fong said.

"No, seriously, I don't need flowers," I said.

"Wait. Was that even on the checklist?" Felix said.

"No. We'd better add it to the checklist for next time," Mr. Fong said. "I can't believe we missed that. We spent so much time crafting that list."

"Zoe, what's your favorite flower?" Felix said.

I muttered "zinnias" although Felix and his dad weren't paying attention to anything but their discussion of Felix's pre-date checklist. Their nattering didn't stop even when Henry jumped in and sat beside me.

The partition rolled down. "Excuse me? Where to now?" the limo driver said.

Neither Fong broke from their conversation, so Henry answered. "Hey, man . . . I'm Henry." They shook hands.

"Dusty. What's the deal? Do we head to the Red Lobster now?"

"Just a couple more stops. Is that cool?" Henry gave him Digby's address.

"No sweat by me, but that cat's credit card's on file." Dusty pointed at Felix's dad. "And we charge by the mile on top of time."

"Um . . . yeah, he'll be okay with it." I tried to sound casual, but my voice went up in that liar way. I pointed at Felix. "I'm his date."

"Riiiiight . . ." Dusty looked dubious, but he drove off anyway. I guess as limo-based shenanigans go, kids mooching free rides wasn't such a big deal.

On the way to Digby's, I gave Henry a summary of what I'd overheard. Henry was worried at first, but his irritation took over.

"Man! You'd think because he knew Musgrave's after him, Digby would at least try to show up to school. See? Remember what I said? How Digby sucks you in? This is it. It's happening," Henry said. "We should be going to the dance to have a good time, but we're in Digby's world now. I mean, I haven't even told you hello or how nice you look. I'm obsessed with Digby's problems. See this tie? It took seven tries to tie it. I was too worried about Digby to concentrate on the instructions. Hello, by the way. You look very nice. Great feathers."

I worried Mr. Fong would notice our little drama. "Okay, calm down," I said. "We'll just tell him Musgrave's coming and we'll get out of there. It'll take a second. Not a big deal."

Henry's phone chimed. He typed a response. "It's Sloane. We're late. She's not happy."

I wished for all four limo tires to go flat.

++++

Digby's was the lone dump on a nice block. It had a shattered upstairs window, a roof with missing shingles, and skinny saplings sprouted in the rain gutters. There was a FORECLOSURE FOR SALE BY BANK sign on the scrubby lawn.

Musgrave was already on the porch when we pulled up.

"We're too late," I said.

"Dusty, can you go around the corner?" Henry said.

Felix barely noticed us getting out. His dad was telling him that on future dates, he should bring chocolates. Allergen-free, just in case.

Henry and I went down the back alley and peeked over the fence from Digby's neighbor's yard.

Digby's front door opened for Musgrave. A woman, very thin, heavily made-up, and wearing a silk turban, answered the door. She held a glass, and had on a full-length muumuu and teeter-totter heels.

"Val," Henry whispered. "That's Digby's mom."

"She's going out," I said.

Henry shook his head. "She's always been kinda eccentric . . . and after Sally disappeared . . ."

At the door, Val said, "Yes, may I help you?"

"Mrs. Digby? Harlan Musgrave. I'm the school resources officer at your son Philip's school. I'm here to talk about his recent behavior," Musgrave said.

"How wonderful! The personal touch," Val said. "Oh, do, *do* come in. How wonderful of you to come all the way here to keep me informed."

Val's entire speech came out in one long shriek. Musgrave took a giant step backward.

"Uh-oh. Val's having a manic episode," Henry said.

"Is she foreign?" I said.

Meanwhile, Musgrave said, "Oh . . . I didn't realize Philip's mother was British."

"Oh, hahahaha! You funny, *funny* little man! It's a shame

234

Americans so often mistake proper enunciation for a British accent," Val said.

Musgrave backed down the stairs, freaked. "Maybe we should arrange an in-school conference instead."

Val lunged for Musgrave's arm and pulled him toward the front door. Musgrave's other hand patted his hip, probably looking for the gun he remembered from his cop days.

"Don't be silly! I couldn't let you go without at least a drink. I was settling in for a quiet evening with the telly, but we could have a party instead!" Val was pulling so hard, her heels crunched into the floorboards.

"Come to think of it, it'd best if we handled this on school property." Musgrave finally twisted out of her grip and ran back to his car. "We'll be in touch, Mrs. Digby."

Before I could digest the weirdness of what I'd just seen, I heard Digby *PSSST*-ing for us to come over to the garage behind his house. I was sad to note I lost two more feathers as I brushed past the bushes.

"Is he gone?" Digby said.

"Musgrave? Yeah," Henry said.

"Come in before someone sees you," Digby said.

We followed him into the garage, where the weirdness got weirder. The windows had insulation taped up against them. The white Chevy we drove to the break-in was parked with its doors open and a sleeping bag spread out in the backseat. Next to a table saw, a lit camping stove heated up a can of beans. There were clothes everywhere—shirts hanging to dry and boxer shorts soaking in the sink.

"Is this what you've been wearing?" Henry pulled out a black suit jacket from a box labeled GRANDPA JOE.

"You live in your garage?" I said. "Does your mom know you're in here?"

"Does she even know you're back in town?" Henry said.

"You saw her. I'm not sure *she's* in town," Digby said.

"Housekeeping problems? This is what you meant?" I said. *"You're homeless?"*

"I'm not homeless. You said it yourself. I live in my garage," Digby said.

I pointed at a shelf with single-serve condiments neatly grouped and stacked. Packs of sugar separated into white and brown, piles of ketchups and soup crackers, a huge mound of fortune cookies. "This is your only food? Is that why you're eating every time I see you?" I said.

"Don't look at me like that, Princeton. Besides, I overcompensated. I think I gained weight."

I had actually noticed that his suits were fitting better these days. And, come to think of it, I'd surprised myself the other day when I'd found myself thinking how much better Digby looked against the typical idiot man-child in droopy pants that trawled our hallways in school.

"What about when it gets cold? When it snows?" Henry said.

"It's cold now. I use the portable heater at night," Digby said. "Seriously, *Daaaaad*. I'm fine."

I thought about him cold and hungry in the garage, sucking down packets of ketchup. I felt like crying. "But you'll freeze . . ."

"You should've said something, dude," Henry said.

"And what? Sleep on your couch again? Every nine months, there's a newborn baby in your house. Nah, this is good. I come and go when I like," Digby said. "I would've asked to stay with you, Princeton, but all the sighing and weeping . . ."

"What are you talking about?" I said.

"You're about to cry right now," Digby said.

"Shut up." Something on the desk caught my eye. I waded through the clutter to check it out. "What's this?"

It was the free map of River Heights the mall's information center gave out. A clump of red-topped map pins were jammed into the tiny downtown part of the map. In fact, the entire middle of the map was just a mass of red pinheads.

"I put a pin into every place my guys said they'd seen Marina." Digby picked up the map and the middle part that was weighed down with pins ripped out and fell onto the floor. "Shoulda probably gotten a bigger map with the streets more blown up."

"Your 'guys'? Like Aldo, whom you paid in cookies? *That's* the quality of informer you have working for you?" I said. "I mean, whoa, that's a lot of pins. Almost looks like Marina's parading around town, keeping appointments. Do you think that's likely or . . . maybe, *maybe* your 'guys' are unreliable and insane?"

Under a stack of stickers of the RIVER HEIGHTS—WE'RE A FAMILY PLACE motto, I found more maps of downtown (this time ripped out of the Yellow Pages) with details penciled in. They were mounted on a corkboard under a tangle of red yarn strung between thumbtacks pushed into the maps.

"What's this mess?" I said.

"One of my guys followed someone he was pretty sure was Marina and I tried re-creating the path he described to me over the phone," Digby said.

"So, she went from the soup kitchen to the library?" Henry said.

"Back and forth over and over . . . and then the 7-Eleven, of course," I said. "What's this? 'Methodist Church'?"

"Actually that's 'methadone clinic' and the next stop was the Dumpster," Digby said. "Yeah . . . about that time I thought maybe it wasn't Marina they were following. Which is also about the time I came to the same conclusion you did that my guys might be a little unreliable . . ."

"I just thought of something," Henry said. "This garage doesn't have a bathroom."

Digby pointed at the utility sink.

"Dude. That's gross," Henry said.

"Urine is sterile," Digby said.

"Okay, but you know what *isn't* sterile?" Henry said.

"Okay, but you know what topsoil's made of?" Digby said.

I noticed the shovel next to the sink.

"Oh, no," I said.

"Yeah. And in related news, the neighbor's pumpkins are running big this year," Digby said.

"Thanksgiving dinner will never be the same again," Henry said.

"God. *Dinner*. Felix has this whole Red Lobster deal planned out," I said.

"Oh, man, Sloane and I have a reservation at La Terrasse. Mom was gonna drive us because Sloane's driver just quit for no reason. I don't know how we're getting there now . . ." Henry noticed Digby's tie. "Dude, you're coming?"

"I even combed my hair."

"So, what, meet up at the dance after our dinners?" Henry said.

"I have a better idea," Digby said.

++++

Sloane was posing for photos when our limo rolled up the long tree-lined gravel driveway leading to her huge castle-style house. The woman behind the camera was in a uniform with an apron and was obviously a member of the household staff. Weirdly, though, Sloane ended the photo shoot by hugging her. The smile on Sloane's face when she did was joyful and totally different from the mocking sneer she usually wore.

"Who's that?" Digby said.

"That's Marta," Henry said. When Sloane kissed Marta, he said, "She's been taking care of Sloane since she was a baby."

"Sloane has a nanny," Digby said. "How fascinating."

When the front door opened and Mrs. Bloom stepped out, the smile dropped right off Sloane's face and she stomped toward us. Sloane jumped in the limo, rolled her eyes when she saw us, and slapped the partition. "Drive."

It took Mr. Fong a moment to summon up the gumption to

say, "I can't help but notice that this limousine's turned into a public bus."

"One more, Mr. Fong, and we can go on to dinner," Digby said.

"Are you kids also eating at Red Lobster? Because I only made reservations for three," Mr. Fong said.

"*Red Lobster?* No! I thought we were going to La Terrasse. What happened to La Terrasse, Henry? I'm not dressed for Red Lobster," Sloane said.

She wasn't. The fringes of beads on Sloane's beautiful silver flapper dress shimmered like water. Her opera gloves had a million silk buttons up the sides that she probably had a maid or a lady-in-waiting to undo. Her yards of pearls clacked in a heavy way that made the plastic-ness of my pearls shamefully obvious. And while I technically had ethical problems with Sloane's silver fur cape, I had to admit it was gorgeous. Next to her, I was a hot glue gun mess. She wasn't dressed for Red Lobster. I was, though.

Henry apologized but refused to give in to her whining with any bargaining or explanations. I was just thinking, Good for him, when I realized that because Sloane wasn't getting anywhere with Henry, she'd have to let off steam elsewhere.

"So, did Walmart carry the feathers for your dress or did you have to shoot your own turkeys?" Sloane said.

"Love is louder, Sloane," Digby said.

"We're going to look stupid all pouring out of this limo," Sloane said.

"Well, we could let you out and you could walk to school."

Everyone—myself included—was surprised when that came out of my mouth.

"Ugh, not in these shoes. These cost a thousand-something dollars," Sloane said.

"A thousand dollars? For shoes?" Mr. Fong said.

"A thousand *something*," Sloane said. "Plus tax."

"For shoes you can't walk in?" Mr. Fong said.

Sloane twiddled her feet to admire her seven-inch heels. The confusion on the guys' faces was comical. Boys don't care about shoes. She wore them for the girls at the dance. I mean, the entire front of the shoe was glass.

"Where are we, anyway? I've never even heard of these streets," Sloane said.

"My date lives on McCaul," Digby said.

"Date? Since when?" I said.

"Huh? Since you set it up," Digby said.

"I didn't set you up," I said. "McCaul? That's where . . ."

"Bill said you did," Digby said.

"She *what*?" I said.

Sloane smirked. "Oh, wait, maybe this *will* be interesting."

Though I was totally shocked, part of me was, like, I knew it! And suddenly, something that happened a few weeks ago made a new kind of sense. I'd been in Bill's room when my phone went missing. Bill and I spent forever searching and then she came out of her bathroom with it.

"You must've left it when you peed," she'd said.

I'd agreed with her even though I knew I hadn't used the bathroom that visit. Taking it to steal Digby's number was

241

low, but to then pretend to help me look for it was downright shady.

To her credit, though, Bill wasn't so shady that she wasn't embarrassed when she opened the limo door and saw me sitting there.

"Uh . . . hi, Zoe. I can explain," Bill said.

"It's cool." Although I made it clear it wasn't.

"I mean, I wouldn't have asked Digby if you'd wanted to go with him," Bill said.

Sloane slow-clapped Digby. "You actually found *two* girls who wanted to go to the dance with you."

Bill's dress, I was happy to see, was meh. Just a regular black dress she twenties-ed up with a jazzy hat and T-strap shoes. I guess her fake fur stole made it a little more *All That Jazz*.

Bill squeezed in and with the limo jam-packed with feathers, fur, and beads, we drove to Red Lobster.

"Look at us. We look so great. It's almost a waste to just be going to a school dance," Felix said.

If I'd known how the night would turn out, I would've knocked on wood.

TWENTY-FIVE

Mr. Fong had been nervous about the seven of us turning up to a reservation for three, but since it was six in the afternoon and there were only four other tables of early birds, we got seated right away. I couldn't decide whether I wanted to face slightly left and watch Sloane sulk into her Shirley Temple or face slightly right, where Bill was interviewing Digby like the big groupie that she was. I couldn't really handle looking straight ahead at Felix, my supposed date who was ordering from the children's menu.

In the end, I chose to face Sloane because at least with her, the evil was all up front.

"What are you staring at? Freak," Sloane said.

"So, Zoe, Felix tells me you might be leaving next year. Prentiss is a good school, but it's very far away from your mother," Mr. Fong said. "Why did you decide to leave?"

"I think we've established that her answer is 'Because Daddy wants me to,'" Digby said.

"You're going to Prentiss? Who's your father? Is he some-body? He's not . . . rich or . . . connected, is he?" It was more than Sloane wanted to contemplate.

"No . . ." Given some time, I might've come up with a decent enough lie to freak her out, but my shoes pinched and I was sweating under my headband.

Sloane started angrily texting. "That's it. This is ridiculous. Literally *everyone* but me is going to private school now."

"So, Mr. Fong, Felix mentioned you're a chemist?" I said.

"I have doctorates in analytical chemistry and neurochem-istry, but I find myself working on nanotechnology these days. Life is a box of chocolates!" Mr. Fong threw up his hands and knocked over his soda, but Henry caught it before it hit the table. "You never know what you're gonna get."

Sloane gaped at a glob of Coke that came incredibly close to splashing her glove.

"So, if I gave you, say, a pill, could you analyze it and figure out if it was produced at the same place as another pill?" Digby said.

"Ah . . . that's the work of a forensic chemist," Mr. Fong said.

"But anyone with a gas spectrometer could do it," Felix said.

"Well, I *could* do it, but why would I? It wouldn't optimize my skill set," Mr. Fong said.

"Wait! Digby, do you have another sample to compare with the drugs I bought?" Felix said.

"You bought drugs?" Mr. Fong said.

"Um . . . no, it's nothing. We're kidding," Felix said. "Hey, my soda looks funny."

"Their fountain probably dispenses too much syrup . . . Come on, people, it's not as though we're asking you to synthesize Acetabularia Rhodopsin II. Let's see." Mr. Fong sipped from Felix's glass. "Yech! That's awful. It tastes . . . fishy?"

"Oh, *gross*. Something's floating around in it," Sloane said.

"Is that a loogie?" Bill said.

Mr. Fong looked and slammed down the drink, horrified.

"It's a clam! It's a *clam*!" Mr. Fong said.

"It's okay, Mr. Fong, I'm sure they'll get you another soda," I said.

"I'm allergic to shellfish! I need to get to the ER! I need to get to the ER!" Mr. Fong said.

I remembered the orientation session Felix gave me for using his EpiPen. "Mr. Fong! I have Felix's EpiPen." I got the EpiPen out of my clutch bag.

Instead of being happy to see it, Mr. Fong jumped out of his chair and screamed, "No! No! No needles!"

"He's phobic." Felix took out his phone and dialed 911.

Meanwhile, Digby and Henry tried to catch Mr. Fong, who was running around the restaurant screeching.

"*Sir*, you're scaring our customers," the waitress said.

"No good, no good! I need a professional! I need a doctor!" Mr. Fong faked left past Henry and ran out the door.

"It's okay, everyone, I'll get him," Felix said.

Felix ran out, leaving the rest of us in shock.

"This is nice," Digby said. "We should get together more often."

Felix came back a few minutes later, surprisingly calm.

"Is he okay?" I said.

"Oh, yeah. His lips hadn't even started swelling yet. We crossed paths with the ambulance a block from here," Felix said.

"Felix, if both you and your dad are allergic to shellfish, why did you choose Red Lobster?" I said.

"Oh, we're also allergic to peanuts, gluten, citrus, dairy, and soy, so pretty much every restaurant's a death trap. Not to mention the non-food stuff that could kill us . . . bees, latex, penicillin," Felix said. "By the way, you guys, *you're welcome.*"

"For what?" Digby said.

Felix pointed at my plate. A clam in the clams casino I hadn't started eating yet was just an empty shell.

"Felix. *No,*" I said. "How? I didn't even see you touch my plate."

"Just like you didn't see the flowers I *didn't* forget?" Felix reached behind my ears and a bouquet of silk flowers appeared in his hand. "Shazzam."

When I took it from Felix, the bouquet's handle caught in the trick holder hidden up his sleeve.

"Is *that* why you're wearing a cape? Because of *magic?*" Sloane said.

"I'm wearing my cape because it looks good," Felix said.

"You think that looks good? You look like Count Chocula," Sloane said.

That crossed the line. Felix looked hurt and that pissed me off.

"And you look like one of your mother's rat dogs crawled up on your neck and died when your perfume hit it. Doesn't matter how much it costs, Sloane," I said. "When you wear too much, it just smells like roach spray."

"Oh, shut up. You can't talk to me about dead animals when you're sitting on an entire flock of turkeys," Sloane said.

"Ooooh . . . meow," Bill said.

I hated that Bill was enjoying this.

"And *you*." Sloane turned to Bill. "Just sticking on a cloche hat doesn't make it twenties, okay? Put on a sombrero and you'd be a Mexican widow in that outfit." Sloane turned to Henry. "What's she doing here, anyway? I thought you said Digby and Zoe were a thing."

Henry looked mortified.

Felix, still recovering from the Count Chocula burn, said, "You're a thing?"

"No!" Digby and I said together.

++++

Felix and I went off on our own when we got to the dance. We got formal photos taken and I let him introduce me to both the backgammon and astronomy clubs as his date. I even put my arm through his.

I had to say it. "This place looks great."

Sloane's mother had impeccable taste. Instead of cheap crafty decorations, we got mini-chandeliers, silver and black balloons, and twinkling Christmas lights. There were seating areas with potted trees and old-timey metal benches. Attendants wearing striped shirts and boaters handed out paper cones of fresh-popped corn.

They even laid down a black-and-white tile dance floor.

The two schools' students were huddled on opposite sides of the room, sizing each other up. Sloane had already found her Chester B. Arthur double: the flirty cheerleader hitting on Henry at practice. They were trying to outdo each other with showy sexy-dancing around their poor dates. Teachers stepped in when Sloane and her competition ran out of ideas and busted into straight-up stripper moves.

It was nice seeing everyone in their outfits. Of course, a group of girls turned up as Barbies because, you know, the theme said "dolls." On the bright side, though, the Film Appreciation Club came dressed in suits and fedoras, carrying plastic Tommy guns, and "smoking" unlit cigarettes (that were confiscated almost immediately).

Henry sidled up. "So, you didn't set Digby up with Bill?"

"No," I said. "It was a surprise to me."

"But you and Digby aren't . . ."

"No."

"I assumed—"

"Don't."

"Because you spend a lot of time together."

"Yeah, but not like that. Our time together's mostly just him mocking me and me getting him food every couple of minutes," I said.

"Okay . . ." Henry said. "Hey, you wanna dance?"

"But . . . ?" I pointed at Sloane.

"She's with her girls. I did my bit already. She won't need me until coronation," he said.

Walking to the dance floor, I tried to stop my knees bending and unbending jerkily. I couldn't look him in the eye while we danced.

"You look nice! Did I tell you that?" He had to shout to be heard over the music.

I bobbed my head side to side to make sure he understood I was remaining humble about the whole thing.

Henry said, "You usually dress more . . ."

"Casual?"

"Butch."

Ouch. "I mostly dress for comfort . . . the weather . . ."

Henry couldn't hear my fumbling response, but before I could clean up my answer, Digby butted in. "Sloane's looking for you."

Henry gave me an embarrassed smile and ran off. Sloane was dancing with her crew. She wasn't looking for Henry or, in fact, looking for anything other than more attention.

"You're welcome," Digby said.

"What?" I said.

"I'm saving you from yourself, Princeton. As a great poet once said, 'Illusion never changed into something real,'" Digby said.

Sloane and her posse finished a choreographed line dance, and a slow song from Britney's golden age came on.

"You know, they're only popular because you make them popular. Those girls live off your hate. Look away and you starve them of their oxygen," he said. "It's a pull-my-finger situation. Stop pulling her finger."

"It's *im*possible to look away. I mean, she made up that choreography and made them learn it. Who *does* that outside of a teen movie?" I said. "And look at this place . . . this is the *gym*. Imagine how her house looks."

"You're really angst-y tonight. What's with you?"

"Everything's bugging me. Plus I'm not excited about Bill's scam."

"So you really didn't set up my date with Bill?"

"No."

"I'm relieved, Princeton. I thought you were sending me a message."

"What message would that be?"

Digby shrugged.

I suddenly realized we'd been slow-dancing this whole time and I felt weird and awkward. I stepped out from our embrace.

"Where *is* your date, anyways?" I said.

He gestured vaguely. "Checking out cigarettes someone found in the faculty lounge trash . . ."

"That's lame."

"Especially since I have a whole pack. She coulda just asked."

"You don't smoke."

"No, but I pay some of my guys in cigarettes." His phone buzzed. "Speaking of . . . one of them just spotted Ezekiel at the 7-Eleven downtown." He showed me the picture of Ezekiel that he just received on his phone. "We gotta jet."

"What? We just got here."

"That whole cult's gonna be gone soon. If we don't find out what the hell's going on now, we're never gonna find out."

"I'm not that curious. And shockingly, I'm enjoying myself. I wanna stay. Sorry if that makes me boring."

"Boring? Who's boring?" Bill rejoined us, stinking of cigarette smoke and chewing gum. "I'm not boring. I'll do it. Whatever it is."

"You're not invited," I said.

"Invited to what?" Felix arrived eating a brownie. He saw my worried face and said, "I checked the ingredients."

"We're going downtown," Digby said.

"We're going downtown? *Awesome*. I've never been downtown. Mom dreamt we were murdered downtown and stuffed in our car's trunk, so we never go," Felix said. "We go to Connecticut for excitement instead."

"See this? This is a bad idea," I said. "No, Felix, we aren't going downtown. Besides, how would we get out of here?"

There was a strict door policy: Once signed in to the dance, students could only leave if a parent or guardian signed them out.

"Mr. Talbot let our pothead limo driver sign us in. D'you think he'll drop the hammer on us now?" Digby said.

"Except Auerbach's doing the sign-outs now," Bill said.

Whereas Mr. Talbot, the art teacher, played Nirvana during class and told stories of peyote-fueled naked painting sessions in the desert, Mr. Auerbach taught government and told us his part-Mohegan grandma still had the scalps of French soldiers in her attic.

Mr. Auerbach stood across the doorway, arms crossed and frowning.

"Kids check in but they don't check out," Digby said. "Felix, could you get Dusty to check us out?"

"Digby . . . Felix should stay here," I said.

"I'm coming," Felix said.

"Maybe you shouldn't . . ." Digby said.

"Well, it's technically my limo, so unless you want to walk downtown . . ." Felix said.

"Welcome aboard, Felix," Digby said. "Now, can you call Dusty?"

"Sure," Felix said. "What's his number?"

"Why would *I* have it? He's your limo driver," Digby said.

"Dad has it, but I put him in the hospital . . ." Felix said. "He's okay, by the way. He texted."

Digby waved at Henry to come over.

"What's happening?" Henry said.

"We're taking off," Digby said. "Downtown."

"I'm in. This dance sucks," Henry said.

"You're not going anywhere." We hadn't even seen Sloane come up to us. "Do you know how much work went into this dance?"

"Your mother hired a decorator and some movers," I said.

Sloane put her hand up in my face. "Henry, *no*. You can't."

"Sorry, Sloane, I'm going," Henry said.

"Fine. I'm sure Mr. Auerbach will want to hear about this." Sloane stomped off.

"Dude. Stop her," Digby said.

Henry ran and grabbed Sloane's arm. We watched them have one of those classic "darling, please" arguments. Even without audio, it was dramatic.

Finally, Sloane came back. "Fine. But I'm coming too. I refuse to be left here without a date."

It was getting ridiculous. "Really? All of us?" I said.

But Digby was already planning our escape. "The way I figure, they'll get suspicious if our entire group tries to leave together or if we go out in boy-girl pairs on account of the whole teen pregnancy thing. So, Bill and Sloane—you two go first. Tell Auerbach one of you got your . . . you know."

Bill and Sloane looked blank.

"Your period," I said.

"Yeah, that . . . and your . . . things are in the limo," Digby said.

More blank looks from Bill and Sloane.

"Your tampons," I said.

"Will that work?" Bill said.

"Look at him. Digby can't even say it. Most guys can't. Yeah, it'll work," I said. "Sloane should do the talking, though."

"Fine. Whatever. Let's go," Sloane said.

As predicted, Mr. Auerbach looked disgusted and waved them through.

"Henry, you and Felix . . ." Digby pointed at Mrs. Boschman, our music teacher, who was so tiny that pushing even an empty drinks cart overwhelmed her. She and the cart were going sideways into the wall.

"Got it." Henry cut off Mrs. Boschman and took over pushing the cart. Then, when no one was looking, Henry grabbed Felix by the scruff and threw him onto the cart's lower shelf.

"Turns out, that cape of his is crucial to the whole operation," Digby said.

It was true. Curled up in the cart, Felix looked like a bundled-up tablecloth. A brief explanation to Mr. Auerbach and they were out the door.

"Genius. But that leaves us. You boy. Me girl. How are we getting out?" I said.

"Man, I keep forgetting you're a girl," Digby said.

"Shut up."

"Kidding. You're dressed like a cream puff. You are all girled out tonight. I saved the best one for us. You and I are climbing out the window."

"In my tight feathered dress. Wonderful."

We went to the windows hidden behind the fake cityscape they set up for the formal photos and Digby gave me a boost. Halfway out, dangling ten feet above the quad on the other side, I realized that, as usual, I hadn't thought things through. Then Digby pushed on my feet and I flew out the window.

Digby's head poked out of the window above me. "You okay? Whoa . . . it's pretty high."

"Yeah, thanks for pushing me out," I said. "Because my fear of death was preventing me from jumping out on my own."

I remember thinking, At least my stockings are okay. But then Digby jumped. By the time he was done trampling on me, my stockings were trashed.

"Ow! Get off me!"

We were tangled up on the ground when someone walked up.

"You kids . . . Zoe Webster? Is that you?"

It was Miss Viv, our sexed-up English teacher, jingling and jangling toward us in an even lower-cut version of what she usually wore.

"Oh-ho . . . and I had you down as a good girl. Sneaking out at the dance, huh?" Miss Viv sighed. "Oh, my . . . I remember being young. Carpe diem, kids, it won't last forever."

"Um . . . okay," Digby said.

"And, Zoe, I expect your participation in class when we talk about what Juliet means when she says 'lovers can see to do their amorous rites by their own beauties.' You know exactly what lovers get up to in the dark." Miss Viv winked and pointed to her cigarette. "I won't tell if you don't tell. Only you'll get caught if you do it here. Go by the parking lot."

Digby and I had accidentally gotten her to let us go and we didn't want to blow the deal by saying the wrong thing, so we slinked off in silence.

"Well, that was a freebie," Digby said.

‡‡‡‡

The idling limo's interior was flooded with a bright green neon light and the music blared as someone rapidly jumped around radio stations. Dusty was on the hood, smoking what was clearly not a regular cigarette. He giggled in between inhales.

"Our sneaky getaway needs work." As we got closer, Digby called out, "Dusty! What are you doing?"

Dusty jumped and dropped his joint.

"*Kid,* man . . . you just almost made me stroke out." Dusty looked at his hand and realized something was missing. "And, *man,* you made me drop my J."

Dusty bent to pick it up just as the limo door flew open. There was a huge bang when it connected with Dusty's head. Felix climbed out.

"*Wow,* that was so *great.* Henry rolled me past everyone. No one could tell." Felix looked around. "Hey, where's Dusty?"

Dusty was facedown behind the open door.

"That's weird. Is he taking a nap?" Felix said.

Henry, Sloane, and Bill climbed out of the limo.

"Is he dead?" Bill said.

"If he's dead, can we go back to the dance?" Sloane said.

"Oh, no! Does that mean the hijinks are canceled?" Felix said.

The nod Digby threw Henry said it all.

"I'd be minus one scar and an arrest record if that were enough to cancel hijinks," I said.

Henry plucked Dusty's chauffeur cap off the ground and put it on.

"Downtown, I assume," Henry said.

I grabbed Dusty's ankles and Digby took his armpits.

"You know it's gonna be one of those nights when you start it with moving a body," Digby said.

Sloane stepped over Dusty on her way to the front seat. "Whatever. But I'm not sitting in the back with you nerds."

"Digby, let's move. He's heavy," I said.

"Are we stuffing him in the trunk?" Felix said.

"*What?* No, Felix. What's the matter with you? In the back-seat," Digby said.

We sort of carried but mostly dragged Dusty into the car. He was totally out and didn't wake up when we banged his head on the roof while we were shoving him in.

"Listen," Digby said to Henry and me. "Maybe we don't tell these guys about the whole Marina angle tonight."

"I thought your guys saw Ezekiel. What does this have to do with Marina?" I said.

"I dunno. Maybe something, maybe nothing," Digby said.

"Hope it's nothing, because Sloane wouldn't be happy if Marina turned up tonight," Henry said.

We climbed in and Henry pulled out of the parking lot.

"He looks dead," Bill said. Dusty slumped over her when Henry made a turn. "Seriously, is he dead?"

Felix put his fingers on Dusty's neck. "Nope. Pulse is okay."

"He's freaking me out," Bill said.

Digby searched his pockets and came up with googly-eyed joke glasses, which he put on Dusty.

I had to admit, "That's weirdly better, actually."

And off we drove through River Heights.

TWENTY-SIX

We got to our destination: the 7-Eleven.

Digby rapped on the partition. "Pull over."

"Ew . . . is this where you emo types go for a good time?" Sloane said to me.

Three goth girls who looked our age huddled around a pay-phone, smoking. One girl had dried blood caked on her cut upper lip. Some old guy rooted through the trash, collecting half-eaten food. Leather-and-chains bikers were partying around a cluster of bikes parked to one side. Even through the thunderous vroom-vrooming of their bikes, we could hear them cursing and shouting.

"They aren't speaking English," I said.

"French-Canadian bikers riding the interstate to the border. Stay away from them. Those guys are serious," Digby said. "In fact, let's pair up and stay close."

"Ooh . . . my bodyguard," Bill said. It was sickening watching her fawn all over Digby.

Digby pointed at the bikers and the goth girls. "Most of this crowd's not local. They hop off the interstate and hop back on again without seeing the rest of town. Bikers, truckers, hitchers . . . people on the Greyhound."

"I bet those girls are hitching." Bill photographed them with her phone. One of the goths flipped us the finger when the flash went off. "They're amazing."

"There's my guy Pedro," Digby said.

"That's your guy?" I said.

Pedro's hood was pulled up over a baseball cap so I couldn't see his face, but he had the height and build of a ten-year-old.

"Geez . . . isn't his mom worried he's out so late?" I said.

"What are you talking about? Pedro's twenty-eight. He has a ten-year-old daughter," Digby said.

"I think he's even smaller than I am," Felix said.

We got out of the limo. Close up and in better light, I saw Pedro was definitely not a kid. He had a stringy mustache and a gold tooth. I couldn't help staring.

"Like what you see, Miss Beautiful?" Pedro sucked air through his teeth and blew a wet kiss. "Hey, Digby, I like your friend."

"She's with me tonight," Felix said.

"This is weird," Sloane said.

"Henry, why don't you guys go ahead? Princeton and I will meet you inside," Digby said.

While they were walking away, Bill tripped and fell inches away from the goth girls. When the one with the cut lip walked toward her, Bill defensively curled up into a little ball.

"Chill." The goth girl was holding Bill's hat. "You dropped this."

Bill made a ridiculous face that I was still trying to describe to myself, when Sloane said exactly what it was.

"You're looking at her like she pulled you from a burning car. It's a *hat*. A fugly one. If she'd wanted to do you a real favor, she wouldn't have given it back." Sloane stepped over Bill, still lying on the ground, and said, "You're an idiot."

"Pedro, you saw my guy? What time?" Digby said.

Pedro held out his hand. Digby patted his pockets, then turned to me. I was familiar with this move. I took a twenty from my clutch and gave it to him.

Digby slapped the bill into Pedro's palm. "When?"

"An hour ago," Pedro said.

"Was he alone?" Digby said.

"He was with some guy, but not one of the ones on your list," Pedro said.

"What list?" I said.

"My persons of interest list that my guys look out for," Digby said. "I can't be everywhere all the time."

"Persons of interest? Who else is on it?" I said.

Pedro looked at me. "Starbucks, yesterday at four thirty, bookstore, then the number six bus at five forty-five," he said.

"*I'm* on your list?" I said. "You have people follow me around town?"

"Just watching out for you, Princeton. You don't always look both ways when you cross," Digby said. "So, Pedro, did you see where he went after he left here?"

260

"Sure . . ." Pedro stuck his hand out again. "But that was overtime."

Digby turned back to me. I fished out the second, and last, twenty from my purse.

"Tropical Hut. Room twenty-three," Pedro said. "Want me to take you?"

"No, man, I know the place." To me, Digby said, "Sloane's driver took Marina to that motel."

Digby and Pedro pounded out good-byes.

"Tropical Hut? You think Ezekiel and Marina are together?" I said.

Digby showed me the photo Pedro texted him of Ezekiel walking out of the 7-Eleven. Digby zoomed in on a package Ezekiel was holding. "Same motel and a huge bag of Corn-Nuts? Maybe that's a coincidence, but it's worth a look."

Digby and I walked into the 7-Eleven, where his order that everyone stay together had clearly never taken. Sloane was checking her lipstick in the sunglasses rack's mirror. Henry was pouring a giant Slurpee. Felix was reading an Archie Comics. Bill was spying on the three goth girls through the store window.

Digby and I walked to the counter.

"Wait. You hear that?" he said.

I froze. Nothing. Just 7-Eleven sounds.

"No," I said.

"Hm . . . it's gone," Digby said.

We started walking. After a few steps, Digby froze again. "There it is again."

"I don't hear it," I said.

"Sounds like . . ." he said. We started walking again. "There."

We stopped. Again, nothing. Then I realized what it was.

"Oh . . ." I tapped my foot. "My tap shoes."

"You're kidding," he said.

"It's not like I thought we were gonna be sneaking up on people. Wait, *are* we sneaking up on people tonight?"

"Well, we know *you* won't be."

A flash went off. Bill had photographed Digby and me.

"Hey," I said. "Why are you taking pictures?"

"What? I'm not," Bill said.

"She's been doing it on the down-low this whole time," Digby said. "I was gonna deal with it at the end of the night, but Bill, looks like your participation in our night's ending right now. Can I see that, please?"

"No." Like the kid that she was, Bill put her hand behind her back. "It's my phone."

"What are you doing, anyway?" I said.

"My guess is she's writing some kind of blog. Only thing worse than a tourist is a tattletale," Digby said. "I'm sorry things didn't work out, Bill. You could've been a good backup for Princeton here—"

"Hey!" I said.

Digby faked left, then reached right and plucked the phone out of Bill's hand.

"Oh, I look good in this one. You can keep it. The rest . . . delete." Digby erased the photos and returned the phone to Bill, who stormed off.

At the counter, the 7-Eleven cashier was opening big sealed envelopes and shaking out stacks of scratch cards. His nametag said he was ASSOCIATE TED, but he didn't look up when Digby called out his name.

"Uh, Ted, we need to ask you some questions," Digby said.

Ted slowly slid the pile of scratch cards into a drawer.

"Are you from New York Lottery?" Ted said.

"No," Digby said. "Homeland Security."

Ted raised his hands, knocking down a display of lighters when he stepped back.

"Dude. I'm kidding," Digby said.

"He's joking," I said. "Really."

"Relax . . . we're in high school, man. We're looking for our friend." Digby showed him Ezekiel's photo.

"You looking for this guy?" Ted said.

"You know him?" Digby said.

"Well . . . yeah. I know him. But if you want stuff, I mean . . . I could hook you up . . . for cheaper," Ted said.

"Oh, yeah? What you got?" Digby said.

"We should probably focus," I said.

"Okay, yeah . . . our friend?" Digby said.

"Sure. He was here tonight," Ted said.

"You remember anything? Did he say anything weird? Buy anything special?" Digby said.

"I dunno. Maybe some food?" Ted said.

"Can you review transactions on that?" Digby pointed at the register.

"That isn't copacetic," Ted said.

"Okay." Digby dumped some candy on the counter. "I gotta pay for these."

Ted logged onto the register and rang up the candy.

"Can we take a look at security footage from tonight?" Digby said.

"Yeah, right," Ted said. "Even if I wanted to show you, these cameras feed straight to the security company."

"Even that one behind the counter? It's different from the rest," Digby said.

"There isn't one behind the counter," Ted said.

"Sure there is. By the cigarettes," Digby said.

Ted's face filled with dread and he turned slowly. When he spotted the hidden camera, he walked into the back room without saying another word.

"Think he's coming back?" I said.

"I seriously doubt it. I mean, if *I* found out there was tape of me committing lottery theft, I'd get straight out of town." Digby got behind the register and hit the BACK button until he saw it. "CornNuts. Two hours ago. Bottled water. Miscellaneous maps. Thirteen ninety-five."

Digby ran to the shelf and pulled down maps to read the prices on the back.

"Too cheap . . . nope . . . too cheap . . ." Finally, he pulled down a book: Road atlas USA, Canada, Mexico. $13.95.

"Makes sense. He's probably driving to Canada with the rest of his cult," I said.

"Except . . ." Digby ran back to the register and looked again at Ezekiel's transactions. "He also bought four things of

Imodium. Seems excessive for a trip to Canada." Digby tapped the cover of the atlas. "He's going to Mexico."

I had to ask. "We're not going to Mexico, are we?"

"Well, the night is young . . ." Digby said.

Then I saw Sloane talking to a shifty-eyed middle-aged man in a cheap suit. "Oh, great. Look."

The guy leaned into Sloane in a way I didn't like. I heard Sloane say, "Do I *look* like I'd know a taxi driver?"

Then the guy's hand reached for Sloane.

"Sloane!" I shouted so loudly that Sloane jumped. The guy's hand froze inches from her boob and quickly retracted. Sloane hadn't even seen it. "Come here. Right now!"

Sloane had the nerve to look irritated when she toddled over. "What?"

"What do you mean, 'what'? That guy," I said.

"He was weird, asking me for a taxi," Sloane said.

"He was asking if you knew *Taxi Driver*. The movie," I said. Sloane's face was blank. "Jodie Foster? Teen prostitute? Because you look kinda . . . you know. Never mind. Just stay close."

"Whatever," Sloane said.

"Where is everybody?" Digby said.

Felix was still reading Archie. He muttered, "I don't understand why I don't have this one." Henry was beside him, sucking on his Slurpee and reading a *Sports Illustrated*.

"Where's Bill?" Digby said.

She wasn't in the aisles, outside the store, or in the parking lot.

"Where'd she go?" Digby looked at the security monitors under the register. "Oh, man. Trouble."

Digby hunted around under the counter. I went to look. There, on the monitor showing the back alley, I saw Bill cowering from a big, bearded man looming over her.

"Digby, she's getting attacked," I said.

"I'm aware of that." Digby kept searching under the counter. "It's gotta be here somewhere."

"What the hell are you looking for?" I said.

On the monitor, the guy grabbed Bill and shook her.

"A-ha!" Digby came up with a baseball bat.

"Whoa . . . you're not even holding that right. Gimme," Henry said. "Sloane, stay with Felix."

"Great, now I'm the nanny?" Sloane said.

⧓

We ran to the alley. From behind a Dumpster, we watched Bill's situation get worse. Bill whimpered. The guy said, "You scream and I'll break your neck."

"Digby, what are we waiting for?" Henry made practice swings with the bat.

Digby pulled Henry back and pointed at the attacker's waistband. "He's got a knife. Clothes are brand-new. Look at his jeans, his jacket. The creases—they're straight off the shelf. The tattoo on his neck. Clock, no hands. That's a prison tatt for doing time," Digby said. "He's probably riding Greyhound on his prison-issued ticket. I'll bet he just got out."

"Then now what?" Henry said.

"We gotta get him off her without a fight. I don't feel like getting shivved. If this doesn't go well, go pull the fire alarm."

Digby took off his jacket and handed it to me. Then he took

266

a running start. By the time he got to Bill and her attacker, he'd built up some speed and was panting convincingly.

"Hey, man, did they come this way?" Digby said.

The ex-con touched the knife in his waistband and covered Bill's mouth. "Who?"

"Two cops chasing me. They come this way?" Digby said.

The ex-con shook his head.

"Then look out, man. If they come this way, tell them you ain't seen me, okay?" Then Digby jumped onto a trash can and hopped the fence.

Alone with Bill again, the ex-con said, "If you tell anyone, I'll find you when I get back out." Then he grudgingly shoved her and ran in the other direction.

Henry and I ran to Bill as soon as he left.

"Let's get you in the car," Henry said.

Bill was crying hard, but from what I understood, she'd been talking to the goth girls after we'd erased her photos. One of them suggested they go out back and smoke something more interesting than cigarettes. When they got there, the ex-con offered the goths twenty bucks to leave Bill. The idea of being sold for twenty bucks was so awful that I hugged Bill and let her cry all over me.

Sloane and Felix joined us in the limo.

"What's the matter with her?" Sloane said. "And where's Digby?"

"He's coming," Henry said.

"Well, I don't wanna wait anymore. Obviously, it's dangerous," Sloane said. "Let's get out of here."

"Technically, this is Felix's limousine," I said. "Felix, do you want to leave Digby here?"

Felix shook his head. "No. That would be a crappy thing to do."

"You could take the bus back if you want, Sloane," I said.

The door opened and Digby slid in, breathing hard from his run.

"We were about to leave you," Sloane said.

"Henry, you should take them back to the dance," Digby said.

"Finally," Sloane said.

"Wait. What are you doing?" I said.

"I'll find my way back." Digby put his jacket on.

"On your own? No," I said. "I'm staying."

"Me too," Felix said.

"That's ridiculous. We're not leaving anyone," Henry said. "Digby, what's going on?"

"I need to go around the corner," Digby said. "A motel called the Tropical Hut."

"That hole? Ew . . . why?" Sloane said.

"You know the place?" Digby said.

"Dad's campaign manager makes disgusting jokes about dead prostitutes in that place," Sloane said. "Why there? Can't you two hook up behind the cafeteria like normal people?"

"Is this about . . . ?" Henry said.

Digby nodded. Henry put the car in drive.

"Is this about *what*?" Sloane said. No one said anything. "Fine. But I'm not going in. There aren't enough vaccines in the world to protect me from what you can catch in there."

++++

The Tropical Hut was one of those theme motels. Neon palm trees and a cardboard grass hut by the front door, and a half-inflated hula girl drooping by the half-drained pool out front.

Some ground-floor doors were open and majorly wasted people randomly stumbled in and out of each other's rooms. A woman's scream sounded partway between crying and laughing.

"Classy place," I said. "Hey, why aren't you surprised she's with Ezekiel? You already knew they were involved?"

"It might've been a coincidence that Marina snorted the same blue generic Adderall Floyd sold Felix, but how many fifteen-year-old girls use the words 'real man'? Ezekiel said the exact same words when we were fighting on your lawn," Digby said. "That, the motel, the CornNuts . . ."

"Marina? Marina *Miller*?" Sloane said.

"Stay out of this, Sloane," Henry said.

"She's in there? But we're not calling the police?" Sloane said. "I knew it. She wasn't kidnapped. She ran away and ended up here? What a loser. And speaking of losers, are those jazz shoes?" She pointed at my feet.

"They're tap shoes," Digby said.

"You sound like a horse," Sloane said. "A loud one."

"You're making more noise complaining than my shoes are tapping," I said.

"But it's the combination of her shoes, your whining, and the two of you fighting about it that's gonna get us killed," Digby said.

269

"Why did he say 'killed'?" Sloane said.

"Just stay in the car," Henry said.

"Listening to this one cry?" Sloane pointed at Bill. "Pass."

Ezekiel stepped out of a second-floor room and stood in the open-air hallway, smoking and watching two drunks fighting in the parking lot below. He was shirtless under his open coat and tattoos crisscrossed his torso.

"There he is," Digby said. "We gotta get him out of there and get Marina out of that room."

"Okay, great plan except for the fact that he knows all three of us," I said.

We all looked at Sloane. Unexpectedly, instead of giving us her usual snotty attitude, Sloane actually looked game.

"Get him away from the room?" Sloane said. "Fine. I'll do it."

"Really? I thought you'd make me beg or something," I said.

"Go ahead if you really want to," Sloane said.

"We have no choice, so I'm gonna pretend I'm not suspicious you're up to something," Digby said. "But you are up to something, aren't you?"

"Do you want me to do this or not?" Sloane said.

"I should probably just take yes for an answer," Digby said.

Sloane got out and toddled to the stairs. Her ankle twisted halfway up her painfully slow climb and she barely caught herself on the banister.

"Those stupid shoes," Henry said.

Whatever she said to Ezekiel when she got there worked, though. He retrieved a wire hanger from the room and was twisting it as he followed Sloane downstairs.

We ran out of the limo and climbed the stairs at the opposite end of the motel.

I had a flash of panic when we got to the room. "Wait, what if she isn't alone in there? If someone else comes to the door?" I said.

"Then we pretend we need help buying beer. But relax. Guys don't sit around together shirtless in November. He and Marina were alone." Digby knocked. There was shuffling inside. Digby knocked again. The lights in the room went off.

Digby said, "Someone called for smokes?"

"Um . . . come back later. He's not here right now." Marina's voice sounded shaky.

"Marina? It's Henry. Open up."

"Henry? Petropoulos?" The door opened and Marina stood in the dark doorway. She had on a bright blue wig and a skimpy bikini and she smoked her cigarette manically. "Why are you here?"

"We'll talk later. Right now, we gotta go," Henry said.

We poured into the room.

"I don't wanna leave. E-Z's taking me to Cabo," Marina said. "He got us a room at the hotel Jennifer Aniston stayed at. He bought me this bikini."

"You can't go to Cabo, Marina. Your parents are really worried," Henry said.

"They don't care. They have Ursula. She's the one they want," Marina said.

I just didn't want to hear it. "Oh, grow up, get your clothes on, and let's get out of here before that psycho gets back."

"No. I'm going to Cabo," Marina said. "I never get to go anywhere."

Digby pointed at Sloane and Ezekiel trying to jimmy open a minivan in the parking lot. "Guys, hurry. She picked a Dodge. I once broke into one of those with a spork."

"Marina, let's go." Henry stepped toward her, hand outstretched.

Marina flicked her cigarette into my skirt's feathers and ran to the other side of the bed.

"Smells like burning hair," Digby said.

By the time we found the cigarette and put out my smoldering feathers, Marina had pulled a knife from the nightstand. Henry leaped across the bed and grabbed the knife. Digby grabbed her other arm. The three of them danced around for a while.

"What are you doing? Get that thing away from her," I said.

They made a few furniture-breaking swoops but no actual progress.

Marina screeched for Ezekiel the whole time.

"Can't do it, dude. Can't hit a girl," Henry said.

"Do it. I can't reach," Digby said.

"For God's sake." I smacked Marina's face and she went limp in Digby's arms.

"Yeah, like I told you. She hit me just like that. But in the nads, dude," Digby said.

"Isn't that basically a vasectomy?" Henry wasn't kidding.

"Do you not have Google at all?" I said.

Digby threw Marina on the bed. "Get her clothes on."

I couldn't get her skinny jeans past her knees. "I miss hoochie sweats."

Digby opened a bag he found under the TV stand. "Whoa . . ."

We left Marina half-trousered on the bed and joined Digby. In the bag were rubber-banded rolls of Mexican pesos and the road atlas from the 7-Eleven. In the dimness, it took me a second to realize there were guns in the bag. Lots of guns. And other stuff that looked like bricks of yellow Play-Doh.

"Are those . . . ?" Henry said.

"Explosives," Digby said.

Digby flipped one of the bricks. The label said: EXPLOSIVE PLASTIC SEMTEX-H.

"Bad news is . . ." Digby held up empty plastic wrappers with the same label. "Where's the rest?"

"That's a lot," I said. "I mean, isn't that a lot? Do you need a lot of this stuff?"

"Dunno. I'm not a demolitions expert . . . yet . . ." Digby counted the wrappers. "Although . . . twelve of anything explosive's probably a lot."

"*Whoa.* Digby, it's time to call the pol—" Henry said.

"Already dialing 911," Digby said.

I glanced out the window. Sloane was in the parking lot waving at us.

"He's coming back. What about Marina? Should we drag her out?" I said.

"Too late. Bathroom. Go," Digby said.

We hustled into the little bathroom and looked at the drop from the window to the alley.

Henry whistled. "That's a broken ankle at least."

Digby looked up and down the alley. He texted someone.

"Digby, do we jump?" Henry said.

"Wait . . ." Digby said.

Ezekiel came back into the room. "Hey, babe? Why are the lights off?" Ezekiel laughed. "You pass out putting on your pants?" He turned on the TV. "Want some, babe?" When Marina stayed passed out, he said, "More for me."

We sweated it out in the bathroom until, finally, we heard a *PSSST* from the alley below. Felix and Sloane were below the window.

"Hurry!" Digby said.

Felix signed *okay*, ran to a wheeled Dumpster at the other end of the alley, and pushed. It didn't move an inch. He re-positioned and tried again. My heart sank when I saw his feet pedaling but the Dumpster going nowhere.

Sloane stomped down the alley in her heels and took her place beside Felix. There was metallic grinding as the two of them pushed the Dumpster until it was right below us.

"Whoa . . . Sloane's strong," Digby said.

"That's weird. Usually, she needs help opening her iced tea," Henry said. "Must be the excitement."

Digby climbed the windowsill, about to jump, when Felix motioned for him to wait. Digby's phone buzzed.

"Nice. Nerds. Very useful." Digby handed us his phone, where we saw a page titled "How to Jump into a Dumpster and Live: Three Steps." It had a GIF of a guy doing it. "Straight down, aim for the middle, land on your back. Easy-peasy."

My brain screamed. I noticed a line of sweat along Digby's hairline and felt better about my slimy armpits.

Digby took a breath and dropped like a rock. It looked terrifying, but on the bright side, it was over in a second. He got up and fluffed the trash for the next person.

"Zoe, you next," Henry said.

I climbed up, thinking of ways to stall, when Ezekiel did the horror movie thing of twisting the bathroom doorknob.

"Hey, babe, d'you lock the bathroom?" Ezekiel said.

All I needed to hear. I pushed off the ledge. I thought I'd have a million thoughts on the way down the way people say your life flashes before you, but really, my mind was blank. Then I landed, my arms still crossed over my chest, my skirt feathers slowly fluttering down onto me.

Digby dragged me out. I barely felt my legs under me as we all ran to the limo. Only the tap-tap-tap of my shoes told me I was moving. I didn't even notice Henry jump down after me.

"What about Marina? Was she there?" Sloane said.

"Just run, Sloane," Digby said.

‡‡‡‡

When we got back, the limo's window was shattered. Dusty was still passed out and Bill was crying again. "He grabbed me."

"He was probably just trying to sit up," I said.

"I pushed him and he hit his head on the window . . . I think I killed him," Bill said.

Felix checked Dusty's pulse again. "Nope. Still alive. But if he wasn't concussed before, he is now. He needs a doctor."

"But how can we leave Marina in there? With that guy?" Sloane said. "Who was a creep. He tried to kiss me! Anyway, let's get her out." The words gushed from her. There was something extra behind the usual shouty rah-rah of her inner cheerleader.

"Um . . . she's not blinking. Like, at all," I said.

Digby grabbed Sloane's face. It looked like he was going in for a kiss.

"Dude. I'm right here," Henry said.

"Criminal, get any closer and I'll knee you in the balls," Sloane said.

"What's up, princess? Not exciting enough for you?" Digby said. "Pupils blown big as dishes, you're panting, it's fifty degrees out, and you have a sweat mustache."

"I do not." Sloane wiped her upper lip.

"What's going on?" Henry said.

"Your girlfriend's high," Digby said.

"She's what?" Henry said.

"I'm what?" Sloane said.

"She's artificially stimulated, dude," Digby said.

It made sense. I imagined Sloane going from diet pills in high school, binge drinking and inhaled powders in college, to clear hard liquors and prescription pills to keep it ladylike after she lands a plastic surgeon husband after graduation.

"Looks like speed," Digby said.

Same thing as diet pills. I did a small fist pump.

"Um, *no,* I don't do drugs. Those things suck the pretty right out of you," Sloane said.

"She looks off," Henry said.

"I do feel kinda weird," Sloane said.

"Hmmm . . . I wonder." Felix took Sloane's pulse. "One twenty. Yup. Probably what happened."

"Felix. Explain," Digby said.

"She twisted her ankle on the stairs and she asked if I had a painkiller . . ." Felix said.

"You gave her the pill Floyd gave you," Digby said.

"By accident." Felix shook out a travel-sized tube of Aleve. "Did it look like these? Or was it more rounded?"

Sloane slapped his hand so the pills showered over us in the limo. "How do I know? They all look the same."

"I think we have our answer," I said.

"She needs a doctor," Henry said.

"Dusty too," Digby said. "Take them in the limo."

"What about you?" Henry said.

"I'm sticking around," Digby said. To me he whispered, "I need to get her out of there."

Dusty sat up, lifted his forefinger like he was about to make a proclamation, and then passed out cold again.

"That can't be good, Henry. Get him to the hospital," Digby said. "In fact, you guys should all leave."

Digby climbed out the limo door. I wasn't particularly excited about trying to convince Marina to leave with us when she clearly thought she was having a ball, but the sight of Digby standing alone on the sidewalk was wrong. Then I saw something like fear momentarily flit across his face.

"I can't just leave him there," Henry said.

"It's okay. I'm staying," I said.

"Me too," Felix said.

We both climbed out of the limo. Henry rolled down his window and said, "Wow . . . no need to worry then."

"I'll make sure he doesn't do anything too crazy," I said.

Beside me, Digby tried to hide the fact that he was happy we were staying behind with him.

"Please, I wanna leave," Bill said.

"Seriously, Henry. Get them out of here," I said.

And even though she'd used me to hang out with Digby, I still felt sorry for Bill. Things are never easy on Planet Digby, but hers had been a particularly difficult initiation.

Watching them drive away, I was terrified. We faced a bag of guns and explosives and a violent runaway, we were downtown without a ride, and Felix's cape was fluttering behind him in the breeze.

"We're dead meat," I said.

As usual, though, Digby had his priorities straight.

"So, Bill's interesting," Digby said.

I rolled my eyes.

"I saw that," Digby said. "So much for sisterhood . . ."

"Turns out we've got nothing in common," I said.

"Henry and I have barely anything in common, and man . . . Felix!" Digby said. "You and I have nothing in common, right?"

Felix shook his head.

"We don't fight like you girls do," Digby said. "But see, Felix likes being the brain."

Felix nodded.

"And Henry's the jock, and I'm—" Digby said.

"The criminal and Sloane's the princess . . . blah-blah-blah," I said. "What's your point?"

"But you and Bill are fighting over the same spot," Digby said.

"And we can't both be in the group?" I said.

"Come on, Zoe, even *I* know there can only be one one-of-the-guys girl in the group. In case you don't know *Seinfeld* or *That '70s Show,* teen movies tell you the same thing. *Euro-Trip* . . . that's why the drummer in *Scott Pilgrim vs. the World* was mad . . ." Felix said.

"Wow, you watch a lot of stuff," Digby said.

"Research. Dad doesn't want me turning out like some weirdo nerd," Felix said.

"Um, first, life is not a sitcom. Second, where are we going? We seem to be walking away from the motel," I said.

"We're gonna check out some storage places nearby to figure out which this belongs to." Digby held up a set of keys.

"Where'd you get those from?" I said.

"Ezekiel's bag," Digby said.

"You stole them out of his bag of guns and explosives?" I said. "What a great idea. How is that going to help us get her out of there?"

"Who?" Felix said.

I'd forgotten we were still keeping Marina a secret from them. Great. More secrets.

"Relax . . . it's all part of the plan," Digby said. He knit his fingers together. "Don't worry, it's very cohesive."

"I can't even tell you how confident I feel now," I said.

"Me too!" Felix said.

"I don't really, Felix," I said.

Digby took out his phone and got on his map app. "All the storage places are close by . . ."

"How do you even know those are storage keys?" I said.

"Clearly, your mom moved the classy way and hired movers. One thing you learn a lot about when you have divorced parents who can't afford movers is self-storage units. The ones in Texas have AC. Upstate, they're heated. Good ones have pest control. Seen them all," Digby said. "This is an RFID keycard and this is a key to a radial pin tumbler lock. I opened one with the shaft of a Bic once."

Felix took the keys. "J22. Row J, door 22?"

"So we just walk to these places and try all the J22s? My feet hurt," I said. "Can I see your phone?"

I didn't really expect to do anything useful, but to my surprise, one name on the list of storage places actually rang a bell.

"This one," I said. "The U-Store on Irving."

"Are you saying that because it's the closest?" Digby said.

"No, but it's a bonus that it is," I said. "When Ezekiel and Floyd were talking by the Dumpster, I thought they were calling someone a 'used whore' but . . ."

"U-Store," Digby said. "Okay. Let's go."

He grabbed my hand and ran, dragging me behind him. I would've begged him to slow down, but I could hardly breathe. My tap shoes sounded like rifle shots on the pavement. Felix ran ahead. Man, that kid was fast. His streaming cape made him look superhero speedy.

We used the keycard to open the U-Store gate. It was an open lot with huge lockers lined up in infinite rows that filled the horizon endlessly. Totally creepy. We found J22.

"What do you think we'll find inside?" Felix said.

"*Silence of the Lambs* scenario? A twisted murder museum?" Digby said.

"I'm excited," Felix said. "I've never seen a corpse that wasn't a mummy."

"Or it could be a roomful of smuggled diamonds," I said.

"We're not in a Tintin adventure, Princeton," Digby said. "These guys are small-town dealers. It's probably a whole locker of chemicals or something."

"At least we know it isn't gonna be Marina's rotting corpse," I said.

"It could be somebody else's corpse," Felix said.

"I'm gonna do it." Digby opened two heavy locks and when he got the roll-up door open, we got a shock of a different kind. "It's an ambulance."

"Maybe the corpse is inside," Felix said.

"You should let the whole corpse thing go," I said.

"It's the ambulance stolen from the Children's Hospital. Remember? Sloane's parents were in the mall raising money to replace it," Digby said.

"An ambulance? They're car thieves too?" I said.

"It's a weird thing to steal if they are," Digby said. "But . . . it's a great thing to have for delivering or picking up stuff without people noticing."

"Maybe there's something inside already," Felix said.

The ambulance doors were locked and none of Digby's stolen keys opened them. Felix noticed a small window on the side of the ambulance was slightly ajar.

"If you lift me up, I could get inside," Felix said.

Digby hoisted Felix through the window. Once he was in, we heard rummaging noises.

"He sounds like a raccoon in a trash can," I said. "Now what? He's stuck."

Through the window, we saw Felix struggling to pull free from something.

"That damned cape, I bet," I said.

"I just realized . . . we probably shouldn't stay here too long," Digby said. "Since we swiped the keys to this locker, they'd have a pretty good guess where they'd find us. I mean, they're probably headed here now."

"That's right, kid. Like, *right* now." We turned. Ezekiel's gun mainly pointed at Digby, but in case I thought my pumped-up kicks could run faster than his bullet, he waved it in my direction a little too. Schell was with him. Ezekiel peered into the ambulance.

"See, I told you . . . she sent them. Look out! There are three of them. The third one will jump us from out of nowhere. That's how they got me," Schell said.

"Shut up, Leo, no one's here." Ezekiel jerked his gun at Digby. We left the locker. "Close up."

I saw Felix's head pop up in the window for a split second before he ducked down.

"Don't make me tell you again, kid. Lock the door," Ezekiel said.

Digby pulled down the door and locked up. I seriously hoped Felix wasn't afraid of the dark.

"Now *move*," Ezekiel said.

Then again, what was I doing feeling sorry for Felix when we were the ones who were probably being death-marched to a body dump by the river? I remembered the no-second-location rule and my knees locked. But then I realized going to a second location that *wasn't* a deserted storage facility in the dead of night would probably improve our chances of survival, so when Ezekiel screamed "Move!" again, I moved.

"Digby, are we gonna die now?" I said.

"Relax . . . I got it." Digby smiled.

"Hand over your phones," Ezekiel said.

We did. And when he waved for us to climb into the trunk of his car, we did that too. The confidence on Digby's face reassured me.

Just before he shut the trunk, Ezekiel went through Digby's pockets. I took a break from my panic to notice the weird jumble that came out. One latex glove, a whistle, half-eaten candy, string, a rubber band ball, more string . . . Then he found Marina's old phone. "Two phones. Bet you think you're real smart." Ezekiel slammed down the trunk lid.

In the dark, I felt like a fist had tightened around my heart. I was glad Digby and I were packed so close, spooning, because having him next to me was the only thing keeping me from losing it totally.

"Now what?" I said.

"Yeah, uh . . . that second phone was pretty much my entire plan, so . . ." Digby said. "I got nothing right now."

"What?!" The fist squeezed in my chest.

"Gimme a second."

"Think fast."

Ezekiel started the car and peeled off, fishtailing around corners. We were quiet a long time. I lay there, trying to calm down. Then I felt Digby's hands patting around the trunk. And other places.

"Hey," I said.

"Oh, was that you?" Digby said. "I was exploring our options."

"They don't include my butt, though, right?"

"Uh . . . I guess not."

"So maybe you can get your hand off it, then?"

"Don't be mad. Ballers be balling."

"Seriously? Now?"

"I dunno . . . I'm a sixteen-year-old guy."

"Should I feel better then? Guess that means you don't think we're gonna die."

Digby patted the taillight by my face. He made a fist and three-inch punched the taillight's housing, but since this was life and not *Kill Bill*, he got nowhere.

"Use one of your horseshoes and kick out the light," he said.

I recoiled and kicked with enough force to do that, but immediately regretted it when a huge cold draft shot up my dress after I did. Digby slipped off one of my shoes and hammered out the light right in front of our faces.

"We're going too fast. The fall would kill us if I pulled the trunk release," he said. "Maybe when he stops and opens the trunk, we jump him."

"I have Felix's EpiPen. I could stab him." I took it out. "God, I hope Felix isn't having an allergic reaction right now."

"He's sitting in an ambulance, so I'd say he's in the perfect place for an allergic reaction. There are probably a million Epi-Pens in that thing. So, that's the plan. You stab him, I jump him." Digby pointed out the view through the hole where the taillight had been. "Check it out. He's headed to your part of town."

"You don't think . . . back to the mansion?" My heart lifted at the idea of getting closer to home.

"Imagine if you died across the street from home," Digby said.

And then my heart sank.

"Then again, he didn't kill us at the storage place, where he had privacy and a place to stash our bodies . . ." Digby said. "So, the good news is that this probably means he's in a complicated situation. Now he's gotta think his way out, and this guy . . . isn't that bright."

The car stopped in the alley behind the mansion.

"Get ready. When the trunk opens, hit him with the pen and I'll grab his gun," Digby said. "You can do this, Princeton. Just focus."

"Yeah, I'm okay. I think."

"Here he comes."

The next bit's a blur, and whereas memories are normally like movies, all I have of the next couple of seconds is sound bites and screenshots.

First, Ezekiel cursed when he saw the punched-out taillight. Then the trunk opened and Ezekiel stood over us. I swung the EpiPen in his direction and pushed the plunger. I felt the needle stab flesh. Then Ezekiel screamed, and I screamed, and, weirdly, Digby screamed too. Then the trunk lid slammed down again. Ezekiel paced beside the car, cursing and sobbing.

"You were supposed to take his gun," I said.

"You freaked me out and I froze," Digby said. "That was gross. I can't believe you stabbed him in the eye."

"I stabbed him in the *eye*? That *is* gross."

Ezekiel punched the trunk. "What did you do to my eye? It's cold. I can't open it." He tried not to shout, but his panic was obvious.

"Maybe you shouldn't have injected an EpiPen of adrenaline directly into the brain of the guy holding the gun," Digby said.

The trunk opened and Ezekiel shoved the gun in my face. Tears streamed from the eye I'd stabbed.

Ezekiel grabbed the EpiPen but seeing it confused him even more. "What is this? What is this?"

Ezekiel pulled me out and threw me on the ground. Digby jumped him and almost got the gun, but Ezekiel wrestled it away. For a second, I thought he'd shoot us right there, but instead, he walked us toward the open cellar door.

"I asked around about you. You're looking for your sister. Bet it's making you nuts. Not knowing what happened to her. Sally. But *I* know what happened to her. Now you'll never know and you're about to disappear like she did." Ezekiel pointed at the doorjamb and said, "Explosions this big, they never figure out how many bodies, never mind whose they were."

Along the inside of the cellar door, the wads of yellow Semtex missing from the motel were wired to a black box. Before I could take in more detail, Ezekiel shut the door and left us in the basement's total darkness. Then, ominously, we heard a beep, and a green light on the black box lit up.

TWENTY-SEVEN

"I guess if that door opened . . ." Digby said.

"Digby . . . I don't wanna die," I said.

"Take it easy, Princeton. No one's dying."

The comforting glow of a phone's screen cut the darkness. Digby dialed.

"How . . . ?"

"I got it from his pocket before he threw us in here."

"You just dialed a lot more numbers than 911."

"There's a bomb on the door. I'm not sitting on hold for fifteen minutes. I'm calling Cooper and Holloway," he said. "Voicemail. I'm sending a text."

I took a step and my feet slid out from under me. I fell but never hit the ground, because I landed against something on the way down.

"Princeton, you okay?"

Digby shone the light on what I'd fallen against: a chain-link fence sectioning off part of the basement and two bodies on the ground behind it. One was a heavyset man. The other was at first only faintly familiar until I recognized her dress. Old faithful. Her Minnie-Mouse-knows-what-Victoria's-Secret-is dress.

"Mom!" I screamed.

"She's not dead, Princeton." Digby clapped his hand over my mouth. "Shut up and listen."

Then I heard Mom snoring. She was draped over the man's body. All around them were huge plastic drums, bales of clear plastic tubing, and crates filled with God knows what. More of that paraphernalia was lying around outside the cage.

"This is their lab," Digby said.

"Did Ezekiel put them in there?" I said.

"Lock them up but leave us out here?" Digby said. "I'd bet he doesn't know they're here."

It took a while for my eyes to make out the police uniform on the man lying under Mom.

"Isn't that . . . Officer Cooper?"

"Meaning whoever put them there and took his phone got my text and knows we're here." Digby cursed. *"Hide."*

Just then, the door between the house and the basement opened. Footsteps thumped down the stairs. Digby and I scurried off and were wedging ourselves behind giant plastic drums, when a bare bulb in the middle of the room came on. Then Digby, Zillah, and I stood blinking at each other in the light.

"Why am I not surprised to see you here?" Zillah said.

"But I'll bet you'd be surprised to hear why we're here. Ezekiel's stealing from you. I mean, you *are* the Bananaman, right? He's selling your stuff in the schools. That's why the cops are on your back and you have to leave town," Digby said.

"I do not know what you mean. We are leaving because this place is no longer suitable for my flock's moral well-being." But from the way Zillah's face contorted, it was clear Digby had nailed it. "The path of the righteous man is beset on all sides by the inequities of the selfish and the tyranny of evil men. Blessed is he who, in the name of charity and goodwill, shepherds the weak through the valley of darkness, for he is truly his brother's keeper and the finder of lost children."

Inexplicably, Digby laughed. "Here's a tip. When you set up in the next town, and you're pretending to be a religious cult and you put in time with the clothes and the weird Amish shtick, make sure you quote the actual Bible and not some fake Quentin Tarantino voodoo."

Zillah's shoulders dropped. She was beat. "Smart kid. I never checked. But do you remember the rest?" She pulled out a huge gun. "And I will strike down upon thee with great vengeance and furious anger those who attempt to poison and destroy my brothers. And you will know my name is the Lord when I lay my vengeance upon you."

The gun clicked ominously. I remembered which part of *Pulp Fiction* she was quoting.

"Digby . . ." I said.

"You're gonna fire a gun around explosive chemicals?" Digby threw the phone he was holding at the lone light bulb. The basement went black. I scrambled behind a plastic drum. Digby's voice whispered from elsewhere in the basement, "Don't miss."

For a long time, nobody moved. Zillah swore, stubbed her toe, swore some more, and then stumbled up the stairway. "I'll be back for you two later. You're not going anywhere." She slammed the door and turned the lock.

"Digby? Now what?" I said.

"I'm thinking," he said.

"We have to get my mom out."

"Shh . . . thinking," he said. "If they cook here, they've gotta have an air vent . . ."

After crawling around, he found the phone he'd thrown and panned its light around the room.

"There." The beam of light pointed at the mouth of a filtration unit at the top of one wall. "How are we getting Mom up that?" I said.

"Sorry, Princeton. We'll have to come back for her." Then, before I could argue, he said, "If we stay, we all die. We'll come back for her, I promise."

We half dragged and half rolled a barrel across the basement and under the air duct.

"This probably leads outside." Digby climbed up the barrel. "Whole neighborhood's been inhaling the fumes of them cooking meth, but everyone assumed it was those girls cleaning."

"What if that vent gets narrower and we get stuck?" I said.

"Beats getting shot," he said.

"Seriously, stop trying to make me feel better."

"Just come up and don't make any noise."

And so I followed him up the rabbit hole.

††††

It was funny where my mind went while I crawled in the dark, going up a smooth inclined tube not much wider than my body, running from not one but two psychos who'd happily take a break from killing each other to kill me.

To distract myself, I registered details like how cold the metal felt under my knees. How the taps on my shoes clacked against the duct's sides. But I also wondered if when Henry said I looked nice, he meant he thought I looked *nice*. I mean, he said it twice. I was there in that duct but also somewhere else. Being split like that was a huge relief. Kind of like my mind was reassuring me, Yeah, we're gonna live. And we're gonna still want to date Henry.

Meanwhile, Digby was doing his best to prove that wrong.

"Turn left," I said when we came to a fork in the duct. Inexplicably, Digby turned right. "The cold air's coming from the left."

"Listen," he said.

A little girl was sobbing.

"Digby, we gotta get out of here," I said. "No side trips."

I tried to grab his pant leg, but he took off. I followed him until we got to a spinning duct booster fan. It was a miniature of an action movie cliché. I heard a *thwack* when Digby tried to stop the spinning blades.

"Ow! That's sharp." He sucked on his injured fingers. "Hey, pass your shoe."

"What? Use *your* shoe."

"I need your metal tap do-hickeys. These fan blades would rip right through my shoes."

And because I didn't want to waste more time arguing, I

gave him my shoe. Moments later, I heard the spinning fan blades chew it up.

"Like that," he said.

"Great," I said.

"Pass me your other shoe."

"I should probably warn you now—I only brought two of these."

"Yeah, ha-ha . . . ever heard of a learning curve?"

"Sure, same time I heard of trying to outrun killers while barefoot in an air vent."

"Just pass me your shoe. It's not like you'll run any faster with one shoe than none."

It was a good point.

This time, he caught a blade with the metal tap and pushed until with a metallic clunk and the smell of burning rubber, it stopped spinning. Digby pushed the fan off its mounts and we crawled toward the sounds of girls talking. I came across my mangled shoes on the way.

Digby pushed off the vent cover and we shimmied into the room. There were eight girls ranging in age from about five to eight years old. One very young one cried while other girls comforted her.

"Who are you?" one little girl said.

"Zillah sent me to check on you," Digby said.

"I don't believe you. No one who *really* knows Amber calls her Zillah," the little girl said. She seemed to be the eldest and the self-designated spokesperson.

"Well, that's one of the things I'm here to check. If you were remembering to use her code name . . . code-name Zillah. She also wanted me to check your arms," Digby said.

"Our arms?" she said.

"She wants me to put stickers on you for tonight's trip," Digby said.

"What for?" she said.

Digby produced Post-its from his pocket. "To help us keep track of you."

She pulled up her right sleeve and let Digby stick a Post-it on her arm.

"There," Digby said.

She frowned at Digby. "Post-its? Gimme a break. Would *you* have believed that when you were eight?"

"What's your name?" Digby said.

"Eve," she said.

"Nice to meet you, Eve," Digby said.

Eve pointed at me. "You live next door. Amber put your mom in the basement. Because she and the policeman were peeking in through the window. I saw the whole thing."

"I know. I was just in the basement," I said.

"Amber's not really religious, you know," Eve said. "Are you gonna put her in jail?"

"You want us to?" Digby said.

"She belongs in jail. She does lots of bad stuff. I know they're bad because I saw it on *Hawaii Five-O*," Eve said. "Plus, she slapped Maddie for crying for her mom."

"Where are your moms?" Digby said.

"All over. Amber watches us when our parents are traveling

for work. Hers is in Philadelphia. Maddie's mom was in Chicago. Amber says she's our mom while we're here," Eve said. "But she's nothing like a mom."

By then, Digby had checked all their arms. "Are there any other little girls in the house?"

"They left yesterday," Eve said.

"What are you looking for?" I said. "Why are you putting Post-its on their arms?"

"My sister had a birthmark on her arm."

Of course, that made no sense since all these girls were way too young to be his sister, but I got it. He needed to look.

To Eve, Digby said, "We need to get Zoe's mom out before Amber sees we're gone. Can you get us to the basement without anyone seeing?"

"Even Ezekiel? Ezekiel has keys to the whole house," Eve said.

"*Especially* Ezekiel," I said.

"Yes, I can," Eve said.

"But I want you all to come with us, okay?" Digby said. "You can come back later, but it's safer for you outside the house right now."

"What about the boys?" I said.

"They're packing up the shed," Eve said.

"So they're out of the house?" When Eve nodded, Digby said, "Okay, now can you show us how to get to the basement?"

It didn't feel great entrusting our lives to a little girl, but off we went down the hall.

How we weren't busted by all the creaking floorboards, I

don't know. On the way down, I saw us in the mirror by the stairs: Digby, me, and the train of little girls. We looked like Peter Pan and Wendy leading out the Lost Boys. Then I saw my skirt of scraggly feathers and realized I was less Wendy and more tumble-dried Tinker Bell.

When we reached the landing, I knew why we hadn't been discovered. Angry shouting came from the sitting room beside the front door.

Eve pointed at a door near the base of the stairs. "The basement."

"Okay," Digby said. "We'll go back to the second floor and get you out the window there."

On the second floor, Digby helped the girls climb onto a tree outside. Soon, the branches were covered in kids swinging down to the ground.

After they were all safe, Digby said, "Last chance, Princeton. You really want your mom back?"

"Shut up."

"Because this'd be a great opportunity to get rid of her . . ."

"Just hurry."

We crept back downstairs. The shouting was still in full force. The slide bolt across the basement door was fastened with an intimidating padlock. Digby took out a black roll-up pouch that unfurled to reveal a weird collection of doodads.

"We need the right-sized shims." He thumbed through tab-shaped cutouts made from Coke cans. He inserted two shims where the shackle entered the lock and jiggled them until it unlocked with a click. "The Internet's a fascinating place."

I followed him down the basement stairs.

When we were halfway down, Mom yelled in a scared, high-pitched voice, "Zillah, you crazy bitch, let me out of here!"

"Mom, it's me," I said.

"Zoe?" she said.

"Yeah. Digby's here too," I said.

"You kids get out of here. That crazy Zillah is—"

"We know, Mom."

"And Mike's here. Officer Cooper," she said.

"We know, Mom."

Digby rummaged around, found a length of pipe, and used it to pry the padlock open.

The three of us wrestled Cooper's unconscious body to the stairs. Mom and Digby took one arm each and I ended up with the legs. Cooper went up the stairs facedown, Superman style.

"Hey, Princeton, you figure it out yet?" Digby said.

"Huh?" I said.

"What your mom's doing with Cooper," Digby said.

Of course I knew. Somewhere, deep in my jumbled mind, I'd cataloged the pumpkin seeds in the trash, Mom's sudden and profound vegetarianism, and her giving up drugstore makeup because of animal cruelty. But this was the first time these facts had presented themselves to be added up. I dropped Cooper's feet.

Digby and Mom lunged forward so Cooper wouldn't slide down the stairs.

"Nice timing, kid," Mom said.

"You'd rather she realized it after we get out this door?" Digby said.

"Honey, I tried to tell you, but you said—"

"Let's talk later, Mom," I said.

"I mean, it isn't like I'm dating one of your teachers or anything. I turned down that truant officer at your school . . ." Mom said.

"These teddy bear types really like you," Digby said.

"Ew," I said.

"Okay, ladies. Now that everyone knows everything . . . to be continued? You know, after all us good guys are safely away from the bomb?" Digby said.

"Did you say 'bomb'?" Mom said.

"Let's just do this." I picked up Cooper's feet and we continued out of the basement. I didn't feel that bad when, at the top of the stairs, I was slow in turning and Cooper's side scraped (painfully, I'm sure) across the doorjamb.

The argument in the living room got louder as we crept up the stairs. Ezekiel was begging Zillah not to shoot him. The urgency in his voice was infectious and hustled us along. Finally, we were back at the window.

Mom and I silently contemplated the task of getting an unconscious 250-pound man down a tree.

"You first, then I pass him to you?" I said.

"Right." Mom didn't sound confident, but she climbed onto the branch anyway, braced herself, and held out her arms.

Digby and I passed Cooper over and I climbed onto the limb. It was an ugly ride down, but after one close call where a branch that caught him in a nut shot was the only thing that prevented him doing a twenty-foot pile-driver straight to the ground, I think he should be grateful just to be alive.

Once we got Cooper down, I realized the reason it had been so difficult was that Digby hadn't been helping us. I'd assumed Digby was right behind us the whole time, but he was still in the house. And I knew why. Ezekiel's taunt before he locked us in the basement. I couldn't blame Digby for wanting to know what Ezekiel knew about Sally.

"Mom, call the police. Tell them to bring the bomb squad. Tell 'em to bring everybody," I said.

"Where are you going?" Mom grabbed my arm.

"Just go, Mom. Don't worry. I'll be right there."

"Are you crazy? You're coming with me."

"Mom, just *go*. Call 911 or we'll all die. I'm just gonna wait here to make sure I see if anyone leaves." When Mom didn't move, I shoved her and said, "The sooner you call the cops . . ."

She finally staggered off with Cooper. Would it be horribly inconsistent if I told you I judged her for actually listening to me and letting me stay?

I snuck toward the living room window, kept my head low, and peeked over the windowsill.

There were four of them in the room: Zillah, Ezekiel bowed down before Zillah's gun, and two gun-toting men backing her up. Ezekiel begged in the please-oh-please way, but it was clear Zillah didn't care. She'd already made him stand on a tarp.

Then, suddenly, Digby sauntered in and plopped down on the couch in the middle of the action. Everyone froze.

"But first, ask him where he put it," Digby said.

Zillah's goon motioned Digby to join Ezekiel on the plastic.

"No, thanks. I'm comfortable here," Digby said. "Whatever you think you're moving, he's already taken it."

Zillah's head involuntarily turned to a steamer trunk in the middle of the room.

"Check it," Digby said.

Zillah unlocked the trunk and triumphantly lifted a bound bundle of bills.

"Look again," Digby said.

Zillah's face darkened when she did. Only the top bill was green. The rest were blank pieces of paper.

"It's one thing to steal product. *That* I can cover up. But do you have any idea what they'd do to you—to *me*—if this money goes missing, Ezekiel?"

"Ohhhh . . ." Digby pointed at Zillah. "The money isn't *yours* . . ." Digby pointed at Ezekiel. "*That's* why he couldn't just steal it. Ask him how he's getting it out of here."

"You have all the answers today. Why don't you tell me?" Zillah said.

"He's gonna put it in the ambulance he stole and drive out of here during the excitement," Digby said. "Straight down to Mexico."

"To Mexico?" Zillah shrieked with laughter. "You were going to *Mexico*? You really are too stupid to live. Who d'you think this belongs to? I'd like to see how long you'd live if you really went to Mexico."

"But everyone'd probably think he died in the explosion," Digby said.

"Explosion?" Zillah said.

"Oh, yeah. The basement's wired," Digby said. "Whole house is gonna blow."

"Show me." Zillah grabbed Ezekiel and pushed him. Both tripped on the tarp on the way out.

Digby was left in the room with just the two goons.

Now's my chance, I thought. I picked up a rake leaning against the wall. Then I thought, My chance to do what, exactly?

Which brings me back to where I started: standing outside a house that's about to explode, trying to figure out the best way to get back in.

TWENTY-EIGHT

I contemplate my options. Throw the rake through the window and climb in? Climb through, drag the rake behind me, and then start swinging? Maybe signal Digby first? Or maybe this is a stupid idea. I look across the street to my house and I'm immediately ashamed of myself for wanting to run home.

But the decision is made for me when hands grab my shoulders and drag me in backward through the window, rake and all. I scream as the windowsill scrapes my back from shoulder to ankle. I look like a cursing, feathered baby being birthed into that room.

The attention momentarily away from him, Digby grabs a table lamp and hurls it. Unfortunately, the lamp stays plugged in and there's a doggie-on-a-chain effect. It's enough of a surprise, though, that Digby is able to jump the guy.

Meanwhile, I swing the rake around, wildly trying to accomplish I don't know what, but I succeed in creating chaos.

Zillah runs back in. She's screaming to her men about the

bomb in the basement when her foot catches on the tarp mid-sentence, and she flies forward. Her gun fires when her hand hits the floor.

We shut up and freeze.

"Where's Ezekiel?" Digby says.

We immediately form a temporary alliance. We are the five people in the house about to explode who have lost sight of the bomb-maker. We descend into slapstick as we all try to squeeze through the doorway simultaneously. Digby gets out first and he tackles Ezekiel, but it takes Zillah's help to wrestle Ezekiel into the living room.

Ezekiel drops his phone while Zillah ties him to the radiator with her scarf.

Digby picks it up. "'Call ended.' That means . . ."

"The bomb," Zillah says. *"Go!"*

Zillah and her goons run to the front door. Digby and I are hot on their heels. Behind us, Ezekiel begs, "Please! Please untie me!"

We keep running until Ezekiel says, "I'll tell you what happened to your sister!"

Digby goes back into the room.

"Digby, what are you doing?" I say.

"Talk," Digby says.

"Untie me," Ezekiel says.

"Then fine." Digby walks away.

"They screwed up. They were supposed to take *you* that night . . . not her," Ezekiel says. "And I know why."

"Princeton," Digby said.

I go back and help untie Ezekiel. Without having to discuss

it, we know our fastest exit's through the window, so the three of us dive out and hit the ground running.

About twenty feet from the house, Digby says, "We should du—"

He doesn't finish because the house blows. I once saw a Discovery Channel show that described being in an explosion as getting hit by a hot steel wall moving at the speed of sound. But I can tell you this is inaccurate.

Being in an explosion is like having that hot steel wall go right through you.

I black out.

⧫⧫⧫

When I wake up, I'm facedown, wondering why the phone's ringing. Then I realize that's my ears ringing and that I'm totally deaf otherwise. The mansion's on fire. My hand's still clutching the rake handle.

Mom runs toward me, her mouth wide open in a scream. She gets down and cradles my head in her lap.

Over and over, I tell Mom I'm okay, but by the time first responders roll up, I feel like hell. Everything I own hurts. Moving my foot an inch sends agonizing pain up my leg.

I see Digby lying near me. My ears clear a little and I'm upgraded from total deafness to hearing everything from under a foot of water. I call out Digby's name a few times and that wakes him up. He crawls to Ezekiel, who's on his back doing an awesome impression of being dead. Digby slaps Ezekiel to rouse him. He's shaking him when paramedics push Digby off and start CPR on Ezekiel.

A pair of paramedics work on me too. I'm blinking in and out of consciousness, seeing only seconds out of every minute that elapses. Every time I come back around, I'm attached to more equipment.

The neighbors are on their lawns. Some take photos when I scream as they lift me onto the gurney. I'm in a plastic collar and strapped onto a board so I can't turn my head, but out the corner of my eye, I see them trying to similarly immobilize Digby. He's struggling, shouting something no one understands.

I look in the direction Digby's straining toward and see medics wheeling Ezekiel away. Somehow, messed up as I am, I know something's wrong. There shouldn't be a big bag on the gurney's bottom rack. Then I see the paramedics' faces. It's Schell and Floyd in paramedics uniforms wheeling Ezekiel and the bag of money into their stolen ambulance.

I yell, but everyone ignores me too. I don't blame them. It's a long story to tell and I don't know where to start, so I yell hysterical nonsense. They're getting away, but when Floyd unlocks the back of the ambulance, the door flies open and smashes Schell in the face.

At first, all I see is the swirl of Felix's cape. My ears are clear enough to hear people screaming when Felix flies out of the ambulance and lands atop Ezekiel on the gurney. Felix is holding defibrillator paddles and from the way Floyd jerks, goes rigid, and then collapses, it becomes clear that Felix has defibbed him in the face.

Felix turns to zap Schell, but Schell sees it coming and

pushes Felix, and the gurney, with Felix and Ezekiel on it, rolls away. Schell grabs the money, climbs into the ambulance's cab, and peels out.

The cops on the scene are too confused to do more than gawp. Schell doesn't get far, though, because a limo—*our* limo—accelerates past us, chases down the ambulance, and hits it hard from behind. Schell loses control, plows across a yard, and smashes into one of the houses. The limo's door opens and Henry tumbles out of the driver's seat. The cops swarm him, bend him over the hood, and cuff him.

Still straddling Ezekiel, Felix says, "Hey, is *this* a corpse?" He touches Ezekiel's neck, but is disappointed. "Nah . . . there's a pulse."

On his gurney, Digby's on a call, fighting off the paramedic trying to take his phone away. As they wheel me into the ambulance, old Mrs. Preston peers into my face and shakes her head. There goes the neighborhood.

It's a huge relief when the ambulance door closes and we finally leave for the hospital. Only then do I realize how much pain I'm in. I scream until I pass out.

TWENTY-NINE

The first thing I see when I wake and look past the machines that go ping is Digby, covered in bandages and sitting on a wheelchair, eating the tray of food left for me.

"How are you less hurt than I am?" I say.

"Oh, I hurt, Princeton. But it hurts a lot less when you pretend it doesn't," he says.

I guess I knock off some sensors when I sit up, because a concerned nurse run-walks into the room. She's peeved when she sees me sitting up.

"Don't pull out your IV. And why are you out of your bed, young man? You kids need to settle down." She replaces my electrodes. "Explosion . . . what were you two up to?"

"You know . . . shenanigans," Digby says.

Just as I'm thinking that the nurse's look of disapproval reminds me of Dad's shame-on-you stare, the door opens and the devil himself walks in.

"Dad?"

He's more bloated than usual. Not even his new tan can hide that he's working too much, eating too crappily, and not sleeping enough.

"An explosion? *My God,* what the hell's been happening here? Explain yourself," he says.

I try telling him, but the story's so long and strange and I'm so battered that I end up spewing gibberish. When I finally not so much finish my story as just stop telling it, Dad turns to Digby. "And you're her accomplice in this?"

"Me? Accomplice? No," Digby says. *"Mastermind."*

Digby rolls his wheelchair until one of his wheels is up against Dad's shoe.

"We haven't been introduced. I'm Digby. You must be Dick."

Dad ignores Digby's proffered hand. "*Mr. Webster.* Only my friends call me Dick."

"Well, with friends like that, amiright?"

"I suppose I should thank you for bringing this farce to an end. It's because of you that the judge finally realized my ex-wife can't be trusted."

"There was a custody hearing?" I say.

"No, but he agreed to schedule a new one." Dad passes me a document and a pen. "Sign this. It'll expedite the process."

"What is this?" I try to read it, but the fine print makes my head swim. "Does Mom know?"

"Your mother is no longer a factor in your upbringing. It's clear she's an incompetent parent," Dad says.

"May I?" I'm grateful when Digby takes the paper out of my hands and reads.

"Do you even understand what you're looking at?" Dad smirks the way most adults do before they realize what they're up against in Digby.

"I've had some experience with these Child Affidavits for Custody. They tried to get me to sign one too." To me, Digby says, "This says that in light of recent events, you don't feel safe in your mother's custody. You sure you wanna say that?"

"I thought I couldn't choose who to live with anyway," I say.

"You can't. Your dad's probably hoping to break your mom's spirit when he shows her you signed it. Or maybe he's hoping to exclude you from the decision process later. I mean, if you sign this and then later say you wanna live with your mom, you'd look like a flake and the court wouldn't take you seriously," Digby says. "I don't think that's what you want to do, Zoe."

I don't know if it's because Digby uses my real name for the first time or if it's because I'm furious at my father for trying to trick me into signing a document like that while I'm in a half-sedated haze, but I start shivering.

"Of course, you could just accuse your father of sexually inappropriate behavior and the court'll get you outta there in no time," Digby says.

"You're a very troubled young man," Dad says.

"Well, you're not wrong there," Digby says.

The door opens and in walks Shereene. She is exactly what a man having a midlife crisis would bring home from the office. Too blond, too tan, blinging way too much, and wearing perfume so thick, I can taste it. She ignores me and spins for my father a web of complaints that spans the hospital's lack of valet parking to the injustice of cutting short their vacation to see me.

Her whining creates a bubble of obliviousness around her and Dad, so Digby and I are able to talk about her without lowering our voices.

"Stepmom?" Digby says.

I nod.

"Seriously, Princeton, you wanna live with this?" Digby asks. I shake my head, no way. "Then may I . . . ?" Digby jumps in while Shereene's midsentence. "What about you, Shereene? Do *you* think Zoe should live with you in New York?" Digby says.

Shereene has a sexy-now-but-oh-wait-until-you're-fifty smoker's laugh. "If it'll save us seventeen percent of our income, then sure. *Liza* should pay *us* seventeen percent of her income. See how *she* likes it."

"'*Us*.' You guys are a tight unit. Such positive family values will really be great for Zoe." Digby points at Shereene's enormous diamond ring. "Wow, that's beautiful."

"It's Van Cleef. The setting's called *Byzance*." Shereene pronounces all its French-y rumbles to make clear how expensive it is.

"I bet the real one's even sparklier. Is it being cleaned? Resized?" Digby says.

"What are you talking about?" Shereene sees Dad's squirrelly look and gets suspicious.

"That's a replica, right? Because that isn't a diamond," Digby says.

"The kid doesn't know what he's talking about," Dad says.

Digby grabs Shereene's hand, swings it, and smashes it ring-first onto his wheelchair's armrest. The "diamond" is pulverized.

Cursing, Shereene yanks off what's left of her ring and throws it in Dad's face. She's halfway out the door when she stomps back into the room and slaps Dad. Twice. And then she leaves.

"Sorry, Dick. I thought she knew," Digby says.

"You'd better bet I'm speaking to your parents about this," Dad says.

"Notify my probation officer too. He hates being left out of the loop," Digby says.

Dad points his finger in my face. "Sign these papers and have a nurse drop them in the mail right away." He throws the pile on my nightstand.

"No." It couldn't have sounded weirder if I'd farted out of my mouth.

"What the hell does that mean?" Dad says.

"I don't want to change the custody agreement. I don't want to live with you guys," I say.

"Young lady, I'm not going to pay for boarding. You either live with me or you don't go to Prentiss," Dad says.

"I'm not going to Prentiss," I say. "Not this January, anyway."

"The dean of Prentiss is a special friend and he's gone through the trouble of making room for you in January. I've already filled in the forms. All you have to do is sign. What's the difficulty?" Dad says.

"Well, maybe I don't have to cheat to get in," I say.

"You don't understand what kind of opportunity you're wasting, Zoe," Dad says.

In the past, the way he spits out my name would've been enough to make me buckle, but my hierarchy of fears have been rearranged.

"I understand perfectly."

"And just how do you expect to get into the Ivy League?" Dad says.

"I guess I'll just work hard," I say.

When he laughs, I realize my father has zero respect for me as a person.

"Let's see how far you get with that." Then Dad comes to his senses and remembers Digby is watching. "I won't have this discussion in front of strangers. I'll speak to you later." He swings open the door so hard, the doorknob dents the wall.

And just like that, the confrontation I'd spent months dreading is over.

"So . . . your dad's nice. Should I expect a Christmas card?" Digby says. "Better tell me now so I don't look like a jerk if I don't send him one too."

"Ha-ha . . . he's going to make Mom and me pay for that in some other horrible way, you know," I say.

"Well, if he does, tell him you know about the money he's hiding in the Caymans. He and his chickie just got back from there," Digby says.

"How could you possibly know that?"

"When she opened her purse, I saw a plastic bag that said KIRK FREEPORT." Digby holds up his phone. "Google says that's in the Caymans and the only reasons people go down there are to visit their pile of dough or sunbathe. Even with his tan, your dad doesn't look like a beach bum to me."

True. I can't imagine Dad stepping out of his suit for a second longer than it takes him to shower. "He's hiding money from Mom?"

"Not just your mom. From Shereene too," Digby says.

"Her too? What does he spend it on? He has no hobbies. His favorite thing to do is yell at people, and that he gets paid to do at work," I say. "I mean, he likes to eat, but he mostly binge-eats Nutella and that's only, like, seven bucks at the bodega."

"He's a dragon with a cave of riches he doesn't wanna share. He's a hoarder, but because he hoards money, it's classy and no one thinks it's weird," Digby said. "You're the princess he wants to drag into his lair. Stealing you back from your mom would really round out his collection."

"Great," I say. "How'd you know about Shereene's diamond?"

"Well, I actually saw that her bag and watch were fakes first, then I worked backward from there," Digby says. "So, what? No Prentiss? When'd you decide that?"

"I didn't say no Prentiss *ever*. I just don't want to go there on his terms."

"So until then, you'll stay here?"

"I guess. At least I won't be bored with you around," I say.

313

"But then, how are you gonna top blowing up a house and busting up a meth ring?"

"I don't know . . . I'll think about it when I get back."

"Get back? From where?"

"I have an appointment in Texas."

"Appointment?"

Suddenly, a burly dude in a suit and a buzz cut pokes his head in the door.

All I'm wearing is a paper-thin hospital gown. "Hey!" I yell. I pull the sheet around my chest even though he isn't looking in my direction at all.

The guy spots Digby, ducks back out, and says, "He's here, Miss Miller."

In comes not Marina (who I expect to see bearing flowers and a THANK YOU balloon), but her hatchet-faced sister, Ursula. Chop-chop-chop in my direction. Her face softens when she turns to Digby. Him, she's happy to see.

"So this is where you're hiding," Ursula says. "I thought maybe you'd left town already, but then . . . you wouldn't get far without this, I suppose."

She's wearing a trench coat and carrying a small metal suit-case. She looks like she's playing I Spy dress-up. I yelp when Ursula plops the suitcase on my legs. She snaps it open to reveal stacks of bills bound and labeled $5000.

Ursula watches me watch her unpack the money into a pyramid. She does the rich person thing of gloating at the astonishment their money elicits. "One hundred thousand."

"It should only be ninety-five," Digby said.

"Mother said to consider your advance a bonus," Ursula said. She picks up one bound stack, runs her fingertip across it, and sucks on the paper cut it gives her. "Ouch. Brand-new, like you wanted. Why did it have to be all new?"

"Because it would be gross to roll around in a bed of dirty bills," Digby says.

"One hundred thousand dollars? For what?" I say.

"Your Girl Friday didn't know about the money? So she got herself blown up for what?" Ursula openly laughs at me. "Oh, I see . . . I hope it's requited."

"What's going on?" I say.

"My mother offered a hundred thousand for getting my sister out of there without anyone knowing she was ever with that scumbag," Ursula says. "We took care of John too, by the way. He'll never tell now."

John. Sloane's driver who suddenly quit his job before the dance.

"Took care of him?" With these people, I had to check.

"He's *my* driver now," Ursula said.

"And Sloane, Bill, and Felix never actually saw her," Digby said.

"But Henry and I did. Are we supposed to lie to the police?" Under my breath, I add, "Again?"

"Not technically *lie* to the police. Erasing Marina doesn't substantially change our story," Digby says.

"Sharesies with your friends, then?" Ursula says.

"I don't want your money," I say. What the hell. I guess today's the day I turn down stuff.

"As you like," Ursula says. "It was worth every cent just to see Marina on a scooter with that ridiculous ape. Where'd you find him?"

"He's kinda like the UPS guy in my economy," Digby says. "He'll deliver anything for anyone anywhere."

"That was Alistair you called when the ambulances came?"

"You know I was always going to split the money with you, right?" Digby says.

"Ohh . . . *that's* why you didn't tell anyone there was a reward," I say.

"I told Henry," he says.

"Why the hell didn't you tell me?" I realize Ursula is watching, loving it. I scrape together all the dignity I have left and ask her, "Is there anything else you need?"

Ursula snorts to convey how ridiculous it is that I think I can dismiss her, but she starts to leave anyway. To Digby, she says, "Maybe I'll call you again sometime."

There's an awkward silence after she leaves.

"I didn't tell you because you have a bad attitude about Ursula and her family. And I knew you wouldn't stick around if you knew I was kinda working for them," Digby says. "But now you get all this money. Well, not all. I was thinking forty, thirty, thirty between us. Okay, maybe fifty, twenty-five, twenty-five. I have expenses."

"Expenses? What, the garage needs new carpeting?" I say.

"You have no idea how close you are," he says.

"When did all this happen? You working for the Millers?"

"Ursula called me the day after we were at their house," he says.

"Listen, Princeton, if I'd told you about the Millers, you would've stopped coming along. And I was having fun . . . with you."

"Ohhh . . . you're saying you lied to me because . . . friendship? Here's a clue, you *ass,* friends don't lie to friends. You lied because you're a liar. Don't pass it off as friendship," I say.

"Look, I don't think it's me you're talking to right now. Maybe you should've said this to your dad when he was here," he says.

"No. I'm talking to the right guy. You're both liars," I say.

Digby is quiet a bit. Then he starts making a smaller stack of bills, presumably setting aside money for me.

"I said I don't want it. You're right. Those people gross me out. I don't want them thinking I took their money." Ouch. I say it knowing it is going to cost me thirty thousand bucks. Oh, wait, twenty-five thousand.

"Well, technically, it'd be my money now that you'll be taking," he says.

"So keep it. And feel free to leave with it," I say.

"Princeton . . ."

"I'm tired. Can you get out of my room now?"

Digby doesn't move. I ignore him and pretend to fall back asleep.

"When I get back from my trip . . ."

"Don't care. Just get out, please."

I don't open my eyes, but I hear him put his money away and lock the case. Then the door clicks shut and he's gone. I have a short anxiety attack about our school project and what I'm supposed to tell the police, but it doesn't last long. I fall asleep for real.

THIRTY

After a week in the hospital and another week on our couch, I'm sick of reality TV's thirty-minute problems and I'm ready to go back to school. I need Mom's help to put on my shoes, but I can't stay home another day.

Every night on the local news for the past two weeks, there's been a report on some other local business getting busted for having connections to Zillah's operation. I'm seeing a lawyer who Officer Cooper convinced to represent me at a huge discount. We're preparing the official statement I'm going to give the police next week.

In the end, both Zillah and Ezekiel were saved by the paramedics. They televised them being put onto a prison transport by the FBI. Knowing they'll be far, far away in federal prison makes me feel better. I plan to be living in Paris, possibly under my married name, by the time those two come up for parole.

Speaking of Officer Cooper. He's still coming around. Mom

wants to give me time to get used to it, so she hasn't made me come down and eat dinner with them yet or anything.

And I was as shocked as Mom when one day, I blurted out, "Mom, why did you let Dad get away with it? All those years cheating on you?"

Mom stared at me, blinking.

"Because you must've known," I went on.

"Well, if we're doing *this* . . ." she said. "I didn't *know*—"

"Lie. You knew. Why else were you so miserable for all those years?"

"I thought I was regular bad-marriage miserable, Zo. I honestly thought it would just pass . . ."

"But you don't understand. You put me through it too, when you didn't deal with it."

"Zoe . . . I didn't know you were miserable too."

"*That* I believe you didn't know."

"I'm sorry, Zoe."

"I'm actually not looking for an apology."

"Then, what are you looking for?"

I'd thought long and hard about this and never came up with a way to say it that wasn't idiotic. "I want you to tell me that there was a reason we stayed. That you had a plan the whole time."

"But I didn't. I really didn't know."

"I just can't believe you."

What else could I say? She didn't know. We sat there like dummies.

"Honey, I'm sorry. I didn't know I made you so miserable . . . I hate myself for that," she said. "And if moving here has made you even more miserable, then . . . I'll waive custody and you can move back early. I mean, since you're probably starting at Prentiss next year anyway—"

I felt my entire body rebel at the thought. "Actually, I'm not so sure Prentiss would be right for me." I checked if I'd really meant it. Yes, I had.

"What? What's changed?"

"I'm starting to wonder how much of Prentiss has been my idea or if it's Dad wanting me to go or me *knowing* Dad wants me to go . . ."

"And?"

"And I don't know. I do know I don't want to live with Dad and Shereene."

"So you want to stay?"

"I want to stay." I told her about Dad and the thing he wanted me to sign, but I didn't tell her about the Caymans. I kept that back for a rainier day.

"Zoe," Mom said. "I—I think maybe deep down, I did know your father . . . that something wasn't right. And . . . I'm sorry I forced you to help me pretend. I just wasn't ready. I needed more time."

To finally hear her admit it. To finally hear her say I wasn't crazy was such a relief. The ferocity of the hug I gave her surprised us both.

"Mom. Just . . . thank you."

‡‡‡‡

First day back at school, I realize that the kids are treating me even weirder than usual. Walking down the hall, I leave a wake of interest behind me that includes both students' and teachers' stares. I take heart, though, when one of the seniors (Claire, I think?) jogs ahead to open the library door for me, and Gabby, my chem lab partner, gives me copies of her notes from the classes I'd missed before I even ask. If I had known this was the response I'd get from my classmates, I would have blown myself up a long time ago.

Henry is waiting for me outside homeroom and he gestures at me to follow him.

"I still don't know how you found out where we went after we split up that night," I say.

"After I dropped off Sloane and Bill at the hospital, I drove around the motel until I spotted a trail of feathers starting at a bush on Rush Street. I figured it was your skirt," he says. "Looked like a bunch of parrots had a pillow fight all the way across town. It got pretty obvious after a couple of blocks he was headed back to your neighborhood."

Some girls walk by and stare at us pointedly.

"What's their problem?" I say.

"Uh, yeah . . . that's kinda what I need to talk to you about. Sloane heard you and I danced together and she's . . . not happy," Henry says. "She thinks . . ."

"What? That's ridiculous," I say, even though I'm thinking, Yeah, you'd *better* worry about me.

"*Totally* ridiculous. I mean, you are totally my friend, but she might as well worry about Digby," Henry says.

And with that, I deflate. "Speaking of. Where is he?"

"He must've left by now. He said you wouldn't answer his

messages." There's reproach in Henry's voice.

"He told you about the money?"

"Yeah," Henry says. "Did he tell you why he needed it?"

"No, why?"

"I should let him tell you himself. By the way, this thing with Sloane . . . don't take what she says seriously."

"What's she saying?"

"Gotta go. I have two late warnings already. Come sit at our table at lunch, okay? It's a little football intense, but . . ."

At roll call, Mrs. Scott stares at me after she calls my name. At lunch, I could swear the cafeteria lady gives me extra fries. Sitting with Henry's teammates turns out to be fun. They all want to hear about what it felt like being in an explosion and I think those boys could listen to me talk about my injuries for hours. The description I give of my concussion starts a particularly horrifying round of one-upmanship. For the rest of the day, no one bumps into me, either accidentally or accidentally on purpose.

I'm curious to see what my new celebrity status will let me get away with, so I return to the main bathroom. Here, the girls have decided to act like I'm nothing special, which is fine by me. They're working so hard to not pay attention to me that one girl backs into me, knocking loose the tampon I'd tucked up my sleeve. It rolls across the floor and another girl walking to the sink tramples it flat. There's a round of giggling that immediately dies when Sloane intervenes.

"Seriously, Heather, you're such a pillowcase," Sloane says. "Gimme one of yours. And don't try to pretend you don't have one. You can't wear fat pants three days in a row and not expect people to notice."

Sloane gives me the tampon, but when I reach for it, she grabs my hand and pulls me close. "Take care of business and meet me outside."

Sloane's waiting for me when I get out of the bathroom. She leads me to the stairwell and after shooing away a couple approaching second base, digs right into me.

"If you think you have a chance with Henry . . ." she says. "Stay away from my boyfriend."

"*He* asked *me* to dance, Sloane."

She's clearly not expecting anything but a denial or apology, so my response enrages her. Which amuses me.

"I will cut you."

"Can't stand in the way of love, Sloane."

Sloane's face reddens and she grabs me by the shirtfront.

"Calm down, okay? He's all yours. *Nothing's* going on between me and Henry," I say. "We're bros. Seriously."

Sloane lets that hang a couple of seconds before she decides she believes me.

"So Digby left town?" Sloane says, like we're suddenly cool.

I shrug.

"And we're supposed to keep our mouths shut about Marina. Yeah, right," Sloane says. "I'm saving that for right after the first debate between our fathers."

Ah, yes. The political rivalry between Marina's and Sloane's dads. "But you didn't even see her, did you? I mean, you never actually *saw* her, right?"

"Well, but . . . she was *there* . . . right?"

I shrug again and enjoy the perplexed look on her face. On that high note, I leave her in the stairwell.

++++

After the final bell, I'm at my locker, packing my books for the weekend. Mom's promised to help with "Convicted in Absence" now that Digby's flaked on me, so I'm feeling better about my chances of actually getting it written.

"Hey, Zoe." Felix comes up holding a blue duffel bag. "Digby said to give this to you," he says. "It's for your project."

The first thing I find when I open the bag is a brand-new laptop still in its box.

"Is this for me?"

"Yeah, he said yours broke?"

Then I find typed notes and printouts of tables and graphs. I skim it and realize what it is.

"It's the research for our project," I say. "Wait. Did Digby make you do all this work?"

"Me? No . . . I mean, that's the exact problem he's helping me with. He's getting Dominic off my back so I don't have to do other people's homework anymore." Felix points at Dominic, scowling at us from across the hall.

"Felix, Digby left town."

"But he's coming back."

The optimism on Felix's face saddens me, and I don't have the heart to tell him Digby probably isn't coming back. So I just smile.

"Okay, then . . . I'll see you later, Felix?"

Now, ordinarily people would take this as a clue that the conversation's over, but Felix just stands there.

"So," Felix says.

"So . . . is there anything else?"

"Isn't there?" Felix says. "Digby told me to wait here. Do you have something for me?"

"No . . ."

We peer into my locker just in case, but, no. Nothing.

Then Felix starts sneezing like crazy. Before I can ask what the matter is, a big dog's wet snout pushes me away and pokes into my locker. It's cute and I want to pet it, but it's wearing an orange vest that says WORKING ANIMAL. DO NOT PET.

"Everybody stand back from your lockers. This is a spot check," the canine handler says.

"Spot check? For what?" I say.

The dog's vest has the River Heights Police Department logo on it and the word NARCOTICS.

I feel a stab of cold fear when I wonder just how sensitive these dogs' noses are, because if they can smell even just a trace . . . well, I don't think it's hard to imagine how many illegal things have left trace material on me.

"Do you think it can smell the explosives?" Felix says.

"Say what, son?" The canine handler yanks the dog's leash.

"He's wondering if it can smell the *egg sandwich*," I say. "My lunch . . . but it's gone . . . because I ate it."

Then the dog starts frantically barking toward Touchdown Alley, the stupid nickname the footballers have given their lockers. Dominic looks guilty and preemptively raises his hands.

"Are those guys dumb enough to keep drugs in their lockers?" I say.

A janitor opens Dominic's locker and the cop retrieves a familiar Ziploc bag labeled BALONEY containing a big pile of shriveled leaves. It's the bag of weed we'd bought from Mello Yello with my twenty bucks.

"Well, that's one way to get him off your back," I say.

Then the cop retrieves a gun from the locker.

"But maybe that's going too far," I say.

The cop cuffs Dominic and leads him out. A bunch of us follow in a slow-moving procession. And then we notice what we didn't before: Just in case it isn't clear that the whole show is courtesy of Digby, there's a mosaic of newly adhered RIVER HEIGHTS —WE'RE A FAMILY PLACE stickers along Touchdown Alley.

"Yes! That frees up a whole lot of my time," Felix says. "Want to celebrate?"

"I gotta work on my paper."

"Oh."

Then, because he looks so disappointed, I say, "Maybe another time." But I'm not much of a faker, and I don't pull it off. "Sorry, Felix, it's just . . ."

"I get it. It's okay . . . I can wait."

"Wait?

"You'll see, Zoe," Felix says. "I'm just a growth spurt and an IPO away from being the man of your dreams."

THIRTY-ONE

Walking home, I notice a black SUV trailing me. I pretend not to see it but watch its reflection in the windows of parked cars I pass. After two blocks, I do an abrupt 180 and walk in the opposite direction. The SUV's window rolls down and a voice I don't recognize says, "Hey . . . Zoe Webster."

I turn around holding a pen in the stab position.

It's Musgrave leaning out of the window of his black gas monster. He looks like a pedophile impersonating a TV-style FBI agent.

"I, uh . . . I wanted to . . ." Musgrave hops out, leaving the car sitting in traffic. He waddles over, red-faced and out of breath. He looks like he's having a heart attack.

"Can I help you?"

"Miss Webster, I just wanted to . . . *apologize* if I gave you the impression I wouldn't grade your assignment fairly . . ."

I would allow my mouth to drop open if I didn't think I'd swallow his flying spit by doing so.

"As for the computer I ruined . . . I could either deposit money into your account every month or buy you a computer six, maybe eight, months from now . . ."

"Keep it. I don't need you to . . ." I say. "I'm sorry, I don't get what's happening here."

"I just need you to know your assignment will be assessed objectively and without prejudice. Do you understand?"

"O . . . kay . . ."

"Now, do me a favor? Let Philip Digby know we had this conversation?" he says.

And it all becomes clear. Sort of.

"Tell him what I said about the computer and be clear you turned me down, but emphasize that I offered."

"O . . . kay?"

"And, obviously, put him down as coauthor even though he isn't technically a student at this school," he says. "Just so there isn't any confusion about getting his credits."

"Not a student at this school? What are you talking about?"

✠✠✠

I climb through the window and past the wads of insulation into Digby's garage. I rifle through the stuff on his table and go through the contents of the car. Nothing. Which leaves just one place. One disgusting place.

I dump out the trash can and wearing shopping bags as gloves, I root through Digby's trash. I find a surprising number of disassembled padlocks. I recognize two that had gone missing from my locker. Finally, stuck to a gigantic wad of chewed gum, I find a clue that both explains Digby's ward-

328

robe choices and tells me where he might be going.

"The student has surpassed the master," I say. It's a pamphlet for the Edgar Allan Poe Appreciation Society's annual conference in Baltimore. Inside, the title of one of the lectures is highlighted. "Bon-Bon and the Man in the Black Suit: A Conversation with the Devil Himself." I say, "Story of my life."

Then a rustling in the corner tells me I'm not alone. With only Digby's disgusting shovel as defense against whatever animal is building a winter den in that garage, I get the hell out.

While I'm climbing back over the fence, I see something and the penny drops. In fact, the piggy bank breaks open and dumps pennies all over my brain.

Digby's mom's on the lawn, swigging a magnum of champagne and cackling as she pours kerosene onto the sign that says FORECLOSURE FOR SALE BY BANK. She pitches a book of lit matches and the sign goes up in a mini explosion.

"The money," I say. "He paid her mortgage?"

++++

I arrive at the Greyhound station in time to see the 6:15 to Baltimore pull out.

"Dammit."

I ask a guy to check the bathroom. Nothing. I'm about to concede defeat, when Digby walks into the station wearing a giant backpack and finger-lickin' from a bucket of chicken in the crook of his arm.

"Hey, Princeton. Original or spicy? I got both," he says.

"You weren't even going to our school? What the hell?"

329

"I never said I was."

"You can't *Sixth Sense* me. Of course you did. You signed us up for independent study. You pretended to be in a bunch of my classes. You *went* to art with me and made a mobile."

"Okay, maybe I did."

"You definitely did."

"So," he says.

"So . . . you could've told me what you needed the money for."

"No, I couldn't. You would've . . ." he says. "Oh, puke. You would've done *that*."

Despite myself, my tears well up.

"Are you gonna cry and kiss me all over because you pity me? Then better put some French in that kiss, or you shouldn't bother," he says.

"You paid your mom's mortgage?"

"I paid off a chunk so the bank'll stay off her back for a while. Also the limo bill. Felix's dad was not happy when he got *that* invoice."

"That was our weed you put in Dominic's locker. But where'd the gun come from? And wasn't that a little much? Getting him thrown in jail for making Felix write his papers?"

"There was nowhere near enough weed in that bag to get him actual time, but that gun was already in there when I broke in. I did a public service planting that weed."

"That's why you signed your work? The stickers are a little . . . Zorro."

"People need to know Felix has a guardian angel. Seeing as

how I have to take off for a while," Digby says. "No one messes with my crew."

"I don't get it. Does that mean you've been AWOL from your school in Texas?" I say.

"Musgrave told you?" Digby laughs. "How was he when he told you? Still trembling?"

"He apologized. Actually, he groveled. At one point, I thought he was gonna call me ma'am. What did you do to him?"

"I found out he bailed on an intervention meeting he'd scheduled with Marina two days before she disappeared," Digby says. "It would've been his third strike on the job."

"He told me to ask you where to send the transfer credit papers."

"Don't need it," Digby says. "I'm homeschooled. I've finished all the material for this year. And next year's, actually."

"What? Are you supposed to be some kind of genius? Then why . . ."

"You see how people treat Felix. No way."

"Your mom didn't know you were here, but did your dad? You talked to him on the phone! Shouldn't he have issued a tangerine alert or . . . something?"

"I don't see my dad even when I'm in the same house. All he cares about is that my chores are done," Digby says. "I kept my Texas phone and paid some kid to do the chores. He never even realized I'd left town."

"So you're telling me that you left home and no one noticed."

"I have an evaluation meeting with the Texas Association of

School Boards in two weeks. If I go to that, no one'll know I was gone. Not to be dramatic or anything."

I show him the Edgar Allan Poe Appreciation Society pamphlet I fished out of his trash. "Dramatic like this? I mean, you want me to come say good-bye but you don't wanna seem like you do, so you put it at the bottom of your trash, which you conveniently forgot to dump out . . ."

"Whoa . . . now you sound like *me*. Paranoia isn't a good look on you. It was just trash, Princeton."

"You didn't take the morning bus, and that was the afternoon bus you just purposely missed. What? You're gonna deny you were waiting for me?"

"Well, actually, I was waiting for *her*." Digby points into the parking lot, where Holloway is walking toward the station. She's wearing sunglasses after sundown and keeps her head swiveling left and right.

Holloway shoves a plastic binder at Digby. "Here. It's a copy, so you can keep it."

Digby checks the binder's heft. "Feels a little light, Stella."

"Double-sided. Now, are we square?" Holloway says.

"Square."

"I took a look, kid. Sorry. That case is as cold as it gets."

"I have a new angle."

"Oh? Something you should share with the police?"

"Are you sure you wanna share so soon after you just got done paying me off for the last time we shared?" Digby wags the binder.

"You're right. I don't wanna know." Holloway grabs a piece

of chicken from his bucket and walks away. "Happy trails. Thanks for the chicken."

I jump at the loud hiss of bus brakes and the slam of the doors opening right beside me. Passengers stagger up the stairs.

"This is me," Digby says.

"This bus isn't going to Maryland. It's going to Atlantic City."

"I'm going to Fort Dix. It's near Atlantic City."

"Fort Dix? What's that? A Six Flags or something?"

"Minimum security federal prison, Princeton. I have to ask Ezekiel about my sister."

"How are you gonna scam your way in there? I doubt you'll get too far with your usual coffee and donuts scam."

"Something will come up," he says. "I better get on. I hate getting stuck near the bathroom. And there's always a chatty old lady who thinks I look like her grandkid—"

"So you're rude to grandmas too?"

"No, *them* I wanna sit next to. They always share their food."

"Food . . . of course."

I don't know whether I should hug him or kiss him or what, so I choose to do the most awkward thing I could've done and offer my hand for shaking.

Digby shakes it mockingly and climbs the stairs. Through the window, I watch him take a seat by some seniors on a weekend slots-and-shrimp bender, introduce himself, and become immediately popular. Someone hands him a sack of popcorn.

The engine starts. There's a sinking, black hole sucking feeling in my stomach. I hid in a friend's apartment the day Dad moved out for this exact reason.

Then, just before the bus door closes, Digby runs up the aisle to the door. "Hey, I almost forgot. *Sabrina Morgan,* then TOOTSIEROLL, one word, all caps."

"What's that?"

"My real estate agent login. In case your dad messes with your mom while I'm gone. Use it to take a virtual tour of the place he secretly bought on the Upper West Side through a corporation that has only him and Shereene as the directors," he says. "Like I said: No one messes with my crew."

Best. Parting. Gift. Ever.

Then Digby suddenly reaches for my face and pulls me toward him. He's staring at my teeth and I know what's coming. I don't need to hear it again and so I say, "I know . . . my retainer—"

But what comes isn't a horse teeth comment. Instead, he leans down and kisses me. I'm so shocked, I don't close my eyes, so I see that he's closed his. Then, before I can decide if I'm enjoying myself, the bus driver blasts the horn, and Digby runs up the steps to the claps and cheers of his new senior citizen friends. He looks out the window at me standing there in a mute cascade of emotions ranging from confusion to anger and a weird embarrassed suspicion that maybe I didn't hold up my end of the kiss. I wonder if he knows it was my first.

Then the bus pulls away and just like that, he's gone.

Acknowledgements

I'd like to thank my agent David Dunton for taking a chance on me and for being my first editor. Thank you, Kathy Dawson, for a world-class education in YA writing and for dispensing exactly the right amounts of kindness and strictness while you helped turn my manuscript into a book. I'd also like to thank the team at Kathy Dawson Books, especially Claire Evans and Regina Castillo for their meticulousness.

Thank you, Mom and Dad. You know what for. I'm sorry I was a pain, but as you can see, it was research. I owe you the same thank you/sorry combination, too, Steve and Stella. Thanks for being my accomplices on many of my adventures and I'm sorry I put your lives in danger as many times as I did. Oh, look, something else I should apologize to Mom and Dad for.

My biggest thanks go to LT and HB, though, for making me strong. All this is for you.

Hey, Stella: no ice.

Mischief continues in

TROUBLE
MAKES A
COMEBACK

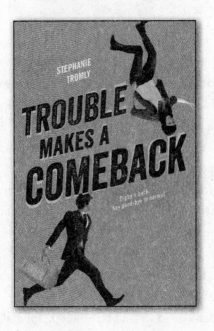

Zoe Webster is looking forward to a quiet spring. Now that Digby has left town, she's finally built a regular high school life for herself. She's dating Miles, the alternate QB; she knows girls she considers friends; she's learning to enjoy being normal and semipopular. Which of course is when Digby comes back: He's got a new lead on his missing sister, and he needs Zoe's help.

Keep reading for a teaser of

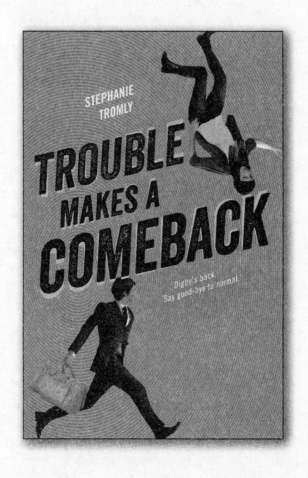

I don't believe in Happily Ever After. Nobody over the age of thirteen with an Internet connection has any business believing in that noise. But the kind of junior year I'm having is seriously challenging the life-saving cynicism I've cultivated for years.

Actually, to be precise, I'm having an epic second semester. My first semester was a series of fiascos, all courtesy of my friendship with Philip Digby. Though, honestly, I'm not even sure Digby ever considered me his friend. Accomplice, sure. But then he kissed me, which made us what? More than friends? Something other than friends? I hate semantics.

Normally, I wouldn't have fallen for Digby's stray-puppy-in-the-rain act in the first place. But I was new in town, I had no friends, and I was still reeling from my parents' brutal divorce. And then I found out that Digby's four-year-old sister, Sally, was abducted from her bed in the middle of the night when he was only seven years old himself and, to add to the tragedy of losing Sally, the authorities thought either his parents or Digby himself was guilty. Even worse, all of River Heights was convinced they'd done it and had turned against Digby and his parents. The pressure tore that family apart. The stray puppy, it turned out, was also the underdog. I was powerless to resist.

By Thanksgiving, he'd gotten me arrested, then kidnapped, and then blown up in an explosion. On the upside, we'd also dismantled a meth operation and found a missing girl. We didn't find Digby's sister, though, so he left town to keep looking for her.

But not before he scrambled my brains with that kiss. And then—nothing. Not a peep from the jerk for the last five months.

Meanwhile, everyone had heard I'd been hanging out with him and that we'd somehow busted up a major drug operation. People in school were curious and I had to act fast if I wanted to convert my infamy into friendships beyond whatever weird crisis-based camaraderie I'd experienced while I was capering around with Digby. I knew I was the flavor of a very short month, so I forced myself past the Digby-sized hole in my soul and Made an Effort.

My first attempts at getting to know new people were disasters. But then I realized that I was boring people with details, and once I basically stopped talking so much and mostly asked leading questions instead, things improved. And then, finally, after a locker room conversation—about the injustice of school going all the way until December 23—with Allie and Charlotte, two of the nicer girls from my PE class, I was in. An invitation to lunch turned into eyeliner tutorials in the good bathrooms and weekends trawling the mall with them. Eventually, I realized that I was enjoying more than just the fact that I was finally feeling included. I was actually having a good time with Charlotte and Allie. They'd been friends since grade school, but I could tell they were trying their best not to make me feel left out. And it worked. Things were looking up.

My luck kept right on improving, in fact, until after winter break, when I got my first official boyfriend: Austin Shaeffer. It happened at the mall. I was with Allie and Charlotte when I saw some guy hauling ass out of the Foot Locker. I didn't have the time—or maybe I didn't take the time—to think. Before I knew it, I'd kicked a wheeled HOLIDAY SALE sign into the guy's path.

The guy hit the sign with a (surprisingly) satisfying *splat*. Digby would've loved watching the Foot Locker employees swarm the thief and pull all the fitness trackers still in boxes from his pockets. For the first time in a while, I let myself feel how much I missed life with Digby. I was so distracted, I didn't notice that a Foot Locker employee had started talking to me.

"Sorry, what?" I said. That's when I realized it was Austin Shaeffer. I didn't have classes with him, but I'd noticed him around school. It was hard not to notice Austin. He was handsome and athletic and one of the few guys who could be funny without being mean. He reminded me a little of Digby's friend Henry, although that might be because Austin was Henry's QB backup on our football team.

"You pushed the sign, right?" Austin said.

By this time, people were clapping. Charlotte pointed at me, yelling, "She's our friend. Our friend did that." Allie stooped for a selfie with the injured thief.

"How'd you know he shoplifted?" Austin said.

I almost said something about the weird bulge in the guy's coat and how his run's head-down urgency seemed more than a late-for-my-movie hustle, but I looked into Austin's big

7

blue eyes and checked myself. *Be normal, Zoe.* Austin Shaeffer doesn't care what you know about body language.

"Actually . . ." I said. "The truth?"

Austin leaned in, forcing me to notice his aftershave. "Yeah?"

"I tripped. The sign kinda . . . rolled?" I tried not to judge myself for the giggle I burped out to sell my lie.

"Zoe Webster, right?" Austin said.

"Yeah . . . and you're Austin—" Then suddenly Austin Shaeffer was holding my right hand. I'd forgotten about my latte and in the course of affecting coolness, I'd let my hand relax so much that coffee was pouring out the spout.

"Careful," Austin said. "So, Zoe Webster, you saved my ass. They would've fired me if my section got jacked again." He pointed at my cup. "You've probably had enough coffee today, but how about this weekend?"

Allie and Charlotte cackled while Austin entered my number in his phone.

"So cute . . . Austin Schaeffer's blushing," Allie said.

"Watch out, Zoe, Austin is trouble," Charlotte said.

"I'm not trouble . . . don't listen to them," Austin said.

After Austin left, Allie, Charlotte, and I talked about him for hours. They liked him, I liked them, I wanted them to like me, Austin Shaeffer apparently liked me, and by the end of the afternoon, I liked him *a lot*. After Austin and I had our first coffee date, Allie, Charlotte, and I parsed every moment I'd spent with him. Being inside that giddy echo chamber was at least as much fun as the date itself.

So now I have a boyfriend and I have friends. I got flowers

on Valentine's Day, I'm invited to sleepovers, and I'm doing decently on social media. Sure, there are moments when I feel alien in my own life, but mostly, it feels good to fit in. Finally, finally, I'm a normal.

But that's all falling apart. Digby sauntered back into River Heights nine days ago, and now my happy ending is toast. Right this second, I'm about to make my entrance at the biggest party of the year. My boyfriend's waiting inside. He'll likely be the starting quarterback this fall, which means I'm dating the official Prince Charming of River Heights High. I'm wearing clothes way above my pay grade and riding in a fancy car with Sloane Bloom, my former nemesis who's somehow turned into my perverse version of a fairy godmother. But here, at the brink of my Cinderella moment, all that matters to me is whether Digby will be at the party. See what I mean? Happy Ending ruined.

But as usual, I'm getting ahead of the story. I need to tell you about the last nine days.

ONE

"April is the cruelest month," Mom said. "Just say it, Zoe. You told me so."

Because my mother worked from home on Friday afternoons, I'd thought I'd save time and get her to drive me to my job at the mall. Mistake.

Mom stood on the gas pedal, but our car was officially beached. The left-side wheels were on the asphalt, but our right-side wheels were up in the air because of the huge snow boulder Mom had driven over and gotten stuck under the car. I felt queasy from sitting tilted as the engine ground away uselessly beneath me. Plus, the car stank of the cigarettes Mom didn't think anyone knew she smoked during her solo commute to the community college where she taught English lit.

"Zoe told me not to park on this snowbank," Mom said to Austin, who was sitting in the backseat. "But it didn't seem so big last night."

"I'll go get your shovel," Austin said.

"Zoe, put those ridiculous things away," Mom said. She took a handful of my vocabulary cards and snorted. "What does this have to do with being a competent reader or writer?"

"Yeah, yeah, Mom. I know. Nothing. But it has everything to do with my doing well on the SATs next weekend," I said. "I am extremely stressed about it . . ."

Austin came back with our shovel and said, "I'm going to start digging, okay, Miss Finn?"

Austin was still in the "Miss Finn" stage with Mom. In turn, Mom still got shy and combed her hair before Austin came over. Actually, even *I* still did. Sitting in Mom's car, watching Austin, all muscles and sheer will, digging us out of the snow, I reflected on how it was probably a *good* thing that I still got nervous before Austin came over.

Austin flung a shovelful of snow over his shoulder, yelled *WHOA*, fell, and disappeared under the hood of the car. Mom and I jumped out.

It was a total movie shot: Austin on his back, his pretty face inches from the spinning tire. We pulled him out, so horrified, we didn't even remember we'd shut the car doors until we heard the auto locks engage. There was our car, hiked up on a snowbank, doors locked, keys in the ignition, stuck in drive with the wheels spinning.

"No!" Mom belatedly threw herself on the car's hood. The car rocked under her weight.

"Careful, Miss Finn," Austin said.

"Get away from the front of the car, Mom." To Austin, I

said, "Quick, put the snow back. But not under the tire!"

"I think there are spare keys in the house," Mom said.

"*Go*. But if you don't find them fast, call 911," I said. "Or a tow truck."

"Oh, God, my life's a farce!" Mom ran into the house.

Austin resumed shoveling in the opposite direction while I kicked snow back under the car. Then a tall figure in black flitted across the field of my peripheral vision and disappeared behind an SUV. Something about his syncopated gait reminded me of something that made me super-happy, and then angry, and then confused.

Suddenly, there he was. Digby. Standing beside me. He seemed taller and broader than when he'd left, but that could've been because of his thick parka. He looked road-weary and his jaw was stubbled. He dropped his backpack in the snow. Clearly, it was the end of a long journey.

"Hey, Princeton," Digby said. "Need help?"

Digby held a screwdriver and a long antenna he'd removed from the SUV he'd passed. He pried a gap along the rubber seam between our passenger's-side door and the roof, fed the antenna through, and pushed the driver's-side DOORS OPEN button. He climbed in and killed the engine.

I got in too, realizing only when we were alone in the car that in the five months since he'd disappeared, I'd collected a ton of confrontational things to say without actually deciding on which to say first.

"Are you back?" I said.

Digby made a ta-da gesture. "Guess where I've been. Wait,

13

don't bother. You'll never guess. Federal prison." He laughed when my eyebrows shot up. "I went to Fort Dix to talk to Ezekiel."

Ezekiel. Just hearing that drug dealer's name made me re-live the horror of his stuffing Digby and me in the trunk of his car and our almost getting blown up in his failed attempt to double-cross his boss.

Digby leaned in. "We've been looking at this all wrong, Princeton. Sally wasn't taken by some pervert . . . it's a whole other thing. When I finally got Ezekiel to put me on his vis-itors list, he told me about his friend—let's call him Joe—who ran a crack squat downtown. Apparently, some guys rented Joe's whole place for a week—exactly when Sally dis-appeared. Joe saw them carry in a little girl in the middle of the night. But when they left . . . there was a whole lot of stuff like *boys'* clothes and video games in the place." Digby paused dramatically. "Remember Ezekiel said they were supposed to take me?"

"Who's 'they'?" I said.

"Exactly," he said.

"Exactly what?" I said. "Who's 'they'?"

"Well, *that* I haven't figured out yet," Digby said.

"Did Ezekiel tell you anything real? Like, what these guys looked like? Or where the crack house *is*?" I said.

"His friend Joe said the guys were in nice suits and drove brand-new black SUVs. Ezekiel never got the address. Nice suits and black cars sounds like government types, and you know what that probably means . . . my dad," Digby said. "I bet it had something to do with his old job at Perses Analytics."

"Where Felix's dad works?" I said. "I thought you said your dad's an alcoholic."

"Being an alcoholic was more Joel Digby's hobby. Alcoholics have to cover their nut too, Princeton."

"He was a scientist?"

"Propulsion engineer," Digby said. "I wonder what he was working on."

"But maybe you're just being paranoid. Or maybe your father gambled, and his bookie took Sally to collect on a gambling debt? Or maybe Ezekiel's evil and he's screwing with your head because you put him in prison?" I said.

"But those are such boring explanations," Digby said. "And, you know, Ezekiel and I got to talking, and he's not such a bad guy—"

"He sold meth to kids and pretended to be in a weird cult to do it," I said.

Digby slapped the wheel. "Ah . . . the ol' Princeton reality check. I forgot how much fun it is."

"You forgot? Is that why I haven't heard jack from you in five months?" I said.

Digby looked genuinely surprised. "I was busy . . ." He pointed out the windshield at Austin, who was still shoveling. "You've been busy too. I assume he's . . . ?"

"Yeah. We're dating . . . we're together . . . he's my boy-friend—"

"Got it," Digby said. "Austin Shaeffer, huh? You teach him the difference between left and right yet?"

Months ago, he'd caught Austin writing an *R* on his right hand and an *L* on his left hand before scrimmage.

"That's a good luck thing he started doing in peewee football," I said.

"Well, I hate to call him stupid, but he's still shoveling and the car's been off . . . what? Two minutes?" Digby tooted the horn, threw up his hands, and yelled, "What's up, buddy? Yeah. Engine's off."

Austin got in the backseat. "Hey . . . you're Digby, right?"

"Hey, Austin." Digby pointed at Austin's gym bag and football helmet on the backseat. "Got a game later or something?"

"That's my workout stuff," Austin said. "Uh . . . we don't play football in the winter, dude."

I cringed at Austin's patronizing tone.

"Way I hear it, you don't play football in the fall either, *dude*. Still riding the bench praying Henry gets injured?" Digby said.

"Okay, Digby," I said, "that's—"

"I'm the backup QB. I play plenty. You'd know that if you knew anything about football," Austin said.

"Got me there, sporto," Digby said. "I'm up nights worrying about everything I don't know about football."

"Should I get the hose?" I said. "Digby, can we talk later? Austin and I were about to go to the mall."

"Afternoon mall date?" Digby said.

"No, we're going to work," I said. "I'm going to Spring Fling afterward."

"Spring Fling? Is that on today? Wait—work?" Digby said. "You mean that stuffed shirt of a father really did cut you off?"

"Dad's a man of his word," I said.

"You didn't use the secret I told you about him?" Digby said. "That information's good."

"You mean that stuff you got on him hiding money from Mom? No," I said. "I'm not a natural-born extortionist like you. I can't suddenly start blackmailing people."

"It's light blackmail," Digby said.

"I'd rather just work," I said.

"What's wrong with working?" Austin said.

"Wait a minute . . . this isn't your mom's car." Digby hooked his fingers on the gunlock bolted onto the dashboard. He found a removable police siren under his seat. "Is this . . . Officer Cooper's take-home car?" He worked it out. "They're still together? Your mom and the cop who arrested you are in a serious relationship? Princeton, your life is *interesting*."

"He moved in last month," I said.

"Wow . . . monotone. That happy, huh? Liza works fast." Digby dove across me and fished around under my seat.

"Hey, man. Not a fan of your face in my girlfriend's lap," Austin said.

There was a loud rip of Velcro and Digby's hand came up holding a mag of ammunition Cooper had stashed under the seat. "Whoa, I wonder if the gun's in here somewhere too."

"Maybe you should put that back," I said.

"Babe, I'm going to be late," Austin said. "We should take the bus."

"Come to think of it, I have mall stuff to do myself," Digby said. "I'll come with."

17

"Good," Austin said.

"Good," Digby said.

"Great," Austin said.

"Great," Digby said. He had that lethal bored expression I wished Austin knew to fear as much as I did.

"Wonderful," I said. "I'd better tell Mom we're not waiting for the tow truck with her."